DAX

Arizona Vengeance

Sawyer Bennett

Find Sawyer on the web!
sawyerbennett.com
www.twitter.com/bennettbooks
www.facebook.com/bennettbooks

TABLE OF CONTENTS

Foreword and Dedication

Dear Reader,

Just a quick note that the start of Dax's book runs concurrently with the end of Legend's, so some events you will see again but from another perspective. I hope you enjoy Dax and Regan's fall into love. If you haven't read Legend, no worries. You'll be able to follow this book just fine without.

I would like to dedicate this book to two very special friends. First to Kristen Carsone... one cool lady, dedicated mom, super nurse, and brave woman who battles the disease paroxysmal nocturnal hemoglobinuria (PNH). Kristen has spent a lot of time educating me on this deadly, rare disease so I could bring attention to it within the pages of this book. Any deviances from fact regarding this disease is purely artistic license, although I tried to stay as accurate as I could. I did change the name of the lifesaving drug she currently takes. In real life, it's called Soliris. Incredibly, it does indeed cost over four hundred thousand dollars a year to receive it. Thank you, Kristen, for sharing your life with me so I could make my heroine, Regan, as wonderful as you.

Second, to my friend Dr. Mark Yoffe. This is not the first book he's helped me on, and it won't be the last. Thank you so much for all you do for me. I'm lucky to have you in my life.

XOXO,
Sawyer

CHAPTER 1

Dax

I RING THE doorbell to Lance's midtown Manhattan apartment, waiting for his sister to answer.

Regan Miles is six years younger than me—which makes her twenty-two—and I've known her for her entire life. Her brother, Lance, was my best friend for as long as I can remember. We lived in the same neighborhood, and our parents put us in the same recreation hockey league. We grew up together in the sport, all the way through major juniors. When we were sixteen, we both got accepted to the Detroit Bears, one of only eight American teams playing in the Canadian Hockey League.

We were together, always, until we both got drafted into the NHL. Lance went to the Vipers where he played his entire career. I went to the Toronto Blazers, then moved to the Vipers where I spent three years before being traded to my current team, the Arizona

Vengeance.

Our friendship never suffered. We talked, texted, and visited when we could. In the summers, we hung out together. Just this past summer, Lance and I spent almost a month together down in Rio, taking advantage of the gorgeous beaches and even more beautiful Brazilian women.

I consider the woman Regan has become over the years. Lance hadn't changed at all, yet I hardly recognized his sister when I flew to New York after he died.

The rattling of the chain on the other side has me bracing. When she swings the door open with a soft smile, I almost have to squint against her beauty. Sometime during the last few years when she was off in California getting her degree, she grew up.

Transformed actually.

The bombshell standing in front of me looks nothing like the gawky teenager Lance had to raise after their parents were killed in an automobile collision when she was fourteen.

My last clear memory of Regan, she had braces, acne, and was a few pounds overweight. She was shy and sweet, adoring her brother for all his sacrifices to keep her with him as he navigated the professional hockey world.

The woman before me isn't the Regan Miles I remember.

This woman is a twenty on a scale of one to ten. Caramel-colored hair, lighter on the ends and styled in waves that hang over her shoulders and down her back. She's sprouted several inches and developed in all the right places. The baby fat in her face has been replaced by sculpted cheekbones and arched eyebrows, framing the most beautiful set of green eyes I've ever seen.

She's a fucking stranger to me, yet there's an underlying truth she's the closest thing to a sister I'll ever have.

She's my only connection to Lance.

It's why I'm here now. Because Lance is gone—killed in a common mugging—and there's something wrong with Regan. I'm here to find out what that something is so I invited her for drinks. We had a game against the New York Phantoms tonight—which we won—and the plane isn't leaving until early morning. I wanted to check in to see how Regan was doing because the few times we've talked since the funeral, I can just tell she's struggling with something. I've tried to cajole it out of her, but she's been stubbornly tight-lipped, insisting everything is okay.

"I'm just about ready," she says as she turns her back on me and walks into the living room. It's a punch to the gut to see it's barren except for a handful of packed boxes I'm assuming contains the contents of Lance's life, which he left to his sister. She has been staying in New

York these past few weeks to handle estate matters and such.

"You got all his furniture sold?" I ask as she stops at the kitchen counter and picks up a pair of earrings.

Tilting her head to put one in, she replies, "Most of it. The rest I donated to a homeless shelter, along with all of his clothing."

I wince. "I know that was hard."

She nods, blinking back what I'm betting are tears as she puts the other earring in. "Rationally, I know it would be stupid to keep that stuff. I mean... what am I going to do with my brother's underwear or t-shirts?"

"But inside, you feel like those are ties to your brother you don't want to give up," I surmise.

With another gentle smile, she nods. "That about sums up how the past few weeks have been. Feeling like I'm losing him over and over again as I scrub his life away from here."

We stare at each other, and I try to swallow past the lump in my throat. My grief over losing Lance is still raw and painful. I can't imagine what it's like for her.

Regan's bottom lip quivers and she sucks in a deep breath, letting it out with a nervous laugh. "Let's talk about something else. I don't want to ruin my makeup."

I don't laugh.

Instead, I hurry across the empty living room and pull her into my arms. She comes without resistance, tucking her face into the base of my neck as I tighten my embrace with one hand on her lower back, the other on the nape of her neck.

It's too much for her, and she gives a little hiccup of a sob before she lets loose. She wept during the funeral but at all other times, she always had the stiff upper lip as she talked to person after person who came to pay their respects. She never lost it, and I felt that was wrong.

Not that *she* was doing anything wrong, but I don't think she was ever given the opportunity to just pour out her emotion. She had to deal with funeral arrangements, burying her brother, and then sorting out all the loose ends that are left to tie up when someone dies.

Regan bends her head so her face is now pressed into my chest. I can feel the heat of her tears soaking into the fabric of my shirt. Tightening my hold, I start to rock back and forth, not saying a word so I don't interrupt the catharsis of her grief.

When she starts to quiet, I pull away slightly to see her. The black streaks of mascara under her eyes and extending down to the tops of her cheeks make her appear even more frail and vulnerable.

I give her a smile, hoping to get one back. Wanting her to acknowledge that was good and freeing to some extent—the security of a good old-fashioned emotional cry.

Instead, she worries at her bottom lip as she tries to wipe the blackness out from under her eyes. It's only a flash, but I see she's incredibly troubled about something. It's gone just as quickly when she shoots me an overly bright smile, which appears forced and painful.

"What is it, Regan?" I ask as my fingers come under her chin to make her look at me. "Something's wrong, and I want to know—"

"It's nothing," she says in a tone so automatic and programmed it's obvious the truth is the exact opposite.

"Regan… it's me. You've known me your entire life. You know what Lance meant to me. I swear to God whatever is wrong, I'll help you fix it. There's nothing wrong with asking for help."

"Honestly," she replies as she tries to make her smile bigger in an attempt to throw me off. "Everything's fine. I'm just tired and ready to get home."

Home for Regan is southern California where she stayed after graduating from college to be a nurse. Lance didn't like her being clear across the country since it impeded his ability to visit with her during the small pockets of time he might have available during the regular season.

But Regan had apparently gone from shy to incredibly independent in the years since I'd seen her. By Lance's account, she was loving her life there.

"You don't have to be so strong all the time," I say,

hoping it will help to break through her stubborn refusal to share what has her worried.

Her lower lip quivers ever so slightly, but she keeps her smile in place. "I'm fine, Dax."

"You're not," I retort, absolutely positive she's lying.

Regan's lips press into a flat line, her eyes hardening. She's shut herself down and erected a wall, and I consider what new tact I should take to break through.

An insanely irrational thought bursts with vivid color in my mind. It's of me grabbing her by the shoulders, hauling her into me, and kissing the hell out of her.

I shake my head, blink, and refocus. We engage in a staring war but given I'm more stubborn than Regan could ever hope to be, I shore my resolve.

Whether she senses it or not, I'll probably never know, but to my incredible surprise, her face crumbles and she practically wails, "Oh, God... Dax. Everything is wrong. Lance ran up a ton of debt, and I have creditors pouring out of the woodwork demanding payment. Lance's accounts are empty, and he didn't have any life insurance. I have no clue—"

"What do you mean he didn't have life insurance?" I cut in.

"I called," she says as a tear escapes and slides down her cheek. She dashes it away. "It had been canceled."

I mutter as I scan helplessly around for the answer to

all her problems. It's not within the packed boxes, which is all that's left of Lance. When I look back to her, I say, "That's not on you though, Regan. You're not responsible for his debts."

"I know," she says without equivocation. "It's just… of course I know that."

I watch her with a critical eye, evaluating her last words. She knows Lance's problems aren't hers now. Yet… something is still weighing on her. I can actually feel it radiating off her.

"What else is wrong?" I ask, crossing my arms over my chest. It's a move to show her I'm not budging until she lays it all out.

She opens her mouth, and I sense the denial. I shake my head. "Don't think to lie to me. Spill it."

For a moment, she stares with blank eyes before her shoulders sag. Regan blows out a frustrated breath, brushing her hair away from her face.

"One of the reasons he was in debt is because of me," she admits in a low voice that's not quite shameful. More like resigned.

"You?" I ask, my brows knitting in confusion.

She nods, smiling sadly. "I've been sick, and he's been helping with my expenses."

"Sick?" I ask, because how sick does someone have to be to drive a person into debt? Especially someone who makes bank the way Lance did. And for that matter… "Don't you have health insurance?"

"I was still on Lance's," she replies. "At my age, I qualified as his dependent, especially since I was starting my master's program. But now that he's dead…"

I blink in surprise. I hadn't known she was going back to school, and I also didn't know she was sick.

How the fuck had I not known that?

"Lance never said anything," I mutter.

Her smile turns understanding. "That was at my request. I didn't want anyone to know."

"Know what?" I ask, feeling an impending sense of doom. "What exactly is wrong with you?"

Her gaze drifts around the empty apartment before coming to me. "A few years ago, I wasn't feeling well. Tired, shortness of breath. Nothing huge but going on long enough I went to the doctor. Lots of tests later, I was diagnosed with a condition known as paroxysmal nocturnal hemoglobinuria."

"What?" I ask, not only feeling lost over that mouthful of words, but also feeling suddenly helpless on her behalf for some reason.

The corners of her lips tip upward. "PNH is a lot easier. But it's a disease that destroys my red blood cells."

"Is it serious?" For a brief moment, I want to kill Lance all over again for not sharing this with me.

Regan's chin lifts, her eyes shimmering with bravery. "It can be. But there's a medication that helps."

"And let me guess," I say dryly. "It's incredibly expensive."

"It costs the average PNH patient over four hundred thousand dollars per year," she says simply.

"Holy fuck," I exclaim. "Who can afford that?"

"Insurance covers some of it, but my out-of-pocket expenses are pretty substantial."

And it's clear why she's so distressed. "And now Lance is dead, your insurance is gone, and you don't have the funds to pay for it."

Rather than affirm what I just said, she backpedals and gives another super bright, overly fake smile. "But that's not your problem. I'm sure I'll figure things out. That's why I didn't want anyone to know, so—"

"Are your bags packed?" I ask, cutting her words off.

Her brow furrows. "Excuse me?"

"You said you were flying back to California tomorrow, right?"

"Right," she agrees slowly.

"Change of plans," I advise her. "You're coming back to Phoenix with me."

"What?" she exclaims in shock. "Are you crazy?"

"Not at all. You're coming back with me, and we're getting married. You'll have my insurance coverage, and I'll pay the out-of-pocket expenses."

"You're nuts," she sputters.

"And you're going to be my wife."

"I'm not," she hisses.

"You are," I say confidently. "Mark my words."

CHAPTER 2

Dax

REGAN IS SICK.

I can't even fucking pronounce what she has but when I Googled PNH, I got all the information I needed to piss me off even more.

Yeah... as I exit the Uber vehicle and make my way up a flight of concrete stairs to her apartment, I'm pissed.

Angry she has an illness that's incredibly dangerous and Lance never even thought enough of me to tell me about it. More than angry at my best friend for dying and leaving his little sister in a lurch. There's also some fury in reserve for Regan as she refused to go to Phoenix with me. Instead, she grabbed an earlier flight to Encinitas, the town she lives in just north of San Diego, and sent me a text just as she was boarding.

It gave me no time to stop her, but it did give me plenty of time to divert from the team plane that was leaving for Phoenix so I could schedule the next available flight out to the West Coast.

Luckily, it's the All Stars Weekend so we don't have another game for five days. We don't even have mandatory practices for the next three days since Legend and Bishop are participating in both the skills competition and the game. I figure that's plenty of time to collect my soon-to-be wife and relocate her from California to Arizona.

I received an invitation to the All Stars as well but with Lance's death, I wasn't into it and declined with regrets. Tacker was invited, too, but I'm sure he wasn't regretful at all when he opted out. It's just not his thing, but then again, not much is these days with that guy.

There's a moment as I reach the landing at the top of the staircase where I realize how foolish and controlling I'm being right now, but I'm being spurred on by absolute fear for Regan's life. A lot of the stuff I read on the plane about PNH was over my head, but some I'd managed to simplify it into understandable terms.

Regan has an incredibly rare bone marrow failure disease that destroys her red blood cells. It occurs because the protein shield around her red blood cells is missing, so it can't protect the cells from attack by the body's own immune system. I don't pretend to understand much more of the mechanics of it, but I read enough to scare the shit out of me. It affects only one in a million people and is a life-threatening disease. What made my legs turn to jelly was when I read the median survival is only ten years after diagnosis. That fucking knocked the wind out of me on the airplane as I flew to San Diego, and I got lost in my thoughts. I wasn't ready to lose Regan so soon after losing Lance.

But then I read more, and I became heartened when I familiarized myself with the expensive medication she needed.

Over four hundred thousand dollars a year to receive Salvistis, which binds to the proteins that destroy the red blood cells. It's a lifesaving drug, and she must have it.

Simple as that.

Therefore, I'm heading toward her apartment door with the sole intention of gathering Regan, returning her to Phoenix with me where I'll marry her on Monday morning, then have her on my insurance by Monday afternoon.

My fist is hammering at the thin wooden door without any hesitation. Within moments, I hear grumbling on the other side before the door is opening to reveal a short Asian man in wrinkled scrubs and his hair sticking up all over the place.

"Yeah?" he rasps as he rubs a hand over his face. I clearly woke him up.

"Is Regan here?" I ask, assuming this to be a roommate. Or fuck, perhaps a boyfriend? He's about Regan's age, although a few inches shorter than her, but that might not matter.

It would to me, but Regan doesn't get stuck on shit like that.

The man coughs and blinks his eyes, focusing on me. "Um… yeah, I think so. I fell asleep on the couch after work last night so not really sure."

He steps backward, welcoming me into the small living room. The apartment is bare bones and cheaply furnished, but the cost of living is high in this southern California coastal town, so I'm not surprised.

I shut the door behind me, and the man disappears into a short hallway where I can see him knock on a closed bedroom door. "Reggie… you in there?"

Reggie? That totally sounds like a nickname a boyfriend would give her. But still… why is he knocking and not just walking in?

My heartbeat picks up when the door opens and Regan steps into the hallway. She gives the man, who I conclude is her roommate and nothing else, a wan smile. "What's up?"

An arm is raised, and a finger extended to point through the living room to me waiting at the door. Regan's neck twists and her eyes round with surprise.

"You have to be kidding me," she mutters.

"You know him?" the man asks, now scratching at

his head before yawning.

"Family friend," she replies, giving him a quick regard before frowning. "Go to bed, John. You look like hell."

Her voice is affectionate and warm. The man—John—gives her a sheepish smile. "On it. See you later."

I watch as he turns on his heel and enters the closed bedroom door directly opposite of Regan's.

Definitely a roommate.

Regan walks toward me, snagging a blanket John must have been using on the couch and folding it up with quick precision. She nods toward the gaming handset on the coffee table. "He plays video games all night after his shift and doesn't get enough sleep. He's a menace to himself."

"A nurse like you?" I ask, with no genuine curiosity but she seems to care for him.

Nodding, she places the folded blanket on the back of the couch. "Works in anesthesia. We've been roommates for a few months now."

"Seems nice," I offer.

"He is," she replies, then narrows her eyes. God, she's so beautiful. I still can't get over why this is something I never really noticed before. "What are you doing here, Dax?"

"You know the answer to that," I reply, strolling over to the couch where I sit. I pat the cushion beside me, beckoning her over. "I realize I may have been a little high handed with you back in New York, and I came so we could talk some more."

"Oh," she says sarcastically as she moves around the other end of the couch to join me. "You mean you're not here to throw me over your shoulder and cart me off to your cave?"

"If I thought I could get through airport security that way, I would," I reply blandly, and she snorts back her laughter.

Plopping onto the couch with a sigh of resignation, she brushes her fingers through the hair at her temple before throwing her arm over the back of the couch. When she curls one long leg up under her, I can't help but admire the smooth flesh in a pair of denim shorts.

"Typical Monahan," she murmurs as the corners of her mouth tip up. "Doesn't know how to take 'no' for an answer."

"Willow is way worse than I am," I defend myself.

Regan laughs, the smile going bigger at the mention of my younger sister by only a year and a half. "That's true. But it's your fault. You were a bad influence on her."

"I am not taking the blame for the way Willow turned out." I hold my hands out defensively. "She's an unexplainable creature."

Which is also true. Willow is fierce, bossy, independent, and a know-it-all. I fear she'll never settle down because I can't imagine a man alive who could hope to handle her.

"She said she's coming back to the States soon."

I nod. My sister is currently working as a photo journalist and travels all over the world. "Late next week. In fact, she's coming to Phoenix to spend some time with me, so you can catch up with her."

Another alpha, controlling move hidden by a vain attempt at subtlety. Regan reacts by raising an eyebrow at me, her lips flattening defensively.

I press forward before she can say a word. "Regan… it's a short-term solution. A paper marriage only. You can have insurance coverage, get your treatment, and finish your master's degree. When you're done and get a job with insurance, we can divorce. It's a simple solution."

She stares for a long moment, and I can tell she's considering what I'm saying but she's not convinced. "I'm the closest thing to family you have now, Regan. And Lance would want this. You know he would."

Her eyes narrow slightly, and she tilts her head. "He'd want me to marry for money and not love?"

My gaze chills and turns chastising. "You know he wouldn't, but he'd recognize I'm making this offer out of love. It's unconventional, sure, but there's nothing conventional about what you're going through. It's a good solution, Regan. There's no reason why you shouldn't accept."

Regan's gaze slides past me and locks on what might be the front door. She nibbles at her lower lip as she considers. "I suppose it's just a piece of paper," she says slowly, bringing her gaze to me. "I've got a part-time contract nurse's job here. I could definitely pay you back as we go along. Once I start the master's program in the fall, we'll just keep a tally and I can pay you back when I land a permanent job. Or I don't have to do the master's program. I could look for a permanent job now—"

"Absolutely not," I cut in. "You're staying in school, and you're not working while in school. You're not paying me back either."

Once again, she straightens and levels a heated glare at me. "I'm not taking a handout."

"Regan… I make a lot of fucking money. Let me—"

"Either I pay you back or no deal," she says primly.

"Fine," I grit out. "Pay me back if you want. But when you're in school, you're studying, not working."

"Yes, Daddy," she snaps with a mocking smirk.

My palm itches. What I wouldn't give right now to land it on her backside. I push that thought aside and stand. "It's settled then. I can stay a day out here to help you get packed up, but then we need to head to Phoenix. I have to be back Monday for practice."

Regan blinks at me in surprise. "I'm not going to

Phoenix with you, Dax. I'll marry you, but I'm staying here."

"Why?"

"Why?" she asks in disbelief as she shoots off the couch to get in my face. "Because this is where I live. My life is here. I have an apartment and a job. It's where I start school in the fall."

"Those things are easy to replace, and you can go to school in Phoenix," I point out. "Do you have a boyfriend or something?"

Okay, that popped out of nowhere and sounded incredibly defensive at the same time. I can feel heat creep up the nape of my neck, but Regan's shaking her head. "No, I don't have a boyfriend, but that's beside the point. I love California, and I'm registered for school here."

"You can register for school in Phoenix. I already checked. Arizona State University has a great graduate nursing program. And you can come back to California as soon as we can get you on your feet," I assure her, ignoring the stab of something uncomfortable in my gut at the thought. "But if I'm going to marry you on a pretense, we're going to make it legit. You have to stay in Phoenix at my place. I'm not about to go to prison for insurance fraud."

Regan blanches and sinks onto the couch, slowly shaking her head. "See… this is such a stupid idea."

"Lance named me as your guardian if he died," I murmur, pulling out my last ace. This won't be news to her as she had to administer his estate. I'm sure she saw it in his will. He'd told me about it when he'd had it done up years ago. Granted... that was if he died while you were still a minor, but his intent was clear. He wanted me to take care of you if he couldn't, and that is exactly what I'm going to do, Regan. Please don't make it so I dishonor that memory."

They're the words that were needed. I can see the capitulation in the way her shoulders sink, and I hate she's so averse to coming to Phoenix with me. But I know deep in my gut I'm doing the right thing. Wherever Lance is, he's nodding his approval right now.

"Fine," she finally says on a huff of resignation. She stands, not putting her eye to eye with me but moving in close enough I can't mistake the determination in her eyes. "I'll come to Phoenix. I'll marry you so I can get my treatment. I'll live in your house."

"You'll love Phoenix—"

"Whatever," she interrupts dismissively, never letting me forget she's not happy about the need for this. "But I want this kept a secret. It's distasteful to me that we're scamming the system."

"We're saving your life, Regan." That comes out in a low, furious growl that has her blinking in surprise. "Fuck the system. They shouldn't make a medication that costs almost half-a-million goddamn dollars a year just so you can live."

She inclines her head, causing some of her lustrous hair to fall over her shoulder. It's so soft looking. I itch to touch it, and I realize all at once… this is going to be a problem for me to have her in my home.

Going to be an absolute monster of a problem.

"Fine," she agrees softly, and my attention goes from her hair to the stunningly soft lips she presses against my cheek after going to her tiptoes. Her hands rest lightly on my shoulders, and I'm not sure I'll ever forget the feeling right now. She pulls away, catching my eye. "We're saving my life, but I still want it kept secret. Tell people I'm taking some time away after Lance's death and just hanging out with you for a while."

"I can do that," I agree.

And it appears that was about as romantic of an engagement as Regan is going to get. A pang of guilt hits me in the chest, but I dismiss it.

Like we just agreed.

We're saving her life.

CHAPTER 3

Regan

I SET THE photo of Lance and me on the dresser, running my finger over the silver edge of the frame as I stare at it. It was taken just a year ago when he'd come out to California for a game and we'd gone out to dinner after. Our waiter took it. Lance and I are smiling broadly, and that's because it looked like my life was turning out a lot differently than what we'd first thought after getting my PNH diagnosis.

Only a few days before Lance had come out to California, Salvistis had received FDA approval and my insurance company had set me up with a case manager to start a treatment plan. Lance was smiling because his little sister would not die, and let's face it... I was smiling mostly for the same reason.

But also because I was simply happy to be with my brother. He and I were tighter than tight, given the fact he took over raising me after our parents died. I'd only been fourteen and he hadn't been much of a seasoned adult at only nineteen, but he'd made me feel safe and secure. My life changed so drastically. Losing my mom and dad and then having to move almost immediately to New York where Lance was playing for the Vipers. I went from a middle-class suburban home to a Manhattan condo—from doting and somewhat stifling parents to a brother who traveled a lot.

During that time, I had a nanny to stay with me to ensure I went to school and ate healthy meals. As I got older, the nanny sort of went by the wayside and I would often stay with friends Lance approved of and who had proper parental units involved. We made it work. Even though I was alone a lot of the time, I never felt that way. Lance and I spoke or FaceTimed at least once a day and texted what seemed like a million times more. Even after I moved to California to go to college, our contact never lessened. He was brother, mother, father, and a best friend to me. Sometimes the grief over his loss hurts so bad I can't breathe.

Like now.

I take four steps back and sit on the edge of the bed, rubbing my knuckles over my breastbone as I look around the spacious guest bedroom Dax put me in. I'll never admit it to him, but I'm grateful to be here. I've felt such an emptiness since Lance died. I truly have no one.

The bedroom is furnished nicely with heavy oak furniture, but the walls are completely bare. Dax told me he'd just moved in a few months ago. He'd been sharing a big suburban house with Bishop when he first moved here, but then Bishop moved in with his girlfriend—now fiancée—and Dax had decided to downsize. He'd bought this three-bedroom townhome in Scottsdale mainly so he wouldn't have a yard to mow.

Or so he said.

I haven't seen him in a couple of hours. Not since we arrived.

It was just a six-hour drive from Encinitas to Phoenix. I only brought my clothes, toiletries, and a few mementos like the photograph of Lance and me. The rest we packed up and put in long-term storage paid for with Dax's credit card. He also left a check with John for six months' rent, apologizing for ripping his roommate away from him. John was sad to see me go, but the check more than made up for it. I called my supervisor, regrettably giving my immediate notice at my part-time job. That hadn't felt good, and I hope I haven't left them too much in a lurch.

After we arrived in Phoenix, Dax carried all my stuff in and promptly left, saying he had some errands to run.

Now here I sit in a room that I'm what... Supposed to live in for the next two years while I get a graduate degree? And what happens to my personal life? If I'm married to Dax, is it even possible for me to have a relationship with someone else?

Not that it's a high probability. My one real relationship had fizzled and faded when I got my diagnosis. I'm not the most overall attractive package out there. I mean, who wants to saddle themselves with someone who has my issues?

A wave of uncertainty floods my senses.

Not the first to happen in the last two days, but the strongest. This was a stupid idea.

"Regan," Dax calls from the living room downstairs. "I'm back, and I have dinner."

Pushing up from the bed, I give a last longing glance at my brother staring at me from the picture frame. "I hope I'm doing the right thing, Lance. If I'm not, you need to give me a sign and really soon."

DAX IS IN the kitchen unloading bags of groceries, and I spy a pizza on the center kitchen island.

"I got a bunch of your favorite things," Dax says as he reaches inside a brown paper bag. He pulls out a package of Oreo cookies, waving them over his shoulder with a grin. The cookies go on the counter, and he reaches into the bag to pull out Cheetos, Chef Boyardee Ravioli, and Pop Tarts.

My eyes widen as he deposits the stuff next to a twelve-pack of Dr. Pepper and box of Lucky Charms.

Dax turns to me, sweeps his hands toward the groceries with a flourish, and asks, "What do you think? Good memory, huh?"

I hesitantly reply, "Um… good memory. Ten-year-old Regan would totally be squealing with delight right now."

Dax's smile falls, his eyebrows drawing inward. He glances at the pile of junk food, then to me with chagrin. "I'm thinking by your lack of squealing, you're eating a bit healthier these days?"

I laugh and move around the counter, poking through all the stuff. There's a bag of Doritos, chocolate pudding cups, and Starbursts. All the things I loved as a kid and my parents had indulged me in, which might have accounted for my slight weight problem and bad skin. But my God, was that stuff good.

Turning toward Dax, I hold my hands up apologetically. "While I appreciate the effort, I truly do eat a lot healthier these days. The PNH has been a bit of a wakeup call to take my nutrition a bit more seriously."

Dax's face turns red, and he groans with a palm slap to his forehead. "Shit. I wasn't even thinking about that, and I should have. I'm sorry, Regan."

I squeeze his shoulder in commiseration. "No worries. Trust me… this disease of mine takes some getting used to. But how about you let me shop and cook? I promise not to swarm you with too many veggies, but

I've got the balanced meal preparations down to a science now."

"Deal," Dax says, returning to the groceries. As I help him load the bags up, he promises to donate them to a food bank or shelter. "Is pizza okay for dinner or want me to run out to the grocery store again?"

"Pizza is great," I assure him, marveling at how at ease I'm feeling in his kitchen right now. As Dax pulls down some paper plates and I nab bottled water from the fridge, I start a mental shopping list for a grocery run I'll make tomorrow.

Dax serves up gooey slices of New York-style pizza, and we sit side by side at the island. He nods toward several plastic bags of varying sizes. "There's a bunch of gift certificates in those bags for you. Target, Bed Bath and Beyond. Stuff like that. I want you to go out and get whatever you need to make your room your own. Decorate it, buy a fluffy comforter… whatever. I want this to be a real home to you."

I freeze with a pizza slice halfway to my mouth, a sudden rush of prickles causing my eyelids to flutter against what I think might be a huge wave of tears. When I don't respond, Dax's head swivels. His eyes are expectant before they fill with concern.

"What's wrong?" he asks suddenly.

I shake my head, still frozen in place and staring at him over the pizza in my hand. I'm vaguely aware of a dollop of melted cheese falling to my plate. Tears start to cloud my vision. Before Dax turns totally blurry, I see awareness in his expression as he starts shaking his head adamantly.

"Don't," he orders with authority, setting his pizza down. I start blinking the wetness away when he growls, "Don't start fucking crying on me, Regan. I can't handle it."

"I won't," I mutter hoarsely, dropping my gaze and my slice of pizza to the plate. A tear drops on the back of my hand.

"Fuck," Dax rumbles. The next thing I know, his arm is hooked around me and he's dragging me off my stool into his embrace. He wraps me up in a huge bear hug, coming off his stool and squeezing tightly. I feel his mouth on my head when he murmurs, "I know things are really hard on you right now, and I've made things even worse by dragging you here. I'm sorry, but this is the right thing to do."

"I'm not upset about that," I say into his chest, then pull my head away so I can look up at him. "Honestly… I'm okay with that. It's just… you telling me you want this to feel like a home got to me. I didn't think "home" was a real concept right now. Not with Lance dead."

"You have a home here with me," he assure me. "You're safe, and you're not alone."

It's a powerful statement. Coupled with the fact

we're supposedly going to hit up the courthouse tomorrow to get married, it strikes me a little more personally than it should.

Luckily, he tempers that by saying, "You have to know, my parents would do the same. So would Willow if she ever stayed still long enough to have a home, and, of course, Meredith would be over the moon if you wanted to stay with her. The whole Monahan family is here for you, Regan, if you let us."

And I know that's true. Deep in my gut, I know there isn't a single Monahan who wouldn't dig deep to help me pay for my treatment or welcome me into their family as if I belonged. Dax's mom and dad, Linda and Calvin, came to Lance's funeral, and while they didn't know my secret, they offered their home up if I wanted to just get away from things for a while. Linda had said, "Come home with us. Let me baby you for a while."

I take in a sharp breath, willing the tears to recede, and damn… why does Dax have to smell so good?

Pushing out of his embrace, I rub my hands over my face. "Sorry. Just… stop being so damn nice, and I won't cry. Okay?"

Dax chuckles, accepting my admonishment as a way to cover up my embarrassment over being a baby in front of him. I point at his plate. "Now sit. Eat."

He winks at me as he does as I say. "You're going to be one of those bossy, demanding wives, aren't you?"

"On the contrary, I'm so grateful for what you're doing, I'll pretty much just be your slave to do with what you'd like."

I meant it in jest—perhaps imagining a Cinderella-type thing where I'd be in rags scrubbing the floor. But something flashes in Dax's eyes, so brief perhaps I didn't really see it at all, and I immediately think of something a lot different.

Naked bodies, twisted limbs, and me doing something incredibly dirty to Dax to show my gratitude for what he's doing for me.

I blink hard and pick up my pizza, taking a mouthful so huge it's a good minute before I'm able to finish chewing so I can swallow. A full minute of silence goes by while Dax continues to eat as well.

Just as it starts to feel awkward, Dax's cell phone starts vibrating on the white-and-gray flecked granite countertop. We both glance toward it, and I see a picture of Willow's face pop up. She has the same mink-colored hair as her brother, but her golden-brown eyes are a few shades lighter than Dax's.

Dax taps on the green button to connect the call, then hits the speaker option. "You're on speaker phone, Will," he says by way of warning, which with Willow is a good move. She has no filter. "Regan's sitting beside me."

"Reg-a-licious," she yells into the phone with bubbling excitement. "I cannot wait to see you. I'll be in on Friday."

"Can't wait to see me either, right?" Dax says, shooting me a grin.

"Nope," Willow retorts. "Pretty sure all my enthusiasm is for the Reg-i-rator."

I snicker and smile at the phone, even though she can't see me. I'm totally warmed by her use of nicknames she used to call me when we were younger. I was the youngest out of all the Miles and Monahan tribes. Willow is four years older than me at twenty-six, Dax is twenty-seven—the same age as Lance had been when he died—and Meredith is the oldest at twenty-nine, the only one married and settled with kids.

But the age difference between me and the others was large. Willow, Lance, Dax, and Meredith were all in a tight group, and I was four years behind them. That meant Willow and Lance dated briefly, Meredith was the older sister who would buy them alcohol before they turned of age, and I was the one who got silly nicknames like Reg-i-moto and Reg-gae Music Girl.

Yes, we all grew up together and our families were tight. We may not share blood, but the Monahans are now all I have left. So while I'm still not sure I'm doing the right thing by agreeing to Dax's plan to marry him, I do know without a doubt Lance would have expected Dax to take care of me.

So I'm going to let him, not only because I know Lance would have wanted it, but also because I'm terrified of what will happen to me if I don't. I'm just going to have to put aside my old-fashioned notions of true love and marriage. Marriage is happening to me for reasons that have nothing to do with romance, and I've accepted that.

Of course, it doesn't help I'm definitely not looking at Dax in a brotherly way these days. He's just too... male. Like a damn romance novel hero, swooping in all buff, successful, and alpha to save the day.

"I'll be in Friday night," Willow says, cutting into my highly inappropriate thoughts. "Dax has a game, so you and I are hanging, Reg-i-bell. We have a lot of catching up to do."

A soft sigh escapes, and I smile at the phone again. Yes, we do. Willow couldn't make Lance's funeral, and it's obvious she feels awful about it. Plus, even though we keep in touch via social media and text, it's been over two years since we've seen each other.

"Regan will be going to the game," Dax inserts cool-ly, and I blink in surprise over what I would term to be a slightly possessive sound to his voice.

"Oh no she won't," Willow snaps. "She can go to another game of yours, and it's not like she hasn't seen you play hockey a gazillion times. But I miss her and I'm sad about Lance, and I just want to hang at your house with Regan and a few bottles of wine. So deal with it."

Dax's mouth snaps shut, a muscle ticking in the corner of his jaw.

"Hanging sounds nice," I say to Willow, hoping Dax isn't mad about that. I have seen him play lots of hockey, so catching up with Willow is totally my preference.

"It's a date then," Willow says, but then I hear someone call her name in the background. "I gotta go. I'll text you my flight information, but I'll handle getting myself to your house, Dax. Later, taters."

And then she's gone.

"She's such a brat," Dax mutters as he snatches another piece of pizza. "Good thing I like her."

"You love her," I say with a laugh, swinging my leg his way and tapping my foot playfully against his shin. "Plus, you know half the stuff she says is merely to get a rise out of you. She's such a button pusher."

"Totally," he agrees, then there's an abrupt change of subject. "Let's leave the house tomorrow about eight thirty. That way, we'll be first in line at the clerk's office."

My throat constricts as the weight of tomorrow starts to settle on me.

"Did you find your birth certificate?" he asks.

I nod, telling him I thought it was in a folder of

papers I had stashed away in my closet and had gone through as I was packing up yesterday.

"All right then." His head bobs in an affirmative nod. "We'll leave in the morning, go to the courthouse and get married, then maybe have brunch. Then I've got practice in the afternoon, so I'll bring you back here. Sound okay?"

Sounds magical, I think in my sarcastic inside voice, but I just smile and nod again. This is the right thing to do, and I need to just get over any disappointment in marrying for something other than love.

CHAPTER 4

Dax

W HILE I KNOW this is the right thing to do for Regan, it just feels all wrong.

Or rather, I feel something "wrong" coming off Regan as she sits beside me in the small lobby of the county clerk's office at the courthouse. It's a ten-by-ten room with four plastic chairs along one wall and a reception window where a bored woman who checked us in sits. Across the room from us, we can see the clerk's office, which has a solid door but a thin-paned window that runs floor to ceiling. Contrary to my original hope, we were not the first to arrive to be married. There is another couple inside with the clerk right now.

A young couple with big smiles on their faces and their arms around each other as the clerk reads what I'm assuming are vows. The bride is wearing a simple white dress that's casual but chosen for the occasion, and she's clutching a small bouquet of flowers. The groom's wearing jeans, a dress shirt, a vest, and a tie. They made an effort for this occasion, whereas Regan and I had not.

While my clothes are designer, I didn't think twice about the jeans and button-down shirt I'd pulled from my closet. As always, Regan looks gorgeous, but I suspect she didn't give a second thought to the black pants and silver blouse she'd chosen.

And yes… I think that might be what feels wrong. Regan is the type of woman who should have a couture wedding dress on such an important day, and she should be vibrating with excitement. Instead, she's slouched onto the chair beside me, skimming through something on her cell phone. She's been polite but quiet this morning, and I get the distinct impression that despite my noble intentions, I'm shattering a dream instead.

That thought almost makes me turn and tell her this is a stupid idea when the clerk's door opens and a happily married couple emerge. They stop, not able to help themselves apparently, then engage in a deep kiss before they bound out the door.

The clerk comes out of her office, glancing across to Regan and me. She's short and plump, I'm guessing early sixties, with a head of tight gray curls. Her eyes are bright and her smile welcoming as she asks, "Are you here to get married?"

I stand from my chair, noting Regan slowly follows. My hands are sweaty, and I give them a wipe on my jeans. "We are."

"Well, come on in," she says jovially, motioning us forward. "Doing these marriages are the favorite parts of my day. Did you see the couple just before you? My word, they were the sweetest. Apparently had been together for almost sixteen years. Have two kids together and just up and decided they should get married today. No other reason than it just felt right, know what I mean?"

I glance at Regan, who stares blankly at the clerk, but she's not paying any real attention to us. She's already turned back into her cramped office and is rounding her desk to take a seat.

We follow her in, and she waves to two more plastic chairs for us to sit in. I let Regan precede me in, then close the door behind us.

As we're taking our seats, the woman introduces herself. "I'm Anita Dougald. We'll handle the license first and then we can do the vows. If you brought your own, that's great. If not, I have a standard set."

The clerk shuffles through a drawer for some paper-work, and then glances at us with another blinding smile. She lays the papers down, then grabs a pen. "So, let's get this filled out? Groom's name."

"Calvin Dax Monahan," I say, giving her a moment

to write that on the proper place of the form. "And Regan Elizabeth Miles."

If my name means anything to Anita, she doesn't show it. But that's not surprising. Despite being one of the hottest teams in the league, most Vengeance players aren't easily recognized out in public unless a person is a super fan.

Anita does not look like a super fan.

"Okay," she drawls before asking, "Dates of birth?"

We provide the information she asks for, which isn't a whole lot. Once the simple form is complete, she takes my payment for the license while the official one chugs out of her printer, upon which she affixes an embossed seal.

When that's finished, she asks, "Do you two have personalized vows written?"

Regan quietly replies, "No. The standard ones are fine."

If Anita feels anything is remiss—as in she has a couple who is unusually subdued on this happy occasion—she doesn't let on. In fact, we are treated with nothing but cheery optimism and happiness from the woman.

"Well, let's stand," she says as she pulls a sheet of paper from another folder.

We all rise from our seats. Without any thought to whether it's the right thing or not, I reach out and take

Regan's hand in mine. It forces her to shuffle two steps closer to me, and I grip it tight. I can feel the clammy sweat of her palm mixing with mine, and I note she doesn't squeeze me back.

"Will there be a ring exchange?" Anita asks.

"No," I say, and I can't help but look at Regan. She turns her head, and I'm given an encouraging smile in return. I can tell it feels wrong to her as well, but she's still committed to this.

Anita doesn't seem fazed by the lack of rings, and maybe it's not all that traditional with this type of marriage. Who knows, but there's no time to ponder.

Anita begins by addressing me. "Calvin—"

A moment of panic hits as I realize I'm binding myself to a woman for all eternity. At least in the traditional sense of why we do marriages, but then that's immediately quelled when I feel Regan finally give my hand a squeeze.

"Dax," I correct Anita. "I go by Dax."

"Sure," she replies with a tinkling laugh. "Dax... do you take Regan to be your wife?"

"I do," I say, my words coming out strong and sure.

Because I *am* sure.

"Do you promise to love, honor, cherish, and protect her, forsaking all others forevermore?"

Fuck, that's a commitment, but there's nothing in there that dissuades me. The word "love" should, but not really. I do love her.

Like a sister, of course.

"I do." And then I give a slight squeeze to Regan's hand, but I get nothing back this time.

Anita turns a bright smile to my soon-to-be wife. "Regan… do you take Dax to be your husband?"

"Yes," she replies quietly, but there's no hesitation. I turn to her again, finding her eyes pinned solemnly on the paper Anita is holding.

"And do you promise to love, honor, cherish, and protect him, forsaking all others forevermore?"

"Yes," she replies. For some reason, a rush of something warm and comforting sweeps through me. Regan angles her face to me. For a moment, we just stare at each other. In the quiet, the enormity of what we're doing seems both oppressive and welcoming at the same time.

"I now pronounce you husband and wife," Anita announces proudly, and we both turn to her. "You may now kiss your bride, Mr. Monahan."

A bolt of what feels like pure electricity slams into me as I never once thought about there being a kiss at the end of these vows. I had considered whether to buy a ring, but ruled it out as unnecessary. I never once thought about there being a proclamation I was to finalize this contract with a kiss.

I turn my entire body to Regan, a question in my

eyes. She stares with a look of utter confusion. I can feel the expectancy and excitement bubbling off Anita as she happily waits for the best part of any wedding ceremony.

Yes, this marriage is fake, but fuck if I want Anita to really understand that. We're getting married so Regan can have insurance, and I'm fairly sure that's no less fraudulent than marrying someone from another country so they can get residency here. And I definitely don't want any of this to blow back on Regan in a negative fashion. I have money and clout, and I could withstand the scrutiny and potential legal ramifications. It would not be fair for her to do so, so I make a command decision.

Putting my hands on Regan's shoulders, I pull her toward me. Those green eyes of hers flare wide as she realizes what I'm going to do, but there's no hesitancy within her posture. Her body is supple and yielding. She lets me pull her in as I bend my head. Lightly but with feeling, I brush my lips over hers.

"Oh, now," Anita scoffs loudly, and we both twist to see her. "Don't be shy. This is a momentous occasion. The kiss to seal your vows is everything in a marriage. Now go on, Dax... give your woman a kiss that says this is the happiest moment of your life."

Jesus fuck.

Regan starts to pull away from me, but I'm not

about to make any type of scene. Besides… can't say the idea of kissing Regan is a turn off. On the contrary, I've given way too many of my thoughts over to the notion of what it would be like the last few days since she reentered my life.

I slide one hand from her shoulder, up her neck, and curl it around to the back of her head. I see a flash of anger—maybe warning in her eyes—but I ignore it as I bring my mouth to hers.

Regan goes stiff as I press my lips against hers. I don't graze. Instead, I take. I use the pressure of my hand to hold her in place, and with a tilt of my head, I kiss my wife.

My mouth locks onto hers and opens, forcing hers to do the same. I can feel her hand on my forearm, fingernails digging in, and I think I might get a knee to my nuts… but then she's kissing me. Her arm winds up and around my neck, her mouth opens and her tongue slides against mine.

And, oh holy fuck is that good. A wave of euphoria washes over me. I lean my entire body into the kiss, wrapping an arm around Regan's lower back. Her other arm locks around my neck as she holds on tight, and the kiss goes so deep I'm not sure I'll be able to surface.

Another wave of warmth and satisfaction overtakes me. Everything just melts away. There's nothing but Regan, her mouth, and her tongue, and just shoot me now… I'd die a happy man.

"Oh my," I hear from what seems like far away. "That might be the best kiss I've ever seen in the thirty-two years I've been in this job."

Regan jerks in my embrace, starting to pull away. My body doesn't like that. I try to lean farther into her, willing that stupid voice I'd just heard to go away.

But then Regan's hands are at my chest, and I open my eyes to find her staring at me with utter surprise. She gives a nervous laugh and pats at me. "Wow, honey… let's save it for the honeymoon, okay?"

Honeymoon? Yes. Consummate the marriage. Sex with Regan. Yes. Yes. Yes.

Regan starts to push at me, just a little more insistently, and I blink several times as I return to awareness.

Shabby office with plastic chairs and a complete stranger watching me kiss Regan for no good reason. The first kiss I'd given her should have been sufficient.

Then why the hell do I want to kiss her again to try to outdo the last?

I release Regan so suddenly she almost falls. With a quick grab onto my arms, she manages to right herself. We both laugh over the awkwardness of it, and Anita joins us.

There's no denying I'm out of sorts as Anita takes us through the last few moments of our time with her by packaging up our license before giving us congratulatory handshakes. I take Regan's hand in mine, leading her out of the office door. There's another young couple grinning at us as we exit. I'm guessing they witnessed that hot-as-fuck kiss through the paned window. Giving them a curt nod, I lead Regan out.

"Sorry about that," I mutter as we start down the hallway to the elevator.

"Not a problem," she replies, understanding I'm talking about that kiss.

I hold her hand all the way until I release it to stab the "down" button.

"Hungry?" I ask.

"I could eat."

"I know a great place not too far from here," I advise as the elevator door opens. Smiling, Regan precedes me in.

And thus starts our life together as husband and wife.

CHAPTER 5

Dax

I'M A BLOCK from the arena. Normally, my head would be in game mode but it's not.

It's on Regan.

My new wife.

Christ, the last few days have been confusing. Yesterday, I got married. While I am convinced it was the right thing to help Regan out, I had not considered what it would mean in real life.

For example, I'd gotten an invitation from a few of the players to go out with them for some beers. I shouldn't have thought twice about it, especially since my closest friends on the team were one by one falling into serious, monogamous relationships.

But it was complicated, and after I'd done some major back and forth in my brain, I declined. It just didn't feel right to leave Regan all alone.

Not when she'd just moved here and was a guest in

my home.

Not when she'd just married me.

Which brought up another complication I'd not considered. I'd recited vows to Regan—promised myself to her and her alone. Does that mean other women are off limits? Not that I'm big into dating, but I do like to fuck and will do so when the opportunity presents itself to my liking. Can I even ethically do that now?

Regardless, beers were out.

For now.

Today was spent in awkward avoidance of each other. Regan spent a lot of time in her room, but the few times I saw her come out, the conversation was stilted. I didn't push anything, because I didn't know what to say. I also figured things would smooth out eventually.

I did invite her to the game, though, as I thought it would be good for her to get out. She loves the sport. To my pleasant surprise, she said she'd love to go. I arranged a ticket for her to pick up at Will Call after suggesting she Uber to the arena since I had to leave so much earlier than she did. I even told her we'd go out with the team afterward to The Sneaky Saguaro to have a few beers so she could meet some of the others.

And Regan seemed happy and excited for our plans. Maybe that's all we need—to get into a regular routine, cement our bonds of friendship while she's staying in my home, and try to forget about this weird mess of a marriage we'd committed ourselves to. That wasn't what was important.

The entrance to the player's parking lot comes into view. I force my thoughts away from Regan. It's time to start focusing on defeating our opponents tonight. I put my blinker on, but just as I'm starting to turn, I see a crowd of people standing around a truck that's crashed into some concrete barriers outside the loading dock.

"What the fuck?" I mutter.

As I pull into the closest spot, I notice a few of the players and dock workers standing around. I exit my car, grab my game duffel, and hitch it over my shoulder.

As I approach, I see Baden Oullet, our backup goalie, examining the damage to the front of the truck. "What's going on?" I ask.

"It's Tacker's truck," he responds, and a chill races down my spine.

"What happened? Where is he?"

Baden nods toward the player's entrance door. "We were told to enter through the dock area, but he's right inside there. An ambulance has been called."

I don't respond, nor head toward the dock area, turning instead toward the player's entrance and marching with resolve.

Throwing the door open, I immediately see Tacker sitting on the floor, propped against the cinderblock wall. Legend and Erik are standing off to the side with their heads angled in toward one another, talking in hushed voices. Bishop is squatted next to Tacker, who is staring ahead with a blank expression on his face. There's a rivulet of blood running down his face, his wrist cradled against his chest.

"What the hell happened?" I demand.

Tacker doesn't even acknowledge me, but Bishop rises from the floor with a grave expression. He starts walking down the hall, away from Tacker, and I follow.

When we reach the end, Bishop stops at the locker room door, turning to me. He's my closest friend on the team. We were roommates and played together with the Vipers prior to coming here. Of course, that all changed since he got engaged to Brooke, but I couldn't be happier for the guy.

Bishop leans in toward me, keeping his voice low so it doesn't carry to Tacker. "Legend, Erik, and I were in the parking lot when it happened. Tacker pulled in, driving crazy. He fucking gunned his engine, didn't slow down, and headed straight for that barrier."

"Was it deliberate?" I ask, hoping Bishop isn't implying what I think he is.

"I think so," he murmurs. "And he's fucking drunk off his ass."

"Shit," I mutter, casting a quick glance down the hall. Tacker hasn't moved. Erik is now sitting on the floor next to him. "How bad is he hurt?"

"I don't know. He was able to walk. Something's wrong with his wrist, but no clue about internal injuries. We had no choice but to call an ambulance."

"Agreed," I say with a clap to his shoulder. "Does Coach know yet?"

"I sent Demere to go find him right before you walked in."

I grimace at Tacker. "He's in so much fucking trouble."

"He's going to be arrested."

Dropping my duffel to the ground, I ask the question that needs to be asked. No one is all that close to Tacker, but Bishop probably spends the most time with him. "Is he too far gone, dude?"

Scrubbing his hand over his face, Bishop lets out a sigh. "Fuck if I know. He asked me a few minutes ago how people could live with themselves knowing they killed someone. Apparently, it was MJ's birthday today."

MJ would be Tacker's fiancée who was killed in a plane crash last year. There had been something wrong with the plane. Tacker was the pilot. It wasn't his fault, but no one can tell him that. He's been one quiet, moody, and disturbed son of a bitch since he started with this team. No one can seem to reach him or get him to open up. While he's probably the best player in the league out on the ice, he has no camaraderie with anybody on the team. He'll talk the mechanics of hockey with us all day long while on the ice, and he'll be a supportive captain to his team. But outside of this arena, he's pretty much closed off.

I had actually thought there might be hope as just last month, Tacker and I spent Christmas Eve with Legend, who had just had the surprise of his life by finding out he was a father. It'd been a low-key evening. Both Legend and I were surprised by how taken Tacker was with Charlie, the newborn baby girl who had just come into Legend's life. I thought Tacker had finally been starting to settle in and become part of our family.

I thought he was starting to leave his pain and guilt behind.

I'm not thinking that now.

The door we're standing beside opens, and Bishop and I both step back. Coach Perron walks out followed by one of the team trainers, Ronnie Nuss. He has an emergency first aid kit in his hand.

He brushes by Coach, then jogs down the hall to assist Tacker.

"What happened?" Coach asks Bishop.

In any other situation, Bishop might think to stretch the truth a little to make things seem a little more positive if it were possible, but there's no sugarcoating this. Besides, Bishop's fiancée, Brooke, just happens to be Coach Perron's daughter, so there's no way he's going to lie to his future father-in-law.

"He's drunk," Bishop says.

Coach flinches while muttering a curse word.

Bishop finishes with, "He drove the truck into the barricade."

"God Almighty," Coach whispers with utter empathy. He's just as aware of Tacker's demons as we are, and while he's a tough-as-nails son of a bitch as our coach, he cares for his players deeply.

We all focus on Tacker. With a fierceness I've never heard before, Coach Perron grits out, "This ends here. That man is getting professional help whether he likes it or not."

Chills take hold of my body when he leaves Bishop and me to stride down the hall toward Tacker. We watch as he squats in front of his star player—the captain of our team. His hand goes to his shoulder and while we can't hear what he's saying, I imagine they're appropriate words of comfort.

When the outer door opens, a Phoenix police officer followed by two paramedics enter.

This just fucking sucks.

"I'm going to go get my gear," Bishop says wearily. "I'll see you in the locker room."

"Yeah, sure." As I turn away from him, I pull my phone out of my pocket and dial Regan.

She answers just as I'm stepping into the locker

room. "Hello."

"Hey." My voice sounds old and tired. Part of me is pissed Tacker is fucking up our team.

"What's wrong?" she asks with clear concern in her tone. She'd apparently realized my mood from just from one word.

"Listen… it's too much to explain right now, but our captain, Tacker Hall, he had a really bad accident just a few minutes ago. He's being taken by ambulance to the hospital. I'm going to go straight there after the game, so we're not going to be able to go out tonight."

"Oh my God," she exclaims. "And no worries. I can take care of myself, of course. I'll just Uber back home. Do you still want me to come to the game?"

"Yes," I blurt out. "Yes, of course. Please come and enjoy yourself. I'm just sorry I can't do anything with you after. I expect the entire team will head to the hospital, assuming that's where he'll be."

"Well, maybe you can head to his house if he's discharged by then."

Or the police station to bail him out, I think, but that's not something to share with Regan right now.

"Dax?" Regan's voice comes across softly, and still concerned. "Can I give you some advice?"

I jolt in surprise, at first not understanding why she feels the need to do so. Then I take stock of how I feel right in this moment. While I don't pretend to understand how she knows it, I feel like shit.

"Yeah," I reply.

"Try to compartmentalize," she tells me. "It's futile for me to tell you not to worry, but at least try to compartmentalize it. Imagine putting that worry into a box. Lock it with a key... envision yourself doing that. Then shove it into a far corner of your mind. Nothing you can do to help Tacker right now. I'm sure he has good people taking care of him. But you have a job to do, so you need to free your mind to be the best damn hockey player you can be tonight. When the game is done, unlock the box and go see your friend."

I suck in a breath through my nose, letting her words settle in. They're surprisingly simple, yet impactful at the same time. They were also given without thought or effort, and I realize something.

"I'd bet a million dollars you've given that speech before," I say as I walk toward my locker. Only a few other players are in here, but no one is talking and laughing, which means the news about Tacker has spread.

Regan returns a light laugh. "Same speech I gave to Lance after we got the call I had PNH. He was really upset and had a game. We had a heart-to-heart before he left the apartment. While not word for word, it was the same gist."

"Did he follow your advice?" I ask.

"He tried. Didn't turn out so well. One of the worst games he'd ever played."

I laugh and Regan joins in, both a little lost in our memories about a man who'd been an amazing professional athlete, and yet had loved his sister so much it reduced him to a bumbling idiot on ice.

"I'll try," I promise. "It's good advice."

"That's all you can do. Now… get your head in the game. I'll be cheering you on."

That feeling comes back. The one I experienced yesterday when we got married. Warmth and security. Regan will be cheering me on, and while she's my wife in name only, the fact she's doing it because it's me means something.

I'm just not quite sure what.

CHAPTER 6

Regan

I T'S ALMOST MIDNIGHT by the time I hear Dax's car pull into the driveway. He'd insisted I park my car in the single garage when we'd arrived on Sunday. It's stayed there minus a quick trip to the grocery store this morning. I figure I've got plenty of time to find my way around the Scottsdale/Phoenix area since I'm not going anywhere soon.

Dax had texted me after the game to tell me that he was headed to see Tacker with the rest of the team, since he'd been admitted. I'd informed him I was waiting on an Uber to take me home, so I'd see him later.

I was tired and should have gone to bed when I got here, but I was too worried about Dax. He'd played horribly tonight. But then again, so had the entire team. There'd been a buzz all around me where I'd sat in the arena, many people wondering why Tacker was on the "injured" list. I'd known—minor details, of course—but

I never said a word. I just watched and yelled and screamed at the game, but in the end, I walked out of the arena with all the other disappointed fans. We'd lost.

Dax's key is in the lock. I stand from the couch where I'd been sitting, placing my half-empty cup of tea on the coffee table. He steps in looking exhausted. Despite that, he's still amazingly gorgeous in the dark blue suit he'd left in today.

He blinks in surprise when he notices me. "What are you doing up?"

"I waited up for you. Wanted to see how Tacker was doing."

Dax tosses his game duffel on a chair with a shake of his head. After he shuts the door, he turns the lock. "No clue. He refused to see anyone at the hospital."

My brow furrows in confusion as I know a little about team camaraderie. "But why?"

Dax pinches the bridge of his nose, closing his eyes a moment before letting out a frustrated sigh. When he looks back at me, he says, "Tacker was drunk. He deliberately drove his truck into a concrete barricade."

"What?" I gasp, dismayed at the way Dax's shoulders droop with fatigue. "Wait a minute… sit on the couch and let me get you some tea. It will relax you."

I get a naughty grin in return. He shakes his head as he moves over to the butler's pantry that sits in a cubby between the living room and kitchen. "This is going to take liquor, not tea. Want a drink?"

"Sure," I reply as I sit on the couch, nestling into the corner with my legs crossed Indian-style. Dax grabs a clear decanter of a dark liquid—presumably a bourbon—and grabs two glasses. He sits them on the table and while he shrugs out of his suit jacket and removes his tie, I take the liberty of pouring us each two fingers.

After he plops down on the other end of the couch and loosens the top two buttons of his dress shirt, I pass the glass to him. Giving me a wan smile, he clinks it against the edge of my glass. "Cheers."

"Cheers," I say, taking a tiny sip that immediately warms me. I'm not a big drinker, but I actually like a slow-sipping drink like straight bourbon or scotch.

"I know you're pretty up on the hockey world, but how much do you know about Tacker's background?" he asks.

It's true, I know my hockey. When Lance got drafted, I was so incredibly happy and proud I immersed myself in it. I knew not only the deep stats on his team, but also on the Vipers' biggest rivals. I was aware of a dangerous amount about many of the other teams, including the league's leading players. Obviously, I was a Vipers fan first and foremost because of Lance, but wherever Dax played, that was my second favorite team. As such, I knew about Tacker's history since he was their best player.

"Little over a year ago, he was in a plane crash. He was piloting, and there was a mechanical issue. The plane crashed, and his fiancée was killed. He was injured and missed the rest of last year's hockey season. Didn't get protection in the expansion draft by the Mustangs, and the Vengeance picked him up. He's been having a wonderful season so far this year. Seems to be playing at his peak."

Dax's eyebrows rise, and he smiles in appreciation of my knowledge. "Not bad but also not that surprising. You do love this game."

"Lance gave me that."

"Yeah," he agrees softly as he swirls amber liquid in his glass. He raises it to his mouth, takes a large swallow, and empties it. Shifting to lean on the edge of the couch, he pours another glass from the decanter I'd left opened on the coffee table. "What you don't know is Tacker hasn't been doing well emotionally. He's been shut off from the rest of the team. He's hard to engage off the ice. He'll show moments where you think— okay, this guy is going to be okay—then he pulls away again."

"Sounds like he's depressed," I offer.

Dax nods. "I'm sure of it. And you saw that fight he got in at the end of November?"

"Against the L.A. Demons. Kneed Lars Nilsson in

the head. He got suspended for—I can't remember how many games."

"Ten," Dax says, then takes another long swallow of the liquor. I take a larger sip to match him, enjoying the burn and the way he's talking to me. Like I'm a confidant he needs to unload on. If drinking bourbon is the way to do it, so be it. It gives me back a little of what I lost with my brother.

"At any rate, it's like he's been a ticking time bomb," Dax murmurs, choosing to stay perched on the edge of the couch. "I've been afraid something bad was going to happen. I pulled into the player's lot tonight just a few minutes after he drove his truck into the barrier."

"How badly was he hurt?" I ask.

"He was conscious with a few cuts and scrapes to his head. I think his arm or wrist was hurt, but past that... we just don't know. His refusing to see us wasn't all that surprising. He's such a loner."

We're silent for a moment. To fill the void, I kick my glass back and finish my drink. Dax doesn't say a word as I scoot to the edge of the couch to pour another.

"So is he... suicidal?" I ask hesitantly, then angle my body to face Dax. Between the last two drinks we poured for ourselves, we'd managed to both move closer to the center of the couch, but there's still a good foot separating us. I'd think nothing of it normally because Dax is like my brother.

Except a lot of the time, my feelings about him aren't sisterly.

"I don't know," Dax admits before taking another long pull. I take a sip as well. "I mean... yeah, he drove his truck into that barricade, but I've just never gotten that vibe from him. I mean... maybe. Fuck... I don't know."

And with that, he finishes his second drink. I tip my glass back. While I had not poured as much into my second, it still takes me two swallows to down it.

Dax lifts the bottle, giving me a questioning look. With a nod, I hold my glass out.

When we both have fresh drinks, Dax settles into the couch and I do the same, tucking my legs under me. I change the subject because Tacker's not going anywhere. Besides, there are no answers to the million questions right now.

"How are you liking the rest of the team? It seems you're all gelling really well on the ice."

Dax smiles, his eyes lighting up. And then he starts to talk.

I get to hear about his closest buddies here. Bishop became recently engaged to Brooke—who is Coach Perron's daughter—after pulling off a fake engagement because Coach had caught them in a compromising position. Playboy Erik falling for a woman named Blue he'd had an "encounter" with five years prior but didn't remember. Now that he's fallen hard for Blue, Dax predicts that even though they aren't engaged, they'll get married before Bishop and Brooke.

Most interesting is what's been going on with the Vengeance star goalie, Legend Bay. Apparently, he came home about six weeks ago and found a newborn baby on his front porch, along with a note from the baby's mother. I actually know Legend as he played one season with the Vipers, and I'm having a tough time seeing him as a father. According to Dax, though, he's taken to fatherhood and is over the moon about his new baby daughter Charlie.

We have another drink while he tells me all about Legend's crazy story.

"So has Legend heard anything more from the birth mother?" I ask.

He nods. "She's popped up a few times, demanding to see Charlie. But Legend is going to make her go through the proper channels. I think he's open to visitation, but no way is he going to give up custody now."

"That's so sweet. It sounds like he's found a really good woman along the way," I murmur. Dax also filled me in about Legend's neighbor, Pepper, who he seems to have fallen for. I look at my glass, frowning when I see it's empty. "Look at that. I'm dry."

Dax chuckles before finishing his drink. "Another?"

"Sure, why not?" I say, even though I'm well on my way to getting drunk. Right now, I'm highly buzzed and feeling good. Pretty sure Dax is, too, as evidenced by the goofy grin on his face as he pours us another drink.

We hold our glasses up and clank them a little too hard, causing some of my alcohol to slosh out. Giggling, I say, "Oops."

"My bad," he replies with a laugh.

After we both take a drink, I can't help but tease him. "All the Vengeance boys are falling. Bishop, Erik, then Legend. And—"

"And here I am a married man now," Dax says with a grin, holding his glass up to me. "To my wife."

I snicker and tap my glass against his again, this time with care so I don't waste any precious liquid. We each take another sip. I'm beyond the liquor warming my belly. Now it just goes down super smooth.

A thought strikes me. "How awkward was our wedding yesterday?"

Laughing, Dax shakes his head. "Poor Anita. I don't think she knew what to do with us."

That cracks me up, and I start giggling. "She was sort of clueless."

"Poor woman," he adds in between laughs. "I bet she's never had a couple as unenthusiastic as us when it came to getting married."

"You totally shocked her with that grandma kiss you gave me," I say with a snort.

"I know," he agrees. "She totally called us out, and I didn't know what to do."

"She was like, 'Oh hell no… you kiss that girl again and you make it good'."

"That woman completely egged us on."

I have to hold onto my glass with both hands I'm laughing so hard now. Dax is as equally as cracked up, but he pauses to take another sip of his drink. He swallows, letting loose a low chuckle. "It was a good kiss, though. Right?"

My laughter dies as my face flushes at the memory of that kiss. It was, without a doubt, the best kiss I'd ever had in my entire life. I can't figure out if it's because I just don't have much experience, or because I'm insanely attracted to Dax. Perhaps it's because I've known him my whole life, and I love him.

In a sisterly way, I mean.

"Shit… it was a bad kiss, wasn't it?" Dax blurts out, apparently not happy with how long I'm taking to answer.

Blushing furiously, I hold a hand up. "No. It was good."

His eyes light up, the expression on his face turning sly. "Yeah? Just how good?"

"Good," is all I'm willing to admit, despite my face

still feeling incredibly warm because I'm afraid he sees through my vague words.

"Admit it," he teases, scooting closer on the couch. He takes my drink from my hand, then sets them both on the table." It was fantastic, wasn't it?"

I sniff with an air of aloofness, my head now swimming with the fact we're actually talking about *the* kiss that so thoroughly rocked my world. "I'll do no such thing."

"You will," he promises, and the ominous tone causes a shiver to run up my spine.

"I won't," I maintain, lifting my chin in the air.

Dax lurches toward me. Before I know it, I'm flat on my back on the couch. He's on top of me, straddling me, his fingers at my ribs, tickling me mercilessly.

"Admit it," he says as he laughs and tickles the hell out of me.

Laughing, I squirm and claw at his hands, shrieking, "I won't do it. You can't make me."

And then, he's not tickling me. He pins my hands against the leather cushions above my head. My chest is rising and falling, and Dax's smile is starting to fade.

We stare at each other for a long moment before he finally says, "If you won't admit it, maybe your memory needs jogged."

My lips part, a slight gasp of surprise and longing escaping. When he hears it, he knows what it means.

Bending closer, he kisses me.

CHAPTER 7

Dax

I AM NOT buzzed enough to even blame this on the consumption of alcohol, fatigue from the game, or worry over Tacker. In my conscience, I know this is so very fucking wrong. Yet, rather than retreat, I squeeze onto her wrists and deepen the kiss.

If Regan would just lie still, try to turn her head away, or even attempt to tug out of my grip, I'd consider stopping.

But she doesn't.

When my tongue touches hers, she moans, and it's not a shy or hesitant sound. It's a fucking invitation, and there's just enough alcohol in my system I won't deny her.

I drop my body on hers, settling right in against the vee of her legs, and there's no hiding my erection. She wiggles under me—rubs and grinds against my cock—and fuck…that just went from zero to sixty in nothing flat. It's enough that doubt takes hold, and I break the kiss to look at her.

"Don't stop, Dax," she orders breathlessly. "You just grab whatever misguided sense of moral duty that's flitting around that head of yours and get rid of it."

As if to make sure I don't misconstrue what she's saying, she lifts her hips to press herself to me. Groaning, I lower my face—not to kiss her again, but to press my forehead against hers. Trying to clear my head, I squeeze my eyes shut. I can feel Regan trembling under me, our chests rising and falling because we're both restless with lust, need, and alcohol.

"Lance would kill me right now if he were here," I murmur so she knows exactly what my hesitation is. "You're his little sister. He'd want me to protect you."

I'm stunned when Regan pulls free of my grasp, puts her hands to my chest, and shoves to get me off her. When I roll toward the back of the couch, she slides out from under me. My dick is aching in protest at the loss of her heat. More than that, I feel a hollow pain in the center of my chest.

Regan rolls off the couch, staring at me with hard eyes. "Lance isn't here, and I have to believe that wherever he is, he's in a place where he wouldn't judge. Now, I know this marriage is fake and I went along with it because you're right… it's the best way to save my life right now. But I'm not going to pretend there isn't an attraction between us. You can look at me like a little sister if you want—can war with your conscience until the cows come home for all I care—but I've learned one thing in the last few years. Life is too short to pass up opportunities, and I'm not going to feel guilty for being attracted to you. So if you want to take advantage of the situation that has presented itself tonight—granted, due to alcohol that's loosened some inhibitions—then I suggest you kiss me again. If not, I suggest a cold shower."

I push off the couch slowly, my lips curving up in an almost predatory smile. "Quite a little speech you just gave there, Mrs. Monahan."

Regan flushes, perhaps at the blunt reminder that no matter the complicated circumstances, she's my wife. Under the eyes of the law, it's totally appropriate for us to have sex. But what really got me—what has me now stalking toward her around the coffee table—was her saying wherever Lance is, he wouldn't judge. As close as I was to Lance, Regan was closer and knew her brother far better than I ever could. I do believe that, just for tonight, I'm going to believe her.

Just for tonight.

Come tomorrow, there's going to be a lot of blame on alcohol, but I'll cross that bridge when we get to it. Right now, I want her too much to listen to my conscience anymore.

Lengthening my strides, I reach her in two steps. Hands to her face, I slam my mouth onto hers. The minute her arms wind around my neck, my hands go to her ass and I lift her. It's an intimate, commanding move, and Regan responds by locking her legs tightly around my waist.

I kiss her fervently as I walk to the door off the main living area that houses the master suite. It's not fully closed so I just push on through and barrel right toward my bed. I manage to crawl up it still holding her, then settle her right underneath me. My mouth moves from hers, across her cheek, and then down her neck. Regan's delicate fingers slide through my hair. When my hips settle down on hers, she lifts her legs and uses her thighs to hold me tight.

Dragging my mouth over her collarbone to the base of her throat, I start to work at the buttons of her blouse, exposing more and more flesh the farther south I move.

When my lips skate over a lump not far under her collarbone, my eyes spring open. I lift my head so I can see and a round protrusion pushing against her skin alarms me. "What is that, Regan?"

Her own eyes spring open, then she glances at her chest. When she laughs, I feel a slight relief.

"That's my port-o-cath," she says. Taking my hand in hers, she presses my fingertips against it. "It's how I get my Salvistis infusion."

"Oh," I say in fascination as I touch it gently. "Does it hurt?"

"Not really."

"So they just stick a needle right in there?"

"Pretty much."

"Wow."

I run my finger over it again, then dip my head to brush my lips over it. The skin is just as soft there as everywhere else, but with a little bit of hardness. It's like Regan herself—soft and strong.

But enough of that. I draw my lips down farther, moving past the port in her chest that receives her lifesaving medication. Regan squirms and writhes, murmuring my name like a prayer.

I keep my eyes open, watching carefully, not wanting to miss an inch of her skin. The swell of her breasts, the lace edge of her bra. Things I've seen a million times before but never like this.

Never like Regan.

Front catch easily unclasps, and I nudge the edges of her bra aside with my nose. When her fingers tighten in my hair, I drag my tongue up the inside of her breast, across the top, and flick her nipple.

"Dax," Regan cries, and I suck on her gently.

She bucks under me, so fucking responsive, and my entire body vibrates with the need to be in her.

But come on, Dax. She's Lance's goddamn little sister.
Baby sister.

Sister to you.

This is fucked up and gross and not meant to be in a million years.

I lift my head slightly, her nipple popping free of my mouth, and I let my conscience break through the passion. Blinking my eyes several times, I still hesitate. While I understand clearly what I was just trying to tell myself, this does not feel gross or wrong in the slightest.

But I should stop. I know I should.

Regan's fingers slide through my hair, come to the top of my head, and then give me a push. A significant push with one lonely word uttered along with it. "Lower."

"Christ," I mutter, my dick now so hard I'm afraid it's going to rip through my zipper. The thought of me going lower, dragging my mouth over her stomach, my tongue through her sex…

I rear upward, a surge of lust locking me into an unbreakable mission to make Regan come. Scuttling backward, I start deftly undoing the button and zipper of her jeans. I vaguely notice Regan coming to her elbows to watch me jerk the clothing from the lower part of her body. Thank fuck she doesn't have shoes on because it will be a hell of a lot easier to get her naked.

It's a mistake to actually glance up at Regan. Her

breasts are jutted forward, the cups of her bra having spilled completely open. Her shirt still hooked on her shoulders, cheeks flushed, and eyes sparkling as she watches me intently. I have her panties and jeans an inch or so below her hips, the promised land just about to be revealed to me. The expression on her face is almost daring.

Do it, do it, do it, her eyes seem to tell me.

I fucking do it. Sliding everything off her long legs, baring it all to my hungry eyes, I step from the bed to the floor. I take Regan's ankles, turn her slightly, and spread her legs wide before I take a good, long look at the beauty in between.

I glance to her face, which is now nothing but wide eyes and teeth nibbling into her lower lip in anticipation. Dropping to my knees, I slide my hands beneath her ass and pull her right into my mouth.

Regan yells my name as my tongue drives right into her, her hips bucking up. I move an arm to cover her belly, pressing her into the mattress, and get to work on eating her pussy like I've never eaten a meal in my life.

I feel her fingers in my hair, clutching and gripping. Her hips rotate, trying to get more from me, so I growl, "Hold still."

Of course, she doesn't listen, so I maneuver my arms to pin her in place. I use my tongue against her clit, licking and grating against it quickly to drive her up as fast as possible. I want her to come now, and I want it to tear her apart.

"Dax," Regan screams as her hips lift all the way off the bed, her legs slamming into the side of my head, ringing my bell good. I slip a finger inside of her, feeling the sucking, pulsing tremors of her orgasm, which causes my lips to curl into a wicked smile.

Lifting my head, I gaze up her body. She's not staring at me but rather the ceiling. She's huffing, her nipples budded tight, and God... I need to fuck her.

I take the opportunity while she's wrecked to start disrobing. Shoes, socks, belt. Her head lifts from the bed as she watches me fumble at the buttons to my shirt, lifting it and my t-shirt underneath off in one fell swoop. Regan lifts her torso slightly, shrugging out of her shirt and bra as I scramble out of my pants and boxers. The entire time, we just watch each other, my tongue still tingling with the taste of her.

It's necessary to turn away from her, but only for a moment as I stride into my bathroom to grab a condom from my linen closet. I know a lot of dudes who keep them in the bedside table, but I don't bring women to my place. Not since that batshit crazy Nanette Pearson decided to sue me after we fucked.

I snag a condom, start for the bedroom, but then pause and turn back.

I grab another.

When I make it to the bedroom, I find Regan has gotten busy with the comforter and sheets, pulling them all down to expose a perfectly blank canvas of white cotton, her naked body stretched languidly out.

Fuck... but she is utterly perfect.

As I make my way toward her, fisting foiled condom packets, her gaze travels boldly down my body to focus on my erection. It's so hard it's standing straight up. My balls feel overly heavy, and I think I'm so turned on with need for her it's going to hurt a little when I come.

That's okay, though. I have a feeling deep in my gut this is going to feel better than anything I've ever experienced before.

I crawl onto the bed, straight up her body where her legs spread in invitation. I bring my mouth to hers, knowing she's fully tasting the orgasm she just had on my tongue. She groans and returns my kiss roughly, hands going to my hips to urge me to her.

Pushing a condom into her hand as I rise to my knees, I say, "Put it on me."

Regan scoots up, leaning against my pillows and headboard. Inching forward, I wrap my hand around my cock, bringing it closer. Within moments, she has the rubber out of the package and lined up over the fat head. The first touch of her fingers on me causes my balls to pull inward.

I dig my teeth down into my lower lip, causing pain

to get more in control of myself. She rolls the sheath over my length, letting her fingers stray down the length and flutter over my balls before she scoots into a prone position.

I follow suit, coming down on top of her. My cock knows the way, instinctually pressing right to her core. Regan's legs spread, raise, and I start to slide in.

Fuck, I'd been right…

This is heaven.

CHAPTER 8

Regan

D AX IS LONG and thick. He stretches me to a fullness
I didn't think was possible. Granted, I don't have a
ton of experience at this and what he did with his
mouth was an incredible first for me, but when I say he
fills me... I'm not just talking physically.

There is some sort of connection between us that
seems... almost ancient. Like maybe it existed before we
were ever created.

Or is that the romantic in me that refuses to die? Is
it a futile hope from a girl who married a man she loves
but not in the way a wife should love a husband, but
perhaps sappily yearns it could turn into something
more? Am I just being a foolish and naive girl instead of
a woman who just had a man put his mouth between
her legs and made her orgasm in like a nanosecond?

I'd possibly continue to ponder these myths and
fantasies if it weren't for the fact Dax bottoms out in

me, and I'm fully impaled by this large man. Completely at his mercy, my body a vessel for him to do with what he wants.

And I want him to do anything and everything. I'm not stupid. If not for the bourbon, we would not be here right this moment.

Dax lifts his hips, starting to slide free. I want to protest, but his mouth returns to mine and I swallow it back. The mechanics of sex comes back and before I can even yearn for his thickness, he's pushing into me again.

Stuffing me so very full.

"Are you okay, Regan?" he murmurs against my lips, hips still moving leisurely against me.

"More than." My voice is soft and dreamy, and it causes Dax to lift his head.

His eyes search mine as if something in my tone causes him to doubt my words.

I merely smile at him languidly, curling a hand behind his neck to play with the ends of his hair. "It feels good, Dax."

"I don't want to hurt you," he replies gravely. "I mean… anything I need to be careful of given…"

"The PNH?" I finish. "No, I'm fine. I promise. The treatment does the job."

Relief washes over Dax's face, and he touches his forehead to mine briefly. "Okay… good. That's good."

I bring my hands to his face, causing him to lift his

head to give me his attention. "I'm not breakable."

"Understood," he says. He rotates his hips, causing my eyes to practically cross. When I focus on him, he's grinning at me wickedly. "Like that?"

"More."

"I can do that," he promises, then puts his mouth to mine once again.

Dax starts to thrust in and out of me slowly. He kisses me with no greater pace, as if he has all the time in the world for us to make love. I'm immediately lost, swept away in the sensation of melding with someone.

Yes, a complete combining.

I realize with utter clarity I've not lost a romantic bone in my body with my sterile marriage. I've found something so unique and special I thank the bourbon gods for giving me the chance to experience this.

"Mmm," Dax groans as he presses deep into me. I gasp, pressure starting to build within me again.

Again. Is it even possible this fast? I've never had a double. Not with a man anyway. Besides, like I said, those opportunities have been rare.

I break the kiss. "Dax," I moan as he goes even deeper. "I'm... I'm..."

"What, Regan?" he whispers, his body somehow responding to the need in my voice and moving faster within me. "What do you need? Tell me, and I'll give it to you."

My response comes in short, panting bursts. "Already. Giving. It."

"Are you going to come again?" he growls, and I nod furiously.

"Fuck," he growls, pushing up to his elbows. Dax puts a hand behind my thigh, raises that leg, and angles in deep. He does that over and over again, his hips pistoning faster. All the while he stares at me with hot eyes. I can't look away even though it feels so good I think my own eyes are going to roll into the back of my head.

The pressure builds and bubbles, straining to get free. I want it to let loose, but I'm slightly afraid I might get lost in it.

"Touch yourself," Dax orders through gritted teeth. There's a vein standing out on his forehead, and it appears he might be in pain, but I can't be sure.

"What?" I gasp.

He halts his movement, grinning in such a way that makes my belly flutter. His voice is low, rumbling. "Take your fingers, put them between your legs, and touch yourself while I fuck you."

Dax doesn't wait for me to comply, but merely starts deeply thrusting again. Immediately, the pressure is building low in my belly.

"Do it, Regan," he orders, watching me like a hawk as I slide one hand slowly over my belly to where he wants me to go.

I know exactly where to touch. That's not a mystery, but I've never done it for a man. There's no doubt he's asking me to do this not only for myself, but also for him. He wants to watch me do this.

When the pad of my index finger finds my clit, it's not like anything I've ever felt before. The thickness of him moving just under it and the friction I give from above causes bright lights to flash in my eyes. Dax starts pounding inside of me. All it takes is one soft swipe of my finger in a circular pattern around my sensitive flesh before I'm soaring.

"Oh, God," I cry, bucking hard against the orgasm that starts to shred me from the inside out.

"Yes," Dax growls triumphantly, planting himself deeply inside me. His body goes tight, then starts to tremble as his forehead once again drops to mine. Despite what feels like a violent rumble of release coursing through him, his voice is soft as velvet as he sighs, "Oh, Regan."

Settling his weight on me gently, Dax pulls me into him and rolls to his side. His hand goes to the back of my head, and he presses my face into the crook of his neck where we just lay quietly for a time.

Even though the orgasm I just had was the most powerful I've ever head, I come down quickly, finding it incredibly easy to cuddle into his warmth. There's a trust factor there I've never had the luxury of with anyone else, because I inherently know Dax would never hurt me. Even if he weren't a cuddler, I am family to him. He'd never push me away for fear of hurting my feelings.

Dax brushes his lips across my head before loosening his hold, pulling away from me slightly. I look up at him, glad to see no regret in his expression. He smiles, leaning to place a kiss on my forehead before saying, "Let me get cleaned up. You need anything?"

I shake my head slowly, a smile playing at my own lips. I'm so well satisfied right now I'm not sure I need anything more in this world.

Turning to my side, I shamelessly watch Dax as he moves from the bed to the master bath. He turns on the light, illuminating every glorious inch of him.

He's a tall man, but most hockey players are. What I didn't know was how cut he was beneath his clothes or layers of hockey gear. Dax's muscles bulge as he moves about the bathroom, removing the condom and running a warm cloth over his cock, ass rounded and paler than the rest of his tan skin. His body is an art form.

Dax turns my way, catches me ogling, and gives me a sly wink. When he turns out the light, I force myself to keep my eyes on his face.

He slides into bed, laying on his side to face me. His elbow goes to the mattress, his head to his hand to stare at me. I settle my head into a pillow, feeling a slight bit of shyness as I return his smile.

"I should have asked you about the PNH before we started having sex," he says, which catches me off guard. So not what I thought our post-sex talk would be.

My eyebrows draw inward. "What?"

"I should have made sure it was okay. That I couldn't hurt you or something. For that, I'm sorry."

"But you're not sorry we had sex, right?" I ask.

Smirking, he taps me on the nose with a fingertip. "Stop changing the subject... what's your 'normal' like now you're receiving the Salvistis?"

Dax has become educated about PNH. I was impressed what he'd learned from reading up on it before coming to my apartment, and we spent a lot of time talking about how dangerous the disease was before Salvistis came along. I had told him how I suffered horrific abdominal pain, headaches, and extreme lethargy. A mere touch could cause a massive bruise. Sometimes I'd be so fatigued and breathless because my red blood cells weren't moving oxygen I couldn't get out of bed. And I couldn't think. It was like my brain wouldn't work. Words wouldn't come, and I'd feel lost and foggy all the time. The extreme dangers were of bleeding out or throwing a clot, and I had to depend on blood transfusions to keep me alive.

Everything had been improved with the miracle of

Salvistis, but it was not a cure. We never got into what it didn't do for me.

"Well, you've been around me for the last few days," I say, letting him learn from his own experiences. "I'm pretty normal. I sometimes get hit with fatigue that comes out of nowhere."

"What does that feel like?" he asks.

"Sometimes, I'll wake up after a full night of sleep and won't feel like I got even a minute. My eyes will be really heavy, and it will seem impossible to get out of bed. And I still have brain fog sometimes. You'll eventually notice it. I might not be able to finish a sentence because the words will get lost. It's like being under the influence of cold medicine or something. But that's pretty much it."

"You're doing it again," he says, and I blink in confusion. "Minimizing things. Like it's no big deal."

I shake my head. "I don't think it's not a big deal. I'm just so grateful I can lead a relatively normal life now. It's nice to get up every morning and be able to go to work. Prior to the medication, I might be able to get up and go to work or I might be in the hospital getting a transfusion."

Dax shakes his head, his expression solemn. "You're pretty incredible, Regan. And to think you handled so much of this on your own, living out in California while Lance was based in New York."

"He was there for me," I say. "We still talked by phone every day and texted more than that. He was a great support, and, of course, I couldn't have afforded the treatment. Even with his insurance, the out-of-pocket was way too rich for my blood."

"It's still unbelievable to me," he murmurs. "How something can be that far out of reach for so many people."

"There's Medicaid insurance. Plus, the pharmaceutical company has private funds it awards to those in need. In fact, I applied to one of their programs right after Lance died and I realized the insurance was gone. I still haven't heard from them yet, but it takes time to get through the process I guess."

"It's moot now," Dax says. "It can go to someone else who needs it since you'll have my insurance. Speaking of which, you should be getting your new card in soon. I had you added yesterday."

"Awesome. I've got my new request for the Salvistis into my case manager. Since you have a different insurance than what I was on, we have to go through the entire approval process. Hopefully, she'll be able to push it through before my next treatment."

Dax's eyes turn dark with worry. "And when is that?"

"I'm due for a transfusion middle of next week," I reply.

"How long does it take?"

"About thirty minutes," I say. "A nurse will come right here to the house to give it to me."

"Do you need me here?"

"Not at all," I assure him.

"Well, the good thing is if you're tired, you just stay in bed. You don't have to worry about going to work and—"

"I intend to get a job, Dax."

"But you don't need to."

"But I want to."

"It's not—"

My fingertips go to his lips, quieting him effectively. "If I'm well enough to do what you and I just did, I'm pretty sure I'm okay enough to work."

I expect Dax to argue because he likes to be right. An annoying little habit I'm sure is going to cause a fight before too long, but to my surprise, he merely pulls me into his arms and settles down into the pillows.

"Fine," he eventually says as I lay my head on his chest. "But just know… there isn't anything you'll want for while you're here with me. I'll take care of you just the way Lance would have wanted me to."

It's nice to welcome the comfort of those words. For the first time since Lance died, I felt incredibly secure. And I love Dax all the more for it.

CHAPTER 9

Dax

I KNOW I should get out of bed since I usually meet Legend, Bishop, and Erik at the arena gym for a workout before our team meeting and practice. At least, that's what I normally do on non-game days.

But my alarm went off almost half an hour ago, and I've been pretty much just laying here with Regan's naked body curled into mine. She's softly snoring and it's adorable. For the first time since the season started, I'm choosing not to workout, putting something else above my priority to hockey. I'd considered waking Regan up with my hand between her legs, but I had second thoughts. I have no clue what types of regrets I'm going to be faced with this morning, and I'd rather figure that out first. So I dozed on and off again, contemplating whether I'm regretful for my actions last night.

I was by no means drunk after having three pretty

quick bourbons while we talked. Yes, I was buzzed, but I'd still known right from wrong. I had the power within my own reasoning to stop what we were doing, but fuck… I hadn't wanted to.

In fact, I can't remember ever wanting anything as bad, so, selfishly, I took.

The covers and sheets are kicked to the bottom of the bed. More than a time or two since the sun started filtering in, I've studied Regan's nude form laying against me. Her upper body is across mine, her breasts mashed softly into my chest. I worry about whether it bothers the port in her chest, but she sleeps on soundly. She has one leg in between mine where my soft dick is pressed up against the silkiness of her skin with the other stretched across the mattress. One arm is curled around her head with her fingertips floating right at the side of my neck. I've got one arm wrapped around her with my palm flat against her beautiful ass. Her breath fans across the top of my chest. I've been in this position a few hours, and I could go a few hours more. She's like a soothing blanket over my body, which I have no desire to remove any time soon.

I think this means I have zero fucking regrets.

Now the question is… does she?

My phone vibrates on my nightstand, and I reach a long arm out to nab it. It's Legend. He's probably wondering where the hell I am. I tap the button that will send it straight to voice mail, then set it on the bed beside me. I don't feel like entering the real world just yet. I've still got a beautiful, naked woman in my arms—whom I'm married to and fucked last night. I would like to keep fucking her, but I don't know if that's possible.

Or even ethical at this point.

Vibrations from my phone ringing again tickle against my thigh. When I realize it's Legend calling again, I know it must be something important for him to call right back. A freezing chill sneaks up my spine as my thoughts immediately turn dark, wondering if Tacker has done something to himself.

"What's up?" I say into the phone when it connects, trying to sound nonchalant. Regan stirs at the sound of my voice, but I merely tighten my hold around her waist. This causes her to lift her head, and she stares at me blearily having just woken from a sound sleep.

I give her a smile and she returns it, which brings me relief. Regret was not the very first thing on her mind, apparently. Regan lays her head down on my chest, and fuck if I want to get out of bed today.

"Just went to the hospital to see Tacker," Legend says, and that causes me to sit up a little straighter. I haul Regan with me.

"He let you in?" I ask.

"Didn't have a choice. I just walked in. He was by

himself when I got there."

"How is he?"

"Banged up. Broken wrist, but that will heal, and he was getting discharged. As I was leaving, there was a police officer there to arrest him."

"Fuck," I growl, causing Regan to push off me. She brushes hair away from her face, which is incredibly beautiful despite her eyes being puffy with sleep and a tiny bit of drool at the corner of her mouth. Her expression is grave in reaction to my tone, and she tilts her head in question. I give a slight shake of my head—indicating I'll fill her in later—then ask Legend, "What does that mean for the team?"

"No clue," he says. "But if I had to guess, I'm thinking he's not going to be a factor on our team."

"Think he'll be cut?"

"Maybe," he muses. "But no sense in worrying about it. I just called to let you know why I didn't make our workout."

"Yeah, I didn't make it either," I admit, glancing at Regan who is still leaning up on one arm, staring at me. My eyes drop to her breasts, to the bump where her port is, then farther to the treasure between her legs. I fucking want that again… and more than once. When I return my eyes to her face, her cheeks are pink, but she holds my gaze.

"You feeling okay?" Legend asks. To his way of

thinking, the only thing that would keep me away from a workout would be if I was on death's door.

I can't really say, *Sure, man... just lying in bed with my wife who I'm going to fuck again after we hang up.*

So I say, "Yeah... I'm good. I'll see you at practice, though."

"Later, brother," he says and then disconnects.

I reach an arm across the bed, place my phone on the table, and turn to Regan. "That was Legend. He saw Tacker this morning briefly. Looks like he's going to be arrested for driving under the influence."

"Oh, that's bad," she murmurs. "I'm sorry."

"Yeah, me too." I take in Regan's posture, still leaning casually with one arm planted into the mattress, her legs curled to the side. Her expression gives nothing away as to how she feels waking up naked next to me after we fucked last night. "You feel okay?"

She grimaces slightly. "Actually... I've got a bit of a headache, which I'm assuming is the bourbon, or maybe I'm a bit dehydrated."

"Could it be the PNH?" I ask, immediately throwing my legs over the side of the bed to exit. I pad into the bathroom, then grab a Dixie cup of water and some headache medicine.

When I return, she continues, "Probably not. This feels alcohol induced."

"Were you drunk last night?" I hand her the water

and painkillers.

She accepts both but before taking them, she asks a question of her own, "Is that what you think? That I didn't know what I was doing?"

"Well, did you?" I can't help the defensiveness in my tone. I feel like I have the right to wonder about these things. There's no offense to her, but I'm probably on edge because I'm going to feel fucking wretched if it was a mistake on her part.

Regan rolls her eyes. "Of course I knew what I was doing. I mean… I think I did."

Fuck, she has doubts. "You either did or didn't. If you weren't in control of—"

"I was in control," she snaps. "I made my choice. Perhaps with some bolstering by the alcohol, but it was still a valid choice."

"But you just said you 'thought' you knew what you were doing," I point out, crossing my arms over my chest. "Not that you 'absolutely' knew what you were doing."

Regan blushes so much the redness creeps from her cheeks to her neck and chest. She blinks for a moment and then rolls off the bed, searching for her clothing.

She thinks she's going to avoid me, but that's not going to happen. Rounding the bed, I step into her path. "Did you or did you not know what you were doing?"

With a resounding growl of frustration, Regan snaps, "I'm not sure. We did things I'd never done before, so I don't know if I was any good at it."

"What?" I ask, taking a slightly stumbling step back as if she'd just punched me in the chest. She doesn't know if she was any good at it? It was only the best sex of my life, and she—

A thought strikes, horrifying me. "Were you a virgin?"

"God no," she exclaims, equally in horror. "But... I'm just not that experienced. And, well, when you... um... went down... Um. What I mean is—"

"I get it, Regan," I murmur, moving closer to her. She tries to lower her gaze, but my fingers go under her chin and I force her to look at me. "Just how much experience have you had?"

She shrugs, but doesn't say a word.

"Regan... you and I did some really intimate things last night. I think we're beyond the shy shit, okay?"

"One guy," she blurts out. "My first and only boyfriend. We met our freshman year in college, and we were eighteen when we first had sex. Neither of us knew what we were doing apparently. And then, well... after I got sick, I mean... who had time for boyfriends or sex?"

"Did he leave you because you were sick?" The anger in my tone comes across with bite.

"Yes, but that's in the past and I don't dwell on it,

so don't go thinking I need some therapy for it. The whole point to this is it's been a while since I had sex, my boyfriend never put his mouth between my legs, and I'm not even sure if there was something else I should have been doing last night to make it good for you."

My entire world about collapses in on itself as my chest constricts over the uncertainty in her voice. This beautiful creature who has struggled against so much should never have a single doubt. "Regan," I murmur as I scoop her up and crawl onto the bed with her. I settle her on my lap, then twist her so she can see me. "You were perfect last night. I just hope I didn't freak you out."

"No, not at all. Okay... maybe a little. I mean... it was, well... I don't know what it was."

"Did you like it?" I ask, and her cheeks flame red again.

"Yes," she whispers, dropping her gaze.

"Regan," I say to get her attention. When she raises her head, I force her to confront it. "Tell me you liked my mouth between your legs last night. Tell me you liked how it felt and the way it made you come."

I get a groan filled with embarrassment in response. She flops forward, then presses her face into my neck. "I said I liked it. That should be good enough."

My arms go around her naturally, and it would be the perfect time to chuckle in amusement over her lack of experience and shyness. But the truth is… it's now causing me to have regrets.

I brought Regan into my home—my life—with the sole intention of helping her get the medical treatment she needed to save her life. The marriage was simply a means to an end, and it conveyed to me no special privileges. I was weak last night, and I took something I wanted.

A woman who doesn't have much experience at all, and certainly shouldn't be cast under the shadow of a man who isn't looking for anything serious but sure does like a whole lot of dirty fucking. Regan is way too good for a man like me. In a way, I feel like I've just tainted her. She's nowhere near ready for someone like me.

And I really don't think I'm ready for someone like her.

I choose my words very carefully. "Look… last night, we both succumbed to loosened inhibitions because of the alcohol, and the last thing in the world I want is for you to be in an environment where things are confusing or awkward for you. Our primary responsibility has got to be your health. I shouldn't have ever gone there with you last night, Regan, and I'm really sorry."

They're the wrong fucking words. I can see it on her face. Pure rejection and hurt reflected in her eyes, even though she puts on an overly bright smile. "Yes. Of course, you're right. I think we got a little crazy last night. We're adults so let's just chalk it up to 'oops, probably shouldn't do that again'. Right?"

"Right," I drawl with a fair amount of uncertainty, torn between wanting to reassure her this has nothing to do with her and needing to be strong enough to put a break between us.

Regan scrambles off my lap, rolls off the bed, and starts grabbing her clothes as she talks. "Last night was great and all. Thank you for having patience with me. But we both have more important things to focus on. You've got hockey, and Tacker is really important. I've got to concentrate on my illness, and I want to get out and find a job. If I'm going to be here a while, I need to assimilate. So yeah—"

And here, she pauses to study me, holding her pile of clothing in front of her chest. Her chin lifts in confidence. "Maybe we should just forget this ever happened and move forward with our original plan. Let's stick to being friends, which we know we're great at. Sound good?"

"Yeah," I reply sort of stupidly.

"Perfect." Her smile is bright, and I don't detect any uncertainty in her now. I do think she's decided to move on. For a brief moment, I marvel at her strength and determination. I respect the fuck out of it particularly because I'm not feeling as positive about all this the way she seemingly is.

I can't even enjoy her perfect ass as she turns on her heel and heads out of my bedroom, too intent on my own internal feelings.

I think I just gave up something really fucking good.

CHAPTER 10

Regan

I WALK OUT of Dax's bedroom with my clothes clutched loosely in my hands and my chin lifted proudly. I know he's watching my naked backside, so I put an extra sway to my hips as I disappear from his sight. The minute I'm out in the hallway, I quickly dash to my bedroom, shutting the door behind me. Once I'm safely away from Dax's pitying eyes, I lean against my bedroom door and sink onto the carpet. My chest is constricted, and my heart is pounding like a runaway train.

Damn it, that hurt.

I didn't think anything could hurt worse than when my ex-boyfriend, Paul, broke up with me because of me having PNH.

"I'm sorry, Regan," he had told me in a sad, almost whiny voice. "But this is too much for me to handle. I can't just sit around and wait for you to die."

I had thought the words were incredibly harsh. They had broken my heart, even though I know he hadn't intended to. I thought when people loved someone, they stayed with them through thick and thin. Their problems and pain became their partner's problems, too.

Paul just couldn't handle it, and I suffered my first major crushing heartbreak of my life. I had immediately called Lance, and he sat patiently while I sobbed on the phone. He was actually in the locker room getting ready for a game, but he never pressed me to hurry. He just let me vent and pour my heart out to him.

Yes, Lance was older and supposedly wiser than me. But he had never had a real relationship with a woman, so I hadn't known if his advice was accurate. He had told me, "Regan... I'm going to propose to you that it wasn't really love with Paul. If it was, he never would have done that to you."

I eventually accepted that advice because I had no other rational explanation for how someone who supposedly loved me could hurt me so badly.

And while Dax and I are nothing but friends, and we were only intimate once, the pain I'm feeling in the center of my chest seems a million times more debilitating. And I don't understand that. Dax and I are not in love. We love and care for each other as friends, but we've never said those words to each other. He's helping me out of the kindness of his heart and a duty he feels he owes to Lance. It's not even actually a duty or an obligation to me. In fact, I think this is his way to keep Lance's memory strong and alive purely for himself.

When I inhale a shuddering breath, it comes out staccato like.

Damn. Damn. Damn.

Why does it hurt so much?

Dax rejected me for reasons that have to do with me being me. Same as Paul.

I sit there a moment with my head against the door, wondering how I'm going to face Dax again. The way he managed to break things off before they even really got started was humiliating. He tried to play it off as if he were doing what was best for me. Telling me he didn't want things to be confusing or awkward for me when I should really be concentrating on my health. But I also saw other things on his face. When I admitted to him how inexperienced I had been, I'd seen what I was fairly sure was pity. Particularly when I told him my boyfriend had dumped me because I was sick. I felt like such a loser admitting those things.

But I have to give myself a slight pat on the back. I recovered, pulled myself together, and gave him the brightest, most unaffected smile I believe I've ever given in my entire life, then told him that we should just forget it ever happened. But I know I won't. I'll dwell on it for quite some time. There's no doubt I will always wonder what could have been.

But one thing I've gotten incredibly good at over the last few years since being diagnosed with PNH is learning how to put on a façade so the people around me would never guess my inner turmoil. I've learned how to keep my pain and vulnerability internally squirreled away from the rest of the world, not because I'm afraid to share it.

But because I don't want to burden others.

So I'm going to do the same thing right now with Dax. I'm going to continue to accept his gracious help, I'm going to find a job, and then I'm going to start school in the fall. Once I complete my masters, I'm going to move back to California. I vow to myself I'm not going to regret a single thing I have been through.

Because when it boils down to it, it doesn't seem like Dax is any different than Paul. I am just too much of a complicated mess for most people. Which means I need to continue to learn how to do things on my own without relying on anyone else.

I take another deep breath. The air flows into my lungs smoothly and comes out just the same. Feeling somewhat fortified and a whole lot determined, I push myself off the floor. Over the next forty-five minutes, I take a shower. To make myself feel better, I even do my hair and makeup. By the time I make it into the kitchen, I'm relieved to see Dax has already left for the gym. He left me a note on the kitchen counter that said he would be back later in the afternoon and would be glad to take me out to dinner. I make a mental note not to be here this afternoon when he comes back. Maybe I'll go out and see a movie. Treat myself to a nice dinner and some ice cream after.

I fix breakfast—granola, yogurt, and a fresh banana—and settle in at my laptop to continue my job search. It can be somewhat difficult to find work since I can only commit part-time hours and have no intention of staying permanently. I know there are many people who would never reveal those intentions to a prospective employer, but I don't feel that is fair. So I've been upfront to every place I've applied. In the handful of interviews I've done over the phone, I was transparent in my future plans about moving back to California and my disease. I need to make sure that whoever hires me does so with the knowledge I come with baggage.

My phone rings. I glance at my phone, recognizing the familiar phone number. The name brings a smile to my face. Dr. Timothy Marino.

I don't know if it's actually Dr. Marino or his nurse, but I answer with a cheery smile on my face that comes naturally because of who is on the other end. "Hello."

"Hey, Regan. It's Mary."

My smile gets bigger. While I adore and have the utmost respect for Dr. Marino, his nurse has become a little bit like a sort of mom to me over the past year since I've become a patient.

When I was first diagnosed with PNH, there was great relief in knowing the name to my problem. But because the disease is so rare, there are few doctors who actually have enough education and training to be able to properly treat it. Lance immediately stepped in and started using his pull as a professional hockey player. In the end, we ultimately decided to have my treatment handled by Dr. Marino at Duke University Medical Center in Durham, North Carolina.

He was highly recommended. When we first contacted him by phone, he didn't talk down to us or over our heads. There was just a natural chemistry, and Lance and I flew to Durham to meet him.

It wasn't a hardship living in California and having my doctor clear across the country. I only had to see him twice a year. My lab work could be handled by my primary care doctor in California. My treatments could also be completed in California. Because of the distance between us, Dr. Marino and his nurse Mary did a lot of communicating with me via phone and FaceTime. Perhaps because of the distance, they put in extra effort, time, and care with me. Over the last year, we've grown remarkably close. Dr. Marino even came to Lance's funeral in New York, which is a testament to that fact.

"So I heard through the grapevine you've moved

from Encinitas to Phoenix," Mary drawls.

I laugh, having expected this call eventually. The first person I had to contact with my move was my case manager with the pharmaceutical company that administers the Salvistis. They would have had to get a new referral from Dr. Marino, which they would submit to my insurance company. With the new insurance I was on, I hoped things would happen quickly this week.

"I just needed a break after the funeral," I explain, giving the story Dax and I agreed on. "I'm actually staying with Lance's best friend, Dax."

"Is he a hockey player?" she teases.

"Yes, he is," I return with a giggle.

"He's probably a little too young for me," Mary sniffs, which I don't think is the case. She's only thirty-five and incredibly pretty. But she has two teenage daughters. For some reason, she thinks that makes herself undatable.

"He's not too young for you," I chide, this not being the first time I've heard her 'woe is me trying to date as a single mom' story. "You're a totally marketable hot chick who needs to get yourself out there. But sadly, this hockey player is off the market."

"Bummer," she drawls, and I don't tell her that Dax is off the market because he's married to me. That would be way too crazy. It's just... why bother when they live on opposite sides of the country?

"But seriously," she continues, ignoring my jab that she's selling herself short. "How are you doing?"

"I'm doing well. Haven't had any major symptoms—"

"No," she butts in impatiently. "How are you doing emotionally? Not physically."

I can't help but snort. "Aren't you supposed to be worried about my physical health?"

"You're avoiding the question."

I sigh as I stare out the kitchen window. "I feel sad and alone. I thought coming to Phoenix and being around Dax would help, but I don't know…"

My words trail off. It's not lost on me that a lot of my turmoil right now has to do with the fact I had a beautiful, intimate experience with Dax last night, yet he wants no part in a continuation. That's pretty much where my loneliness is stemming from.

Pure rejection.

Mary launches into a thousand comforting words about grief and healing. I listen because I know they'll be beneficial to me. When she winds down, she lets me know Dr. Marino has signed all the necessary paperwork for my new insurance company to approve the Salvistis.

"Now just so you know, it doesn't mean they're going to approve it just because Dr. Marino has signed all the paperwork."

"I know. I expect most insurance companies are

going to balk at paying that kind of money for a drug."

"If they deny it, Dr. Marino is ready to step in on the appeal process. Just know it could take a little bit of time. So we need you to keep careful watch on yourself, Regan. You know the signs and symptoms to look for, so get your butt to a hospital if you suspect you need a transfusion."

With a resigned sigh, I say, "I understand. And I'll be careful. I promise."

I hate being back in this situation. Over the past year, I've become so reliant on the Salvistis that I had forgotten the day-to-day terror of knowing I could be one thrown blood clot away from dying. If I don't get my treatment next week as planned, I'm going to be right back in that same situation.

CHAPTER 11

Dax

"**W**HAT THE FUCK, dude?" Bishop says as I miss the rack and almost drop three hundred and fifteen pounds onto my chest. Bishop grabs the bar and helps me get it over the lip, then I roll off the bench. "Where's your head at?"

I shake it, feeling it attached at the neck, but I sure as shit wasn't concentrating the way I should while pressing that load.

"I'm good," I mutter.

"Worried about Tacker?" he asks as he takes my spot on the bench. We're both doing the same weight, working a load of five by five.

I move in behind him. Although it's not where my thoughts were just now—as they were on Regan—I admit, "Yeah. But I think if anyone can help him get through this, it's this team. We've already proven we've got some kind of magical mojo together on the ice."

Even though we're a brand-new expansion team in the league, we're currently favored to take the Cup away from the Cold Fury this year. We've just clicked that well together.

"Truer words," Bishop says before he pushes the weighted bar up and off the rack to start his set. I stand at the ready in case he needs help, but he won't.

"I'm going to invite him over to dinner one night after Willow gets here." Bishop easily finishes his set, re-racks with no fumbling issues, and rolls off the bench. "If anyone can force Tacker to interact, it's her."

"I don't know," Bishop drawls with a laugh as I straddle the bench. "Your sister can be so irritating. She might push him over the edge."

I laugh because that's true. Willow has never met a stranger. She will start up a conversation with Tacker, totally missing any anti-social cues from him. "At least Regan will temper her somewhat."

"How is Regan doing?" Bishop asks as I start to lay back on the bench. I'd like to tell him she's doing wonderfully, but I just don't know. Ever since our "heart-to-heart" talk yesterday morning, we seemed to have lapsed into a familial-type friendship. Conversation is easy and light. There's laughter. No awkwardness.

Unless I counted the fact my dick gets hard when I'm around her sometimes, I can't stop thinking about the night we were together, or that I jacked off in bed last night thinking about the way she tasted, or...

"Bro... you gonna lift or what?" Bishop asks. I startle, focusing on him to find him staring at me over the bar.

"Yeah," I mumble, getting my grip set. Then I think about the man who is hovering over the bar, there to help me in case I falter, and I remember Bishop is my best friend. It's fucking moronic not to get his advice, since I'm clearly out of sorts over Regan. Legend had been working out with us, but he doesn't stay as long as we do, having baby duties and such. The gym is nearly deserted. It's the perfect opportunity to get this shit off my chest.

I release the bar and roll off the bench, immediately launching into my story as I turn to face Bishop. "So... well, I sort of did a thing."

Bishop just stares in confusion. "A thing?"

"A big thing."

"What kind of big thing?"

"I got married," I blurt out. Bishop's eyebrows shoot so high they disappear under his hairline.

"You got married?" he asks slowly, as if he's missing out on the joke.

"To Regan," I clarify.

"Lance's sister?"

"Only Regan I know."

"Jesus Christ." Bishop sighs, then takes a seat on the

bench I'd just vacated. "Start at the beginning. I'm way too lost."

So I do. Pacing back and forth before him, I recount the shortest engagement ever. I inform him about Regan's disease, taking the time to explain what that means. His expression goes from exasperated I'd do something so foolish to gravely concerned when I tell him about the Salvistis and how expensive it is. By the end, he's nodding along with me, agreeing I hadn't a choice but to marry her to get her on my insurance.

"You did the right thing," he says encouragingly. "I'm sure Regan is grateful."

Shaking my head, I grimace. "I sort of did something else."

"What?" he asks, the approving smile sliding off his face.

"I slept with her," I admit.

"You stupid motherfucker," he says slowly, but that's not unexpected or offensive to me. It's totally legit.

"See, but here's the thing," I continue, getting to the crux of what's bothering me. "It was fucking amazing, Bishop. I mean… she's like no woman I've ever been with, and I have no clue why. And I can't figure out if what we did was right or wrong. I can't stop thinking about it. Obsessing, actually. But she's sort of moved on, I think. I mean, she acts like we're just friends and like it wasn't that big a deal, but trust me when I tell you… I feel like a big fucking girl right now admitting it to you, but it was a big deal."

"God, you're fucking screwed, Dax," Bishop mutters as he stands.

"That's it? That's your advice?" I ask incredulously.

"No, my advice is to talk to her about it. Clearly she means something important to you—"

"She did before we fucked," I growl. "Yes, she's important and there's a long-standing love and care there. But I'm talking about sex, Bishop. I'm talking about something different."

"I think it's different," he says with a sage and pointed look, "because there was already love and care there."

His words hit me with the force of a nuclear explosion, and my entire body rebels at the thought. I'm not ready for that type of "love" in my life. I'm still young and want to be free. I want to have fun and not be committed. That type of love and sex mixed together is a recipe for a relationship that is beyond what I want right now.

I start to tell him that, too, but his phone rings, which is sitting on the floor next to our towels. Legend's face is on the screen.

Bishop bends, nabs the phone, and answers, "What's up?"

I stand there, impatiently waiting for him to finish his call with Legend so we can get back to what's important. Me and my lust for Regan, or whatever it is I have.

But the expression on Bishop's face turns to horror, his skin going pale. All of my senses fire and my stomach rolls.

My immediate thoughts are of Tacker. Now, my impatience is waiting to hear what the terrible news is.

Bishop doesn't say anything to enlighten me. He ends the short call with, "I'm on my way to your place now."

When he disconnects and turns to me, I'm not prepared for his shocking words. "Lida shot Pepper and took Charlie."

"What?" I bark out, my head actually spinning. Lida is Charlie's birth mom and has been doing some crazy stalkerish stuff, but I never expected this. "Is Pepper okay?"

"Legend doesn't know," he says with a short shake of his head as he hurries to the locker room. I follow while he fills me in on the pitifully short details. "He's at his house right now with the police, and Pepper's on her way to the hospital by ambulance."

"Jesus," I curse as we scramble to get into our lockers.

Bishop pauses. "I think we need to organize a search

party."

"Come again?" I ask, beyond puzzled. "I'm sure the police—"

"Yeah, I know they'll be out looking for her," he interrupts. "I'm sure with the idea in mind she's running with Charlie. But fuck, Dax... she shot Pepper. Legend said she also pistol-whipped Lucy, the nanny. What if..."

Bishop's voice falters, and he gives a cough to clear it. Leaning in, he whispers, "What if that crazy bitch did something to Charlie? I mean... she's fucking crazy, right?"

"You think we need to be searching for Charlie?" I ask slowly, because although I understand exactly what he's saying, I absolutely don't want to consider it as a possibility.

Bishop rubs at his head. "I don't know, but this is going to be leaked to the news fast. I'm confident we're having no team practice today. I'm going to Legend's, so he has someone with him. I think you need to rally the team together, then get out there and start searching. The more eyes, the better."

A jolt of adrenaline zings through my body. "Yeah... got it. Can totally do that. And I know exactly who to recruit to help me get it going."

IF I THOUGHT I wasn't prepared to hear the news about

Lida shooting Pepper and kidnapping Charlie, I am most certainly not prepared for the haunted man who stands before us when Tacker opens the door to his apartment. It's only been a few days since his accident, but he looks like he's lost fifteen pounds. Or maybe that's just because he's shaved his entire head down to a mere stubbly buzz, which makes his cheekbones stand out gauntly.

His left arm is in a short cast, and he has scrapes and scabs all over his face from the air bag. Both eyes have a little bruising under them, and there's a cut across the bridge of his nose.

Tacker doesn't offer any greeting, just stares at me blankly. I survey the shabby apartment complex he lives in, which is shocking given the amount of money he makes. Clearly, he doesn't care about spending it.

"Team needs your help," I say, just to gauge his reaction to the word "team" because I'm not sure if he ever really felt he was a part of us. He's kept us all at such a distance, and he hasn't asked any of us for help over the course of the last several months since the season started.

And let's face it… technically, he's not part of the team. Coach told us the day after the accident that he was indefinitely suspended, and no one has heard any follow up as of yet.

"How so?" Tacker asks neutrally, not even bothering

to invite me into his place.

"Lida shot Pepper and kidnapped Charlie," I say bluntly. The guy has had it rough, but there's no time to spare him.

His eyes bug out of his head. "What?"

"Pepper is at the hospital. The police are out searching for Lida and Charlie, but the team is all out canvassing the area, too. And I figured you'd want to be in on it."

What I'm implying without actually saying is Tacker is unable to actually go out and look by himself as he is currently without a vehicle and has a pending DUI charge. Not to mention the whole broken wrist and concussion thing.

But I judged my teammate correctly, since he nods vigorously. "Yeah… of course. Let me grab my wallet and phone."

He's not gone but a minute before he returns, locking his apartment door behind him. As he follows me, he asks, "How is Pepper?"

"I haven't heard yet. Last info I had was Legend was heading to the hospital, so I expect we'll get an update soon. Bishop is going to start a group text."

After I unlock my car and we get belted, Tacker twists in his seat to face me. "Do you think Charlie is okay?"

Just last month, Legend had invited Tacker and me

to spend Christmas Eve with him and Charlie. Not much gets our big, silent, and brooding captain out of his shell, but he bonded with Charlie. Spent a good portion of the night holding her, and it was the most hopeful I'd ever been about the man.

Or at least I had been...

Until he drove his truck into a concrete barricade.

But I can see the angst in his expression. Recognize it deeply. I'm terrified Pepper might die and Charlie—

Nope... can't think like that. I'm afraid I'll vomit. "I think," I say carefully, "that Lida is a mom first and foremost. Despite the fact she's done some crazy stuff, all she's wanted since she reappeared in Legend's life was to have time with her daughter. I have got to believe that means something. That Charlie is at least safe with her."

Tacker swallows hard, then gives me a curt nod. "Then let's get going. Sooner we get out there, sooner we can find her."

"I want to go walk around Legend's neighborhood," I say. "If she doesn't have a car, she could just be hiding somewhere there."

"Sounds good," he replies as I start my car.

It's a twenty-minute drive over to Legend's neighborhood, and I don't want any of the time Tacker is my captivated audience to be wasted. At our team meeting yesterday, the entire team discussed how it was going to be a major group effort to get Tacker's head back on straight. We all committed to it. After the meeting, Bishop, Erik, Legend, and I talked about it some more. So far, we'd seen Tacker react positively to people who needed care or protection. Specifically, he's developed a pretty good bond with Blue's brother, who is disabled, and, as mentioned, with baby Charlie. It was a no brainer we'd exploit that angle.

But we'd also discussed just pressing interaction on him whether he wanted it or not. He was going to be getting a lot of pressure from all of us, and my gut said it would be a battle.

So now... while he's strapped into my passenger seat, I'm going to take advantage of the situation.

"Coach told the team you'd been indefinitely suspended." I give him a quick glance, noting his face is as stoic and expressionless as ever. "And that you got charged with a DUI."

I wait for him to respond, but he doesn't.

"So...," I drawl, indicating he should say something.

He turns his head my way, and I flick my gaze from the road to him. His voice is dry and taunting. "Was there a question in there somewhere?"

Okay, he wants to play it that way?

I'm diving in.

"How do you feel about it?" I ask.

Tacker snorts in response. "I feel shitty, that's how I

feel."

"Care to elaborate?" I press.

I get an exaggerated sigh in return and an apathetic tone. "What the fuck do you want me to say, Dax?"

It pisses me off. "I want you to acknowledge you're going to try to overcome this shit because we're all worried sick about you. I want you to say you're going to work hard to get through your issues, get your head on straight, and come back to this team because we need you. That's what I want you to say."

"Yeah?" Tacker says with a mirthless laugh. "Well, if I ever figure out what the fuck I want in life and I decide it falls in line with what you want, I'll let you know."

He's being a dick, and there's no sense in pushing him on it. Besides, it wasn't my goal to have him miraculously decide to care about things again.

I merely wanted him to know I cared, and I think I accomplished that.

CHAPTER 12

Dax

IT'S NOT EVEN seven and I'm exhausted. I pull into my driveway, stopping just short of the single car garage where Regan's car is parked. My shoulders are knotted from the tension of the day, and I'm going to be glad to eat a frozen meal and head to bed.

Granted, the day started off about as bad as it could with the news Pepper had been shot and Charlie kidnapped, but it had ended with the best possible outcome. Lida had been captured just a few hours after she took Charlie. But, most importantly, Legend's baby daughter was safe and unhurt. Pepper had come through her abdominal surgery. Luckily, the bullet caused no major damage, although she'll be in the hospital for a few days recovering.

I had been out with Tacker driving neighborhoods and lonely dirt roads during the entire time Charlie was missing. The stress of what we might have found was horrendous. We barely said a word to each other the entire time, both dreading like hell we'd find something unimaginable. When Bishop sent a message Charlie had been found to the team group text, I wanted to weep with relief. Had I not been driving at the time, I would have hugged the shit out of Tacker, but I was at least satisfied he was grinning the entire time I drove him home after hearing the good news.

Of course, I kept up my unrelenting plan to draw him into the fold. I invited him to come over for breakfast on Saturday, figuring Regan and Willow could work on him, too.

He declined.

I asked if he was going to come to the rookie party on Saturday night, which would be a great time for him to reintegrate with the team. Granted, he's suspended and technically not part of the team, but the party is not a team-sanctioned event. It happens every year on every professional team, but the management turns a blind eye to the utter hedonism of the event.

It's when the rookies of each team throw a party for the veterans, and the rookies have to bear the expense and the brunt of anything bad that happens. It's usually held at an expensive restaurant, and nothing is off limits to the veterans. That means they can order every damn item on the menu for themselves and have just a tiny bite of each thing, and drink as much alcohol as they want. And if the after-party involves women of a certain ilk, well, that expense is borne by the rookies, too. I've heard of some tabs running over a hundred thousand dollars when it's all said and done, but that's not going to happen amongst our team. It's not that we won't go out and have a wild and crazy time. We'll absolutely order the most expensive steak and supreme liquor, but we're too close to the playoffs to screw with the magical mojo we've got going on, so the veterans are not going to try to break the rookies. It's not worth it for one evening of fun.

Regardless, Tacker said he wasn't interested and turned down my invitation twice. It was time to pull out the big guns and have Erik and Blue invite Tacker on an outing with them and Blue's brother, Billy. Or have Legend ask Tacker to come over to help with Charlie while Legend visits Pepper in the hospital. I doubt he'd say no to those requests.

After dropping Tacker off, I'd gone to the arena and worked out, then we actually had a short skate practice that wasn't mandatory, but I wanted the distraction. Apparently, everyone else had, too. Only Legend was absent, but that was understandable. The informal practice had been followed by a short meeting where Coach Perron praised us for coming together as a team today, making sure we remembered we were so much more than just a bunch of talented skaters.

It was totally inspiring.

So yeah, we ended on a good note, but my shoulders are still tight with tension that probably has everything to do with Regan. I'd gotten just a few minutes to bare my soul to Bishop today about my predicament before it all went by the wayside. Rightly so, my focus was on Charlie, Pepper, and Legend—and Tacker to some degree—and I had not had much time to reflect on what he'd told me.

His advice was way too simple.

Talk to her.

Yeah, fucking fat chance of that. That means discussing feelings and emotions and other shit I'd rather stay away from. I've dealt with enough of that crap between Lance dying and finding out Regan could die without this treatment.

I think I'll just leave things alone.

Surely I'll stop obsessing about her eventually.

After exiting my car and locking it, I trudge up the steps with my workout bag over my shoulder. I'd been able to grab a quick shower at the arena after our skate, but I'm dying for a longer, hotter one to help give my shoulders and neck tension some relief.

The key slides easily in the lock. When I let myself into my townhome, I'm assailed by the most amazing aroma. I inhale deeply, eyes closed, and let out an appreciative sigh.

"Pot roast, carrots, and potatoes." Regan's voice floats toward me, and I open my eyes to see her standing in between the open-plan living room and kitchen. "I called your mom, and she walked me through how to make it. I remember it being your favorite growing up."

Christ, the squeezing in my chest rattles me a bit, knowing my body is reacting to a simple kindness a woman has done for me.

No, not any woman.

Regan. My wife—who's not really my wife—after I've had a really tiring day.

"Hope you're hungry," she continues, giving me an uncertain smile. "I wasn't sure if you'd had time to eat."

"I haven't," I say, dropping my workout bag in the foyer and placing my keys on the small round table there. The dry protein bar I had after the team skate didn't count.

"Well, sit down," she instructs, pointing to the breakfast nook table before turning into the kitchen. "I'll make you a plate."

It's at this point I should insist she doesn't have to— that I'm clearly capable of serving myself. But I don't. Instead, I sit at the table and let someone who made my favorite meal because she was concerned for me serve me as well. For these next however many moments, I'm going to pretend I have a doting wife because, right now, it feels too good to let it go.

I watch Regan carefully as she puts my meal together. There's a large pan on the top of the stove from which she serves up slices of roast beef along with caramelized carrots and potatoes onto a plate. My eyes drop to her shapely ass molded into a pair of faded jeans, sliding down to her bare feet. I'm thoroughly enjoying not only this purely male fantasy of an awesome home-cooked meal, but also of the fact I've got a hot-as-hell wife who has done so for me.

In conventional marriages, I'm wondering how appropriate it would be for the husband—that would be me—to walk up behind his gorgeous wife—that would be Regan—and take the plate from her hand.

Set it to the side.

Turn her in his arms and kiss the ever-loving hell out of her.

A kiss that would turn deep and sexual, which would lead to clothes coming off and a quick hard fuck with her bent over the kitchen table.

"Here you go," Regan chirps as she sets the plate in front of me. I blink, having been lost in the fantasy, hoping to God she can't see I've got a hard-on now. "What do you want to drink?"

"Um… water is fine," I mutter, diverting my eyes to my food because no telling what expression I have on my face right now.

Regan brings me a water, fixes herself a plate, then

sits on the opposite side of the table. We stare at each other a moment before she levels another overly bright smile at me. "Well, dig in."

Food. Right.

When I put the knife to the pot roast, it falls apart, shredding with the slightest bit of contact. The steaming aroma hits my nose again, and I have a vivid flashback of mine and Regan's families sitting down to this same exact meal for my birthday one year. I was about fourteen or fifteen, somewhere around there. My parents' dining table only had seating for eight. There were nine of us in total, so we just pulled a kitchen chair in and Regan squeezed into the corner of the table since she was the smallest.

It's a good memory, but it fades away as I take my first bite of the pot roast. It's perfectly seasoned and tastes exactly like my mom's. I'm touched Regan went to the trouble. She could have easily Googled a recipe, but she went the extra step to call up my mother, who I'm sure was all too thrilled to help her out.

"This is amazing, Regan," I say as I use the edge of my fork to split a piece of potato in half. "Thank you."

Shrugging, she spears a carrot. "It gave me something to do. I'm bored."

"You'll find something soon, I'm sure," I reply. She's used this week to put in applications to several medical facilities in the area. She's being up front about starting school in the fall, so she'll get passed up by companies needing committed, full-time nurses. "Were you able to set up your next treatment?"

"I've got an appointment with a case manager on Monday."

"And then you'll get your treatment?"

Another shrug while she pushes her food around on her plate. "Maybe. She said it could take some time to get through the approval process since I'm a new insurance subscriber."

"How much time?" I ask, putting my fork down.

"A few weeks to a month."

"Oh, hell no," I exclaim, shaking my head. "You can't wait that long."

"Yeah, well… I'm sure the insurance company will jump on it faster since you say so," Regan replies dryly.

"I'm coming to your appointment on Monday," I say as I pick up my fork. "What time is it?"

"Nine," she replies, eyes wide with surprise. "But you don't need to. It's just to go over forms and my history. Stuff like that."

"I'm going." My tone makes it clear I won't be dissuaded. "I'm not going to let them sweep you under the rug. You're getting your treatment next week."

Regan's mouth falls slightly open in shock. She wants to argue—I can see it in her eyes—but then she drops her gaze to her plate. Spearing another carrot, she pastes a resigned smile on her face. "How are Pepper and Charlie?" she asks.

I'd called Regan this morning on my way over to pick up Tacker at his place. Explained about everything that had been going on and told her I'd be out searching. She wanted to come and help, but I put her off, mainly because she'd be a distraction. I also wanted some alone time with Tacker to try to get him to open up on his own.

I'd called her once again when Pepper came out of surgery, then for a third time when Charlie had been rescued. She knows they're both good, so she's just trying to make conversation by steering us away from prior events.

But that's fine by me. I'm not going to argue with her about whether I should come to her appointment on Monday. Regardless of the fact I'm her husband, I'm the man her brother trusted most in the world to look after her, so that's exactly what I'm going to do.

CHAPTER 13

Regan

THE KNOCK AT the front door has me springing from the couch where I'd been settled in with a glass of wine. I fling it open, then take in all that is Willow Monahan as she stands at the threshold.

Despite looking travel weary, she is still one of the most gorgeous women I know. She looks just like her siblings, Dax and Meredith, but with a slightly more exotic tilt to her eyes. It makes her appear a tad foreign with her dark hair, golden-brown eyes, and sun-kissed skin, like she's the princess of some desert sheik.

Her eyes appraise me critically. It's the first time she's seen me since Lance died. She'd been on the other side of the world under some perilous conditions, and she hadn't been able to make it back for the funeral.

"I'm good," I say, answering the unwritten question in Willow's eyes that wonders how I'm dealing with my brother's unexpected death. "I promise."

The concern washes away, although it's really just tucked down deep so I can't see it, and she breezes in the door. Willow pulls an olive-green canvas duffel on wheels behind her, which I'm sure carries all of her clothing and travel necessities. Her precious camera and lenses are in the battered leather backpack resting easily on her shoulders. With her khaki cargo pants, olive-green tank top, and heavily pocketed tan vest, she looks every inch a traveling photo journalist. Almost a cliché.

What I don't see under all that clothing are the physical scars from being hit by grenade shrapnel in Syria last year. She was so proud of her injuries, sending me not only photos of the wounds but also of a tiny plastic jar that held the metal shards that had been pulled from her body. It was something she felt safe in showing me, but I was positive she never would have showed her parents or siblings, because they already have a modest amount of fear over her job. I do, too, of course, but she also knows she can be a bit freer with the sister who's not actually blood, and more of a close friend and confident.

"I need wine, a hot shower, and pizza, but not necessarily in that order," Willow announces as she releases the duffel handle and shrugs her backpack off, gently setting it next to the entertainment unit in the living room. "Then we can turn on the hockey game to cheer Dax on."

"Wine first," I say with authority as I walk into the kitchen to pour her a glass from the bottle I'd recently opened. "And I've already ordered the pizza. It should be here soon."

"Now you're talking," she replies with a grin, plopping into a chair at the kitchen table.

I top off my drink and take the glasses to the table, pulling a chair out opposite of Willow. I last saw her two years ago at Christmas when she happened to be home visiting her parents for the holidays. Lance and I had made a trip to visit the Monahans. Our time there had been short, my diagnosis with the PNH new. We chose to keep it between ourselves, a decision Lance sort of followed my cue on.

Now as I study Willow, I'm wondering why we kept it a secret. Technically, it had been so we wouldn't throw a pall over the holidays. I also hadn't wanted Linda and Calvin to worry about me. But I also think it was partly because Lance and I had bonded so tightly after our parents died that we seemed like an unstoppable unit together. He'd promised he would take care of me when we became orphaned, and he'd kept his word. He'd been all I really needed.

And now he was gone, and I'm still keeping secrets. Willow takes a sip of her wine, sighs, then smiles, not knowing I have a deadly disease or I'm married to her brother.

Shit... we're actually related now. Sisters by marriage... and she has no clue.

A wave of guilt courses through me, but it's quickly extinguished when Willow sets her glass on the table, making a clucking noise. "Christ, Regan... you look like shit. Are you sick?"

My eyes round with wonder. How in the hell could she know about my PNH just by looking at me? But then I remember I had a rough morning. I woke up from a sound night's sleep utterly fatigued with dark circles under my eyes. It happens sometimes—luckily, it's infrequent—and I hadn't thought twice about it. I barreled forward with my day, doing some light cleaning and laundry before attending a job interview for a part-time position at a local pediatrics office.

Sidestepping her question, I turn the tables. "Look who's talking. You're a total travel rat, and you smell, too."

Willow laughs, her bright white teeth flashing as she inclines her head in a touché moment. But then her face sobers, and she asks, "Seriously... how are you doing with everything?"

She means with Lance dying as she has no clue about the other upheavals in my life. Because I am not about to tell her I'm married to her brother, I stick to the limited scope of her inquiry so I don't have to lie. "It's tough. I reach for my phone at least ten times a day to call or text him. I turn the TV to sports the day after a Vipers game to see the highlight reel so I can get a glimpse of my brother. I'm not exactly sure when he'll stop being my go-to thought of the day, but for now... it's just tough."

Willow's eyes mist up. "And still no leads on who did it?"

My brother had been mugged. He'd also been stabbed, possibly for fighting and refusing to give up his wallet. The cops aren't really sure, but the case is cold and unsolved. Not having justice meted out to his killer is another source of pain.

I shake my head. "It appears to be a random incident, a classic mugging gone wrong. His wallet and watch were missing. His shirt was ripped, so they think there was a struggle. No witnesses. No other leads."

"Fuck," she mutters as she stares glumly into her wineglass before she focuses back on me. "I'm so sorry."

"I'm dealing," I assure her. "And Dax has been great by letting me stay here."

"Yeah," she drawls. "Not sure I saw that one coming. I mean... Dax isn't the most dependable—"

"But he is," I rush to defend him.

Chuckling, Willow holds her hands up. "Let me finish there, sassy pants. I merely meant he's not the first person to notice there's a problem. He's just so damn busy and always traveling. But once he does see something, he's the first to act."

"He caught me at a low point in New York," I admit, thinking about how I'd dissolved into tears in his arms when he sort of strong-armed me into telling him all my woes. "And you're right... he definitely springs into action. He didn't give me much of a choice but to come here with him."

"He's a caveman," Willow commiserates. "But I think it's good for you. You shouldn't be alone, and there's nothing our family wouldn't do for you. Especially Dax."

Including marriage, I think, but then decide to change the subject. "What about you? I can't even keep track of your travels anymore."

Willow's eyes light up, a clear indication she's still madly in love with her job. "I'm getting ready to head to Kosovo. It's been twenty years since the war, and I got a contract to take photos of some of the survivors with updates on what they're doing now. The only downside is the reporter assigned is a real douche. Thinks he knows everything and will try to control my shots, but still... it's going to be an epic news piece."

"Wow," is all I can say because I'm not even sure where Kosovo is or what really happened there. I give a small shake of my head in awe. "You're such an adventurer. Don't you ever get nervous about all the places you travel to, not to mention the ones that are actual war zones?"

"Not really," Willow says with a shrug. "I mean… if I think about it too much, then I'm sure I'd have some moments, but I just try to focus on the job and trust the people around me to keep me safe."

Tables are turned again as we try to get updated. Willow asks, "Are you still dating that guy—what was his name—Pete? Pablo?"

"Paul," I supply with a laugh. "And no. That fizzled."

I turn the tables away from my love life, since digging deeper could potentially reveal I'm a married woman now. "What about you? Are you dating?"

"Not sure what I do is called dating, but I had an extended booty call relationship with another photographer going for a while. Biggest dick I've ever seen. Like to the point of being uncomfortable at first, but then he had a mouth that would get me loosened up and it was the best dick I'd ever had—"

My mouth drops wide open, and I stare at Willow in abject fascination. We've never talked sex before. Maybe it's because she felt I was too young, but now we're in penis size and oral sex territory, and it's all very new to me.

Stopping midsentence, she blushes. "I'm sorry… was that too much information?"

I shake my head hard and fast, wanting to hear

more.

For comparison purposes, that is.

Grinning, Willow leans forward. "I'm talking easily nine inches. I mean… it was actually frightening the first time I saw it, but then he assured me he knew how to use it. Well… he did, and really… it's sad. Because he was so boring and utterly dull, except in bed. I'm not sure I can keep that going. I need my brain stimulated, too, you know?"

I really don't know. I'm still stuck on exactly how large a nine-inch penis is while wondering how big Dax's is, because it seemed pretty monstrous to me. My hands involuntarily separate as I measure an approximate distance that might be nine inches. Willow laughs as she watches me.

"Nine inches, huh?" I say in amazement as I study the distance between my palms.

"It doesn't all fit in," she clarifies.

"Wow," I say in amazement. "You really *are* an adventurer."

The doorbell rings, and I jump up to grab the pizza. When I return to the kitchen, Willow has refilled our wineglasses and is searching around for plates.

"To the right of the sink," I instruct as I plop the pizza on the L-shaped kitchen island.

We load our plates up before moving to the table where our wineglasses are, then spend a few silent minutes stuffing our faces. Willow groans over her first three bites, and I'm betting pizza like this isn't something she gets often in her travels.

She wipes her mouth, a sparkle in her eye as she peers at me. "What kind of trouble are we going to get into while I'm visiting?"

"Trouble?" I ask, eyes blinking.

"In case you haven't noticed, you've actually become of legal age since the last time we were together. So you and I are going out partying tomorrow night. Dax can come, too, if he wants."

"He can't," I say, knowing his schedule well. We have it taped to the fridge, so I know his travel days. "He has their rookie party to go to."

I don't have to explain what a rookie party is to her. When in a professional hockey family, the parties are legendary and widely known about, although I'm sure we haven't heard the real dirty stuff that goes on at them.

Willow's eyes practically flash with mischief, and she grins even bigger. "Oh, we are so crashing that party."

"We're not allowed," I say, feeling like a damn nun as the words come out. "I mean... you know it's only for players."

"Which is why I said we're crashing," she replies deviously, and a tiny spark of reciprocal naughtiness flashes within me.

"Dax will be mad," I say, although I'm not sure if that's true.

"Don't care," she replies. "It will be epic. We'll crash, get lots of good free food and alcohol, then you and I can go out clubbing after."

And it's at this point I realize my life has actually been quite dull, particularly my four years of adulthood so far. I'd been so focused on school and my relationship with Paul, then my diagnosis and losing Lance, that I've just never gone out and done something crazy before. Sure, I've gone to parties.

But I've never crashed a professional hockey team's closed-door party before. I've never done anything overtly crazy, and right now... I think I need to start living a little bit outside the box. Besides, I'm tired of moping around wishing Dax could be something more to me that he clearly doesn't want to be.

Yes... we'll crash the party.

She's right. It will be epic.

My return smile comes slowly, but it's just as wide. "All right... let's do it."

CHAPTER 14

Dax

ROOKIE PARTIES.

People either love 'em or hate 'em, and most players love them. I think they're great. Not only because I'm guaranteed an exceptional meal and all the best and most expensive booze I want, but it's also a way for me to kick back with my teammates and just enjoy being with them. Sure, us veterans like to give the rookies a lot of hell. That's why we run the dinner and bar tab up as high as we possibly can. It's an honored tradition on virtually every professional hockey team, and it occurs every year.

They had gone all out and rented an entire restaurant and bar. My belly is happy with the bone-in ribeye with lobster tail I had, and now we are congregating in the expansive bar area with its sumptuous leather seating, dark lighting, and top-shelf liquor.

The bartender approaches me as I step up to the

polished wooden bar with brass railing. I scan the bottles on the shelf behind me. "Let me have the Balvenie forty-year-old Speyside."

One of the rookies, Vance Gather, comes to stand beside me. At the end of the night, all the rookies will pony up an equal share to cover the exorbitant cost of our evening of camaraderie.

I go ahead and rub it in a bit. "How much is that?" I ask the bartender, knowing the answer will make Gather a little green around the gills.

"One hundred and seventy-five dollars, sir," the bartender replies smoothly. I can see Gather grimace in the reflection of the mirror behind the bar.

"Perfect," I say with a wide smile.

When the bartender brings my drink, I take a grateful sip, savoring the complex flavor of peat mixed with possible vanilla and a hint of cherry. I've got a pretty sophisticated scotch palate for a middle-class dude from Michigan. Lance and I had gone to Scotland over one of our summer breaks. While there, we'd done a scotch-tasting tour. It'd been fucking fantastic—even made the haggis taste better.

I prop an elbow on the bar, surveying the room. The night is just getting started now that the niceties of dinner are done. The drinking and women are next on the agenda. About twenty minutes ago, the doors had opened and scantily clad women started pouring in. Not sure where the rookies got them, and I mostly definitely don't want to know either.

There are a few people noticeably absent from our team gathering. Legend wasn't budging from Pepper's side since she's still recovering in the hospital. I'll just make sure to drink an extra Balvenie for him.

Tacker is also absent. Although he has been indefinitely suspended, everyone would have loved for him to show up tonight. Hopefully the fact he didn't—despite many of us extending the invitation for him to come—is not indicative of his lack of desire to stay with the team.

Also missing are the members of the coaching staff and the front office. That's because they were purposely excluded. This is purely a player event. Which is good, because things will get wild tonight. Most of the single dudes in here are going to get laid, probably by more than one woman. Some of that will most definitely occur right on the premises.

"What are you drinking?" Bishop asks as he comes to stand beside me at the bar.

"Scotch," I reply, then nod toward my glass. "Ask for forty-year-old Balvenie. You'll love it."

"Sounds great," Bishop replies with an evil smile, knowing it costs some serious bank. "And just keep them coming for both of us."

Gather swallows hard, then turns to leave. Bishop and I tap glasses once his drink arrives.

"Here's to bankrupting the rookies tonight," I say before taking another sip. Bishop does the same, hissing in appreciation.

"That's good stuff," he rasps.

"Told you."

We move from the bar area and step off to the side, taking in the players—comrades, really—congregating. Laughing. Joking. Talking strategy. Talking shit.

Brotherhood stuff.

Bishop sidles in closer, tilts his head in, and asks in a low voice, "How are things going with Regan?"

I hunch slightly over my drink, not wanting to talk about her. I'm fucked up in my head in about a million different ways whenever I think about her. Part of me is telling myself it's wrong to pursue something with her. I'm a brother figure. Some lines shouldn't be crossed.

The other part is telling myself to be a selfish son of a bitch and take her. I hurt her with my rejection, but I know Regan is into me *because* she was hurt. This makes me realize something potentially wonderful could develop between us.

Then there's another part that says, "Don't fucking go there. Commitment is not what you want, and it's a lot of damn work."

"Are you going to answer me?" Bishop asks.

I twist my neck to regard him. "Nothing to say, brother. Things have settled, and we're back in the friend zone. It's all working out well."

"Lying motherfucker," he says with a chuckle, shaking his head.

There's no sense in arguing with him. He can totally tell when I'm laying down bullshit. But if I refuse to take the bait and keep my mouth decidedly shut, then we won't have a conversation about this, which is what I prefer.

Bishop's large hand comes down on my shoulder. He gives me an affectionate squeeze, which actually hurts a bit since he's trying to make a point.

I give him my attention because I would never disrespect his advice.

"Take it from someone who has recently realized the benefit of falling in love with a wonderful woman. Don't pass up something that could be amazing just because you have a few doubts. Something great is worth the risk, my man. Without risk, there is no reward."

"Yeah? What if I take the risk and then decide it's not for me? What happens then? I'll tell you what… Regan ends up incredibly hurt. And I sure as shit don't want to do that to her."

That expression on her face when I told her what we'd done was a mistake had been enough to last me a lifetime.

"Maybe that's for Regan to decide," he suggests

slyly. "It's not all about you. She should have a say so."

I know the bastard's right, which causes me to growl in frustration before I down my drink. Turning toward the bar, I immediately catch the bartender's eye. I hold my glass up, indicating I want another, and he gives me a thumb's up in return.

If Bishop is going to insist on warm and fuzzy talks tonight, I'm going to need more liquor.

"Well, will you look at that?" Bishop says, his eyes on the bar entrance.

Angling my body, I glance that way, stunned to see Dominik Carlson walking in, which is shocking for many reasons. The first and most obvious is he's the team's owner. As far as I know, a team owner has not only never been invited but has also never dared to crash such an event in the history of professional hockey and rookie parties. Another reason this is eyebrow raising is because he lives in Los Angeles. He doesn't spend a lot of time in Phoenix, despite the fact he owns our team. He has so many other diverse business holdings originated in California he isn't frequently seen in this area.

The final thing that has my jaw hanging low is how he walks in with his head held up and his chest thrown out with the confidence of a man who knows he's going to be welcomed even if he wasn't invited. Not one of us would dare try to kick him out.

I actually wouldn't want to. Everything I've seen about Dominik Carlson tells me he's different from any other team owner out there. I could cite example after example where he has gone out on a limb or done something special for one of the team members. He's personally invested in us. He may not be on the ice doing battle with us day in and day out, but I think it's safe to say we all feel his presence there with us.

Carlson makes the rounds, stepping in on subgroups of people, shaking hands and clapping backs. He's got a billion-dollar smile that keeps him rolling in hot women. I'm sure the fact he's actually a billionaire doesn't hurt, either. While I'm a dude and normally don't notice such things, I would have to say he was blessed with good genes.

He's a total stud.

Erik comes up behind Bishop and me, throwing his arms around our shoulders. "Can you believe Carlson showed up?"

I take my attention off the owner, grinning at my teammate. "He certainly marches to the beat of his own drum."

Erik nods, then glances at his watch. "I think I'm going to head out."

Under his breath, Bishop mumbles, "Pussy whipped."

"Goddamn right I am," Erik says with a cheesy grin.

"Why would I want to hang out with you losers when I can be at home with Blue?"

Bishop sighs, then empties his drink. "I guess I should head out, too."

I glare at my best friend. "Don't you even think about it. Bros before hos."

"Call Brooke a ho again and I will punch your teeth down your throat," Bishop growls.

We stare at each other a long moment before we both burst out laughing.

"Come on, dude… Stay out with me tonight," I cajole. "We never hang like this anymore."

This is absolutely true. While I'd never begrudge Bishop and Erik falling in love and settling down, it sucks being the lone wolf these days. I could try to bond harder with Tacker—who I believe will remain single forever given his past—but that seems near impossible to me these days with the way he's acting.

Before Bishop can answer, Dominik Carlson himself walks up to our small group. He smiles, shakes our hands, and asks if we're having a good time.

"It's the best of times," Erik replies with a grin. "But what are you doing here?"

I cringe slightly, and Bishop rolls his eyes. Erik isn't known for his tact.

Carlson laughs—a big, booming one that tells us he is amused by his player—and shrugs. "I heard through the grapevine the rookie party was going down tonight, and I didn't have any better plans. Thought I would check it out."

And there it is.

As simple as that.

Our team's owner didn't have anything better to do so he hopped a private plane—he owns several—and flew from Los Angeles to Phoenix to have a few drinks with his players.

When I look at it like that, it doesn't seem to be that big of a deal. Although I certainly hope if any of the rookies have paid prostitutes in here tonight, they keep that shit on the down low. I'll go out on a limb and say Carlson would most definitely not like that.

"Well, let me finish making the rounds so I can order up the most expensive drink they have," Carlson says with an evil smile.

We all laugh because that's exactly what's expected at rookie parties.

But then he leans in so no one else hears and murmurs, "But between us, I'm probably going to put a little money on the tab to help the lads out."

Erik chuckles, not afraid to ask the nosy questions. "Oh yeah, how much?"

Dominik's teeth flash, and he gives a slight shrug. "Ten thousand? Twenty thousand? How hard do you guys party?"

Erik throws his hands up in mock surrender. "I have no clue these days. I'm a taken man. And with that, I am out of here."

Carlson reaches his hand out and shakes Erik's, who then makes a prompt exit.

"I'll catch you guys later for a drink," Carlson says as he looks around for his next group of players to go talk to.

After he walks off, I turn to Bishop. "Stay out tonight, dude. Don't turn all grandpa on me."

Bishop's gaze flicks past me a moment, eyes widening slightly, and then his smile turns practically gleeful. "Oh, I'm not leaving now. I wouldn't miss this for the world."

"Miss what?" I mutter as I turn to take in what has his attention.

And just fuck me.

Into the bar comes Willow and Regan, both dressed in incredibly short dresses. I ignore Willow because she is her own woman and if I ever tried to get her to wear something more sensible, she'd kick me in the nuts.

But my entire body flames hot when I fully take in Regan. She's got on a teal-blue dress that's cut so low I'm surprised her belly button isn't showing. It's also cut wide, the inside swells of her breast on magnificent display.

For. Everyone. To. See.

My vision turns red, a phenomenon that has never occurred in my entire life, and I have the insane and overwhelming urge to throw a blanket over the top of Regan so no one can see how gorgeous and sexy she is.

"Easy there, buddy," penetrates through the buzz that's taken up residence in my ears, and I realize Bishop actually has a restraining hand on my arm. I'd taken three steps toward Regan. "I think you need to calm down and stay right here beside me for a few minutes until you get your shit under control."

My head snaps his way, and I growl in fury and frustration.

He grins, poking me in the chest. "Dude… you have it so bad for her. Just give the fuck in and make something with her, okay?"

Returning my gaze to Regan, I stare. She's fucking stunning.

And young and innocent.

She's also mine if I just fucking take that last step.

My attention is interrupted by the bartender coming out from behind the bar to hand me a refill. I take it, graciously downing about half the drink in one swallow. I have got to get my shit together, so I don't act like an idiot tonight.

CHAPTER 15

Regan

S UBCONSCIOUSLY, I PULL at the hem of my dress. I swear I feel air on my ass, but I don't remember it being exposed in the dressing room mirror when I tried it on earlier today. Willow had talked me into this scandalous garment. She took me out to lunch, plied me with wine, and then took me shopping. I couldn't have afforded the extravagance of a designer dress for one single night out on the town, but Willow could. She insisted she pay for it because she makes damn good money at her job and essentially has no bills to pay as she doesn't even own a home. When she's in between assignments, she just crashes at her parents' house in Michigan and otherwise hoards most of her money.

I should have figured I'd be in trouble hanging around with Willow. It was the wine that ultimately led me to purchase the damn dress. In the safety of the dressing room, it hadn't seemed that revealing. But as I take in the looks of the hungry hockey players checking out the new women who have entered their lair, I feel incredibly underdressed.

I also feel like a fraud. I don't do sexy well.

"Come on," Willow says with excitement as she takes me by the hand. "Let's get a drink."

We make it no more than two steps toward the bar before a large, hulking hockey player plants himself in front of us.

"Ladies," he says in a smooth, honeyed voice. "Welcome to the fun."

Growing up in a hockey family, I have learned to know the players. It didn't take me long at all to pretty much memorize the entire Arizona Vengeance team just from some simple roster research before the game the other night.

Before us stands Trace LaForge, a third-line rookie defenseman. He's more my age than Willow's, but he looks between the two of us without a care as to such things.

I can tell by the sparkle in his eye and the leering smile on his face he thinks we're part of his entertainment tonight. And I don't mean that in an offended or prudish way. I'm a sister of a hockey player, so I'm well aware of what happens at these parties as I listened in on conversations between Lance and his teammates when I was younger. I don't begrudge it.

But I'm not on the menu tonight, and he's gazing at me like I'm the main course. He clearly has no idea Willow is a family member, or he would get that look right off his face before Dax takes it off.

"LaForge..." The deep, slightly cultured voice comes from behind me, and I turn to find an incredibly handsome man standing there. He's tall with raven-black hair and even darker eyes. He's dressed in an impeccably cut suit that's obviously designer, although I have no clue about the label. I can tell just by his bearing he is big money. "They're asking for you to go to the maître d' stand. Something about your credit card being declined."

Trace's eyes bug out of his head, and he mumbles in apology as he brushes past us.

I glance at Willow, who is openly checking the man out in an overly appreciative away. When I turn to the man who just scared off the young rookie, he's regarding Willow with the same open appraisal. I swear I can feel the sizzling vibe between them as they eyeball each other.

The man drags his attention off Willow to shoot me a warm, genial smile, then sticks his hand out. "Dominik Carlson. I own the Arizona Vengeance."

Holy shit. He not only owns the Vengeance, but he also owns a professional basketball team in Los Angeles. This guy is more than just wealthy, and I fear my hand is sweating profusely as I place it in his.

"I'm Regan Miles," I murmur.

Mr. Carlson gives me a gracious incline of his head before regarding Willow.

The expression on his face turns almost predatory as he sticks his hand out to her. She places her fingertips gently against his palm. He naturally curls his hand around hers, pulling her knuckles up to his lips where he brushes a kiss there.

It's old-fashioned and romantic, although I don't think either of those describe his intentions. "And you are?"

Willow boldly holds Mr. Carlson's gaze, the corners of her lips tipping upward before she gives him a dazzling smile in return. "Willow."

It's not lost on me that she doesn't give her last name, which would likely out her as Dax's sister. It's clear she'd rather not be identified.

Mr. Carlson knows she's being evasive, too. I can see it on his face, and I expect him to challenge her for more information, but he releases her hand instead.

"I'd love to buy you ladies a drink," he merely says.

"That would be lovely," Willow replies huskily. "How about we find a table?"

"Perfect." His voice is rumbling, his eyes gleaming. "What would you both like?"

We both ask for wine, then Willow has my hand in

hers again. She tugs on me as she winds her way through the crowd to find a table. I keep my eyes on the ground, following behind her and hoping we can just avoid Dax. I assume he's here. He told us before he left he'd be really late tonight and for us not to wait up.

Admittedly, I was slightly bothered by that, and I'm not sure why. He owes me no allegiance, and he's free to do what he wants.

It makes me wonder why in the hell I've got my head bowed in avoidance of him. I owe him nothing as well.

Just as I tip my head up, Willow comes to a crashing halt, causing me to run into her back. I freeze when I see Dax in front of her, imposingly blocking her path with his arms crossed over his chest. Bishop Scott stands just off to his left, watching with interest.

I know Bishop as he played with the Vipers—my brother's former team—although I can't say I know him well. Dax told me Bishop is his closest friend on the team, and Bishop and my brother were tight. His eyes cut briefly to me, and he gives me a warm smile.

I don't smile back, instead bringing my gaze to Dax as I move to Willow's side. He's glaring at his sister, and she's just grinning at him. She knew he'd be pissed we crashed, and I think part of her is relishing this.

"What in the hell are you doing here?" he asks. He doesn't even spare me a glance.

Willow rolls her eyes at her brother. "That's a stupid question, Dax. I'm here to party."

"No, you're not," he replies with a solid shake of his head. He then points his finger to the door and says, "You both need to leave."

Still... he doesn't spare me any attention at all.

"I think not," Willow replies cheekily. "Besides... your nice owner, Mr. Carlson, is buying us some drinks. It would be bad form to skip out on that and all."

"Willow," he growls, leaning into her. "I swear to God—"

"Is there a problem here?" Dominik Carlson asks as he comes to stand on the other side of Willow. He has a bland, expectant expression on his face, but I can tell he knows he just stepped into something tense and on the verge of blowing.

If I'd expected Dax to bow to the owner in any way, I was sorely mistaken. Dax merely slides his gaze to his head boss and replies, "I believe you've met my sister. And I was just explaining to Willow that this is a private party and she cannot be here."

Mr. Carlson is surprised by that news. His eyebrows jet upward, and he tilts his head at Willow with a chiding expression on his face.

But he only spares her a moment before turning back to Dax. "Oh, come on. I think you can make an exception. And I was just going to take your sister and

Miss Miles over to a table where we can enjoy a drink. I promise to protect them from any debauchery that's been rumored to take place at these events."

I can see Dax gritting his teeth, a muscle jumping at the base of his jaw. Lips pressed flat, all he can do is give a curt nod to Mr. Carlson in agreement of this plan, although I think he'd like to punch the guy out.

Willow slips her hand into the crook of Dominik Carlson's arm, giving a cutesy air kiss to her brother that pretty much translates into "kiss my ass," before they start walking away. I spin to follow, getting one foot planted, then I'm brought to a halt.

Grasping me by the upper arm, Dax mutters, "Oh no you don't. We need to talk."

He spins me away from Bishop, then marches right out of the bar area into what is now an empty restaurant. Dax keeps heading deeper into the restaurant until the sounds of the party recede.

When he releases me, he glances around wildly, scrubbing his hand through his hair. He looks far more upset with me than he did with Willow, and I don't understand why. Surely he knows his sister is the ring leader here.

Finally, his eyes travel down my body, up again, then back down before snapping to me. He motions at my dress with his hand. "Just what the hell is that, Regan?"

I glance at my dress, get met with a whole lot of cleavage because of the cut, and then raise my head. My voice is almost nonexistent when I weakly offer, "A dress."

"Really?" he replies with utter sarcasm. "Because it looks like a few scraps of material thrown on your body. Did you really think that was appropriate to wear?"

And then it hits me.

He's judging me. Immediately, I'm over the concerned brother act. I certainly hadn't put up with that from Lance when he was alive, and I sure as shit wasn't going to put up with it from Dax.

I step into him, go on my tiptoes, and poke him in the chest with my index finger. "What I choose to wear—or not to wear as seems to be the case—is none of your fucking business, Dax Monahan."

"It most certainly is my business," he yells.

Actually bends his head down and yells right in my face. And then his hand is on my arm again. "I'm taking you home."

I jerk my arm out of his grip. "You most certainly are not."

"You are begging for the palm of my hand, Regan."

"What in the hell is going on here?" Willow's voice cuts over our spat, and Dax and I jump apart from each other. She's standing there with her hands on her hips, glaring daggers at her brother.

I open my mouth, but nothing comes out. When I glance at Dax, he's scowling at his sister.

Willow's eyes are soft when they land on me. "Are you okay?"

The air comes rushing out of my lungs as I rush to assure her. "Yes. I'm fine. We were just—"

Willow spins on her brother, eyes narrowing and as cold as ice. "Why were you yelling at her? Manhandling her? And threatening to spank her? Have you fucking lost your mind, Dax?"

I almost feel sorry for the man, because Willow seems like she's about ready to throw down. My mind races, figuring out how I can diffuse this situation, but Dax beats me to the punch, although so not in the way I would have handled it.

"She's my wife," he tells her smugly. "I think I have every right to do those things."

Of course, Dax isn't a Neanderthal. He's an incredibly progressive man, and he wouldn't think marriage conveys that type of power to anyone. He is, however, a smartass who's trying to set his sister back on her feet as well as knock me down slightly since he's getting ready to be attacked.

I brace, knowing he's doing the same.

"Wife?" Willow wheezes as her hand goes to her chest. She wildly swivels her gaze between Dax and me. Back and forth. Back and forth. "Somebody better explain."

Dax knows the best way to piss his sister off is to clam up, so he just casually runs his hands down the front of his dress pants and rocks on his feet with a smug smile. He's not saying another word.

Asshole.

I rush toward Willow, then take her hands in mine. "It's nothing really. In name only until I can afford health insurance on my own. Lance was pretty debt ridden when he died, so Dax is helping me out financially."

I hate throwing Lance under the bus like that, but I don't want to put too much emphasis on the health insurance aspect of it. I'm just not ready to get into that with her, although she deserves an explanation.

Willow's expression morphs into a mixture of empathy and slight confusion. I take advantage and press on, turning her slightly away from Dax and lowering my voice. "Listen… why don't you go back in and have some drinks with Dominik Carlson? He's totally into you. I'm going to grab an Uber home. We'll sit down and talk about all this tomorrow. I promise."

"I don't want to go back in without you," she replies, but I know that's not true. She knows it, too.

I point toward the bar area. "Go. Have fun tonight."

Willow stares at me for a long, thoughtful moment before leaning in and giving me a hard hug. She whispers in my ear, "I know damn well there's more to the story, but tomorrow... you and I are going out to breakfast and you're telling me everything."

"Promise," I murmur, squeezing her back.

After I pull out of her embrace, I head for the exit doors, not wasting a moment's attention on Dax. He can kiss my nearly bare ass.

But then his hand is on my arm again, this time more gently. Jolting, I twist to look up at him.

"I'll take you home," he growls as he pulls the door open.

"I can get home fine on my own," I snap. "I'm not a child."

"Fuck if I haven't figured that out with you in that dress," he mutters, tightening his grip slightly. "But I'm taking you home. I was about ready to leave anyway."

"Fine," I grit out, snatching my arm away.

He gnashes his teeth in frustration, but merely holds the door for me. I get a mocking bow as he motions me through. "After you."

My chin rising high, I brush past him and march out into the evening, definitely feeling cool air on my ass.

I also feel his eyes there, too, and it gives me a small measure of satisfaction.

CHAPTER 16

Dax

THE RIDE HOME from the rookie party is silent, which is fine by me. Gives me plenty of time to think.

Like why in the hell had I gone berserk over seeing Regan dressed that way? I've dated plenty of women who have worn outfits just as sexy and never once batted an eye. Yeah, even got a kick out of other men ogling the half-naked woman on my arm. It's a source of pride.

But with Regan in that dress—that has ridden up incredibly high on her legs as she sits in the front passenger seat of my car—I'd been filled with certainty I didn't want any other man to see her in it. It felt like it should be for my eyes only, and it was a treasure I would never share. As it stands, I feel the insane need to beat the fuck out of Trace LaForge for eyeballing her when she first walked in. His eyes were glued to her tits, and—

I tighten my hands on the steering wheel, feeling like it could snap under the force of my fury.

All because Regan bared her gorgeous body to the world, and I was jealous of anyone else getting the gift of seeing her in all her glory.

And for that matter, why am I taking her home? I could have just as easily waited outside with her until an Uber arrived. It would have been the gentlemanly thing to do, then I could have returned to the party, gotten drunk on expensive scotch, and fucked any number of beautiful women there.

Except I didn't want to do that.

I only want to be in this car with Regan—to take her home where I can lock her safely away for my pleasure only.

No.

No. No. No.

Not for my pleasure. She can't be that to me.

Something great is worth the risk, my man.

That's what Bishop had said. He'd pushed me to take a chance with her.

I know one thing for sure, though. My cock is on board with that. It's been half hard since I first saw her in that dress, and it hasn't calmed down yet.

Fuck.

I pull into my driveway, coming to a stop just inches from the garage door. Regan's car is safely closed inside.

I barely have the car turned off before Regan bolts. She trots up the porch steps, her keys already in hand to unlock my front door. My eyes are glued to her shapely ass as it sways. Is it my imagination, or can I actually see the rounded swells of said shapely ass peeking out from under her hem?

Goddamn her for wearing that and goddamn my cock, which is now thickening even more.

My strides lengthen so I can catch up with her, and I'm at her back just as she's stepping over my threshold. She ignores my chiming alarm, for which I take a few seconds to punch in the disarm code. It lets her get all the way across the living room and to the staircase that leads up to her bedroom.

"I'm going to bed," she mutters, raising her leg to take the first step.

"Wait," I call.

She stops, one high-heeled foot perched on the step. Regan turns, eyebrows raised in question.

I have no clue what to say. She has my insides so jumbled up that rational conversation seems improbable. Besides, what can I possibly say to her? I can't tell her the truth—that I want her desperately. That it would be selfish as hell to take her, but I might be willing to risk it all for just a fucking taste of her again.

Yeah… can't really come out and say that.

But maybe I can provoke the situation. Make it

where words aren't necessary.

Best way to do that is to pick a fight.

The words are out of my mouth before I can stop them. "I think we need to talk about that dress you're wearing. What in the hell were you thinking coming out to a team party—my team's party—with so much of your body on display for all to see?"

My intent is to anger, not shame, because her body is so fucking beautiful. I mean, why wouldn't she be proud to show it off? It seems I hit the mark because her eyes flash with unholy fury as she comes charging at me.

I hold my ground, but she stops inches from me and hisses, "You are not my brother, Dax. You are not my husband, despite what a fucking piece of paper says. You have no right to tell me what to wear. In fact, if I want to dress like this every night... I will. If I want to spread my legs for a different man every night... I will. You have no say in anything I do so keep your fucking opinions to yourself."

I pretty much lost my shit the minute she'd suggested she could spread her legs for any man she wanted to. It was at that moment I envisioned myself committing murder to any faceless, nameless man who would ever even think about touching Regan.

I take a step into her, and she immediately retreats. I match her movement, moving in closer, but she only continues backpedaling. We do this for several strides until I have her against the wall beside my entertainment unit.

I dip my head, locking my eyes onto hers. My voice is calm, rational, but there is no mistaking the strength of the declaration I'm about to make. "Let me make this clear, Regan. No man gets to see what is rightfully mine. And no man is fucking you while I'm fucking you. Understood?"

When she rolls her eyes, I vow her ass is going to pay for that. "You're not fucking me," she sneers. "So I will—"

I effectively cut her words off by crushing her mouth under mine. My hands go to the wall, pinning her in, and I fucking ravage that smart-ass mouth of hers. The kiss claims ownership, but it's short because words are more important right this moment.

I lift my head. "I'm getting ready to rectify that 'not fucking you' thing right now. You have one chance to tell me 'no,' and—"

"Yes," she blurts out, her small hands fisting into my dress shirt.

Yes.

Christ… she said yes.

Exhaling a sharp breath, I let my forehead drop to touch hers. With my eyes squeezed tight, I tell her a dirty secret. "I'm not sure I can be gentle with you right now, Regan. That dress has me all kinds of twisted, and

I'm beyond pissed other men saw you in it. Got this strange need to fucking mark you."

"Damn, that's hot," she breathes, and that's all I need to center me again.

I snicker, lifting my head to smile at her. "I'm so going to spank your ass."

When she grins, it's the most beautiful thing I've ever seen. More beautiful than her breasts threatening to pop out of that dress and her ass that's begging me to do all sorts of things to it.

Just… that smile.

It also helps center me, puts me a back in control of the raging fire burning inside.

"Shall we go to your room?" she suggests.

My teeth flash in a feral smile, and I shake my head. "Can't really wait that long."

Regan's eyes turn curious before they pop wide with surprise as I turn her roughly around to face the wall. With my body, I press her into it.

My cock, thick and fully hard, digs into her lower back, causing her to moan. Regan's face is turned, cheek pressed to the wall, and her breath comes out in little pants.

"Don't move," I murmur against her ear before putting space between us.

She looks fucking fantastic. Legs slightly spread, palms flat against the wall, and ass tipped up slightly as if she's expecting me back there. The dress indeed shows the bottom globes of her butt. Fingertips itching to go there, I slowly raise the hem to reveal even more creamy skin.

Higher to reveal a white string thong nestled into the crack of her ass.

Damn. My dick is actually throbbing in pain now.

I press into her, slide my hand around to her front, and dive my fingers into her panties. She's already soaking wet, and I slide two fingers in deep.

Regan groans, presses her ass into me, and gyrates her hips. The friction against me feels amazing. My balls are already tingling.

I nuzzle my face into the side of her throat, sinking my teeth into her earlobe. "Keep doing that, little girl, and I'm going to unload in my pants."

That, of course, makes her rub against me even harder. I quell her motions by adding a third finger to her pussy, then pump them in and out roughly. Regan makes a noise deep in her throat that sounds like she's starved for even more. But I don't give it to her that way. Instead, I run just the tip of my index finger over her swollen clit, which causes her entire body to jerk against me.

"Yeah," I praise, applying more pressure and speed to my finger. As I strum her like a guitar, her head slams into my chest, her back arching. She pushes her palms into the wall, slams her body against me as tight as it can go, and comes all over my fingers as she moans her release.

"Fucking beautiful," I mutter, dipping a finger back inside her wetness and relishing the feel of her inner muscles contracting all around it.

Regan is gasping for air, trembling, and my cock is feeling sorely ignored. Putting my hand on her upper back, I push her into the wall, then pull her hips toward me.

"Spread your legs a little," I order, and she complies. Her head turns, cheek against the wall, her long eyelashes fanning out against the skin just below them as she closes her eyes in anticipation.

My fingers are quick and assured as they work at my belt, then my zipper, before releasing my cock. It's painfully hard, precome leaking from the tip.

I can't fucking wait... I just dip my knees, bring the head to her entrance from behind, and rub it through her folds to get it coated with her juices.

"Mmmm," she moans, wiggling her ass.

Tilting my hips, I press against her, feel her flesh quiver, tighten, and finally loosen just a fraction as the head of my cock slips in.

I grit my teeth, letting my breath rush out slowly from the overwhelming sensation of her heat against me.

I press harder into her, feeling the slide of my skin

against hers. Feeling the tug as if she's sucking me in deep, or is that from me plunging? I have no clue.

All I know is the journey into her is the fucking best thing I've ever felt in my life, and my balls throb in relief when I bottom out. Snaking my hands up her stomach, I reach into the deep cut of her dress and fit a palm around each breast.

"Christ, you feel good, Regan," I mutter as I give her tits a squeeze.

She responds by pushing against the wall, tipping her ass up higher, and trying to make just a little more room for me. I sink in just a fraction more, but then my pelvis is pressed hard against her ass, and I'm finally all the way in.

I'm almost afraid to move, suspicious Regan is better than anything I've ever felt before, and I don't know if my self-control can take it. It's not lost on me that I'm fucking her without a condom, which is an absolute no-no for me.

But then again, I've never fucked someone I've cared for or known for their entire life.

The only thing I do know is I'm not stopping because this feels so very right.

Unless…

"Are you on birth control?" I murmur, nuzzling into her neck.

"Yes," she gasps, then moans low as I pull back in

relief of her answer, only to punch in deep.

I push my head against hers as I start to move inside her. Putting my lips against her ear, I promise her the moon. "Hold tight, Regan. I'm going to show you just how crazy this dress has been driving me."

CHAPTER 17

Dax

THE BOURBON I'M sipping isn't helping as I sit in my dark living room waiting for Willow to get home. I've just left my bed, leaving a warm, naked, and completely wrecked Regan there. I'd thought I'd had my fill when I'd fucked her up against the wall, but by the time I'd carried her to my room, I'd wanted her again. That's when the clothing came all the way off and nature took its course.

It wasn't how I envisioned things happening, but I was soon flat on my back with Regan riding me. She was so sweet. Shy and hesitant when she asked if she could be on top. I'm not sure she quite understands, but there isn't any wish I wouldn't grant her. I'd let her do anything she wanted to me, perhaps even break my heart at some point.

She was fucking spectacular. When I came inside of her, my hips bucking hard and almost dislodging her body from mine, I realized it was even better than before. Maybe it was her own concurrent orgasm that caused mine to go nuclear. Or maybe it's just going to keep getting better and better each time.

Who knows, but one thing is certain... I'm not giving this up.

Not any time soon at least.

Which means I have to sit in my dark living room and wait for my sister to come home because I need to talk to her about why and how I have a sleeping Regan in my bed.

Willow deserves to know the full truth about what's going on, particularly since she witnessed me going all jealous commando on Regan and she'll be walking out of my bedroom tomorrow morning. I asked Regan permission to tell Willow about the PNH because it makes the fact we're married a little more palatable.

In addition to filling Willow in on the entire situation, I also need to tell my sister to back off before she decides to get on my case about the fact Regan is in my bed at all and will stay there for the foreseeable future. I know my sister. She's a busybody, and she'll also feel super protective over Regan. Willow will feel the need to protect Regan from any supposed misdeeds or harms I might impose. Yeah, I know my sister well.

Lights flash through the blinds of my front windows, indicating a car has pulled into my driveway. I stand from my chair, then cross to the side of the window to peer through the half-closed slats. My jaw locks when I see a limousine with the running lights on and the engine rumbling. Dominik Carlson doesn't wait for the driver to open the door for him. Instead, he steps out of the rear door. He's without the dress jacket and tie he'd been wearing earlier tonight, and the top two buttons of his shirt are undone.

He helps Willow from the limo. After she steps elegantly out, he pulls her hard into his arms and kisses her. It's deep and hot. I avert my eyes, my teeth now grinding against each other. Trying to rein in my protective instincts, I head to the chair and flop down.

And I wait for my sister to come in.

And wait…

And wait…

And wait…

It's a full five minutes before I hear the spare key I gave her this morning turn in the lock. She breezes through, not appearing any worse for the wear from what I can see. Instead, her eyes are sparkling and there's a smile on her face.

It's not the dreamy smile of a woman who has just had a romantic date with a nice man. Rather, it's a victorious, self-indulgent smile, and I don't want to know what that means.

Or do I?

"It's almost three. Out kind of late," I growl from the gloom before turning on the lamp that sits on the side table.

She jumps slightly, having not seen me sitting there, but then rolls her eyes. "I'm an adult, bro. I don't answer to you."

Leaning forward in the chair, I plant my elbows on my thighs and clasp my hands hard. "Dominik Carlson, Willow? Seriously? Could you pick anyone more complicated than that? He's my boss for fuck's sake."

Glaring, Willow puts a hand on her hip. "Who I choose to spend my time with is none of your business, Dax. But no worries... I'm not going to see him again."

My chin jerks inward. "You're not?"

"Nope," she replies, setting her purse on the coffee table.

"Why not? Did he treat you badly? Think you're not good enough for him?"

Willow snickers, shooting me an incredulous look that I'm defending her. "No, I declined his invitation to come to LA next weekend."

Eyebrows furrowing, I ask, "What's wrong with him? Did he do something to you?"

"Not at all," she replies with a shrug as she moves to the couch. She plops down, then leans forward to take off her shoes. "He's great even. But I've got another assignment coming up in a few weeks, so why even bother? Besides… I'm not into dating."

"Neither is he from what I hear," I mutter. Dominik Carlson is a known player.

"Well, there you go," she drawls with exaggeration. "It's not fated to be. Wait…why are you up?"

"We need to talk." My words hang heavy in the air.

"Is this where you set me down to explain why you married our childhood friend behind your entire family's back?"

"Yeah… that's about right."

Willow curls her legs up under herself, then throws an arm over the back of the couch. "So she needed health insurance or something? Surely there was an alternative to marriage for something as simple as insurance."

There's no good way to break this to Willow, and I don't know how to minimize the impact. So I just launch into it. "Regan is sick, Willow. And she has to have the health insurance because her treatments are incredibly expensive."

"Oh, my God," she practically moans, her face crumbling. "Does she have cancer or something?"

"No, not cancer, but something just as bad," I say gravely. "She has a blood disease. It's incredibly rare and dangerous, and it probably would have killed her sooner rather than later. But there's a new treatment out that's been effective in helping her. The problem is it costs more than four hundred thousand per year, so health insurance is essential."

"Jesus..." Willow gasps as she sits forward on the couch. "Who in the hell can afford that?"

"The out-of-pocket portions are still pretty high even with the insurance. Without insurance, it's practically unobtainable. The only way to help her was to marry her and put her on my coverage."

"What's the disease called?" Willow inquires.

I relay everything I've learned in the last two and a half weeks since I found out about Willow's PNH. My sister peppers me with questions, and I'm proud I have most of the answers. The research I did *was* pretty extensive, and I've grilled Regan on a lot of things as well.

When Willow is satisfied she understands as much as she can, she regards me with a tinge of hero worship. "You did the absolute right thing, Dax. But why didn't Lance leave her with anything?"

"Lots of reasons." I explain that some of it was because of her expenses, but a good chunk of it was also just plain mismanagement of his money. We all know Lance loved Regan more than anything in this world, but he suffered the same delusion most people do when they're young and at the height of their careers.

That nothing bad will ever happen to them.

"Unbelievable," Willow murmurs, her gaze drifting

off as she worries at her bottom lip. "But why couldn't she just tell me?"

"She doesn't feel good about marrying for something other than love and for something as basic as insurance."

"That's understandable," Willow replies, her eyes searching mine. "But why keep her illness hidden?"

I shrug. "It's not like we saw each other a lot. I think she was just trying to deal with it as best she could. I'm sure she would have at some point."

But that comment sounds hollow to my ears, although Willow nods her understanding.

She stretches her legs, plants her feet on the floor, and starts to stand. "Well, I better head to bed. It's been a long night."

"There's one more thing," I say. She freezes, hovering above the cushion a moment before she eases down. I've told her some pretty bad news tonight. By the tone of my voice, I'm sure she's thinking there's worse to come.

"What?" she whispers.

"Regan and I are sleeping together," I say without trying to tone down the challenge in my voice.

"Oh, fuck no," Willow hisses as she shoots off the couch. She wags a finger while scowling. "No, no, no, Dax. She's not cut out for you. You'll traumatize her."

"Flare your dramatics much?" I mutter sarcastically.

"You'll hurt her," she warns, not being dramatic. Even I realize there's a chance that's going to happen.

"I hope that's not true," is the best I can promise.

"If you're not in it for the long haul—or for reasons other than just because the sex is good—you're going to really, really hurt her, Dax. Regan is not built for casual relationships."

"You don't know that," I growl from low within my belly. Willow's assertion is a direct threat to my immediate happiness, and I'm selfishly going to defend against it. "You don't know Regan any better than I do."

"You're wrong, Dax," she murmurs, taking a step closer to me. Standing over me, she says, "I'm a woman, and that means I know her in a way you don't."

"But you're nothing like her," I point out. "You only do casual relationships. You don't like commitment. So you being a woman doesn't mean you have any greater insight into Regan's mind than I do."

Willow's mouth snaps shut. Her eyes flash with anger, but I can see by her expression I've hit the mark. She can't argue with my very spot-on assessment.

She huffs in frustration, scrubbing her hand through her hair. With a sigh, she admits, "She's been through enough, Dax. Losing Lance… being sick. She deserves to be happy."

"And what if I can make her happy?" I ask curiously,

having no fucking clue if I'm the man for the job. I just know there's something unique between us that transcends the amazing sex. I've got a bond with her I've never felt with another person.

Willow doesn't answer me, which is discouraging to say the least. Instead, she bends at the waist to place a kiss on the top of my head. "Be careful, Dax. That's all I'll say."

That is good advice, which I intend to follow.

CHAPTER 18

Regan

I HEAR THE clink of dishes and low voices as I tiptoe down the stairs. I woke up in Dax's bed with him beside me. He was already awake, just lying on his side watching me. I was a bit surprised I'd stayed in his bed all night. I'd have expected him to have regrets like he had the first time and come up with some lame excuse to boot me from his room.

Instead, he'd merely pulled me into his arms and kissed me. Not in a sexual way, but not sweetly either. I'd describe it more as an affirmation.

Dax then proceeded to tell me how things were going to go between us. It sounded a bit practiced and rehearsed, but I'd listened intently.

"Regan," he'd said, still holding me around my waist but with his head tilted so he could look at me. "I don't have a lot to promise you. I have no clue what this attraction between us is, but I don't regret acting on it this time. I don't know where this is going to lead us, since I've never been good at relationships. But I can promise if we're being intimate, then I won't be with anyone but you. That's about all I can offer you at this time. So either tell me to leave you alone or keep touching you. I'll respect whichever decision you decide on."

Deep down, I realize Dax doesn't want a committed relationship and isn't ready to settle down. It's hard to envision a long-term future with him because of that. But he makes me feel things I've never felt before, and I want to explore these feelings. My brain tells me to put a stop to this but my heart, which thinks Dax might actually be capable of more than he gives himself credit for, is calling the shots.

I'd responded by kissing him.

He'd made love to me, quietly and with consideration of the fact his sister was in his house.

Afterward, Dax rolled out of bed and got dressed, promising his world-famous chocolate chip pancakes for breakfast. He has a game this evening, and he'd said something about carb loading. I took my time coming downstairs—getting dressed, brushing my teeth, and putting my hair up.

I find Willow at the nook in the kitchen, sipping on a cup of coffee. As soon as I step onto the cream tile floor, her eyes soften as they appraise me. I'd been prepared for this since I'd given Dax permission to tell her about my PNH, which he had early this morning when she got home.

Willow stands, rounds the table, and gives me a long, warm hug. In my ear, she whispers, "You've got this, girl. You're fierce, brave, and as stubborn as your brother was."

I squeeze her back. "I know. And I'm sorry I didn't tell you."

When Willow pulls away, I receive an encouraging smile that tells me it's water under the bridge. She pats my arm, then returns to the table and her cup of coffee.

Coffee seems like a great idea, so I make my way over to the pot, which gives me a moment to appreciate Dax in his breakfast-making glory. He's wearing nothing but a pair of sweatpants that hang low on his hips, revealing the slanting vee muscles that disappear from sight. It's hard not to get distracted by his rippling muscles. His hair is mussy—courtesy of my fingers— and he turns slightly to give me a wink and a grin.

"How many pancakes do you want?" he asks as he mans a griddle he'd just dropped butter on. A huge bowl of batter sits next to it.

"Two," I reply as I open a cabinet to grab a mug.

As I pour, Dax moves past me. He does this not by giving me wide birth, but by brushing his body against me. His hands settle on my hips, and he squeezes affectionately. It's a brief touch before he grabs a spatula from a drawer and sidles back to the griddle, but it was enough of a statement that I immediately cut my eyes toward Willow.

She's watching with an expression on her face that I don't like.

It's worried, but it's also not surprised. Dax must have told her we were sleeping together.

My face flushes with the awareness she knows everything. All my dirty laundry. I'm sick, I'm committing insurance fraud by marrying to get coverage, and I'm sleeping with her brother while knowing it's nothing but casual sex to him and probably means more to me.

I wonder how much she pities me.

"I'm heading out tomorrow," Willow says, addressing us both. "Going to head home and hang with the parents for a few weeks. Assume you'll be able to swing by and spend some time there around your Detroit game this coming Friday?"

"Yup," Dax replies as he pours four perfect pancake circles on the hot griddle. "And I was hoping Regan might be interested in coming on the trip, too."

I jerk as I pour milk into my coffee, spilling a little. "Excuse me?"

Dax spares me a glance before slipping the spatula under a pancake. "Come home to Michigan with me. Stay at my parents. They'd love to see you."

"I don't want them to know I'm sick or we're married," I blurt out.

Willow's head tilts. "But why? We're your family now, even if you weren't married to that bonehead making pancakes."

I don't speak or raise my head until Dax says, "Regan... you should. There's no reason not to."

Pivoting, I face him. "But now it feels like I've been deliberately deceitful for keeping my illness from them. And then marrying you. They'll be disappointed in me."

"They most certainly won't," Willow says firmly. That it comes from her instead of Dax makes me feel better. I think Dax would say anything to try to put me at ease.

"I don't want them feeling sorry for me," I say desperately.

"Of course they'll feel sorry for you," Willow replies with a wicked grin. "You're married to Dax, after all. But seriously... you know they'll understand. They'll believe Dax did the right thing just like I do. Now, whether you want to tell them he's boning you at the same time—"

"Willow," Dax barks, turning from the pancakes to glare at her. "Just cut it out. Regan feels uneasy about all this to begin with. Lay off what's going on between us personally. That's for us and no one else."

Something about his words—his tone—reassures

me. It comes off as protective and reassuring instead of patronizing.

"Fine," Willow says, throwing her hands up in surrender. "I'll let it go."

Sighing in what sounds like relief, Dax returns to the griddle. But I can tell by the expression on Willow's face that she has more to say about it.

But not to her brother.

AFTER BREAKFAST, WILLOW and I cleaned the kitchen. She didn't say a word to me about my illness, being married to her brother, or the fact I was sleeping with him. Dax had gone to take a quick shower before he had to head to the arena. He wouldn't normally go this early, but he and Erik have to meet with the team's lawyers because of a lawsuit that's been filed against the team.

Back in October, a woman apparently filed a sexual harassment lawsuit against Dax, Erik, another guy in the front office, and the team as a whole. Dax told me about it one night while we were eating dinner last week. One of Brooke's friends—well, ex-friend—is the woman at the heart of this matter, and she might be on the high end of the crazy spectrum. Dax emphatically denied there was any type of sexual harassment, although I didn't need him to defend himself. I know him well enough there's no doubt in my mind that he'd *never* do that to a woman.

He's frustrated by the process, though. Supposedly, this will be a mediation where all parties' attorneys meet to discuss a settlement. I have to wonder why there's even going to be discussion if the players did nothing wrong, but that's none of my business.

We're just putting up the dried dishes when Dax reappears in the kitchen. He's wearing a suit, and he looks damn good dressed up. I remember having an inappropriate thought at Lance's funeral about Dax, but my head had been all kinds of messed up, so I gave myself a pass.

Regardless, the guys are required to dress up when going to the arena on game days, and it'd been the same when Lance played for the Vipers. Probably an industry-wide sort of unwritten rule. The players are professionals after all.

Dax has his game duffel slung over one shoulder. He glances between Willow and me. "Do you two need anything before I leave?"

"We're good," Willow says.

"Got the tickets?" he asks.

"Yes, Dad," she intones in a faux whiny voice.

Dax ignores her, focusing on me. "You good?"

My brow furrows. "Um… yeah. Why wouldn't I be?"

"Can't a guy wonder?" is all he says with a quirk to

his lips.

"I guess."

Willow coughs, and I don't miss the evil flash in her eyes. "Um… listen, dude. If you want a moment alone to kiss her or something, I can get lost if that makes you feel more at ease."

Those were the wrong words. I know she's trying to shame him—further proof I was definitely picking up on an air of disapproval from her earlier when he grabbed my hips—but it seems to have the opposite effect on Dax.

Instead, he lifts his chin and his jaw locks, eyes hard with determination. He stares at his sister as he strides across the kitchen. Just keeps his eyes locked right on Willow as he makes a beeline straight for me.

Without slowing or doubting his mission, he doesn't stop until he's flush against my body.

Finally sparing me a triumphant glance, he then kisses the hell out of me. I'm talking about one hand shoved into my hair, the other settling on my back, before bends me backward over the sink kind of kiss.

It's hard, swift, and meant to claim.

To send a message to Willow.

He's not going to back down.

I'm blushing and at a complete loss for words when he straightens us. I get the flash of an unrepentant grin before he's heading for the door, calling over his shoulder, "See you both after the game. We'll go out to The Sneaky Saguaro."

After the door closes, I cautiously peek at Willow. She's staring at the door her brother just exited with a thoughtful look on her face.

"Penny for your thoughts," I say with a nervous laugh.

She eyes the door for another long moment before shaking her head and sending me a vague smile. "If I didn't know any better, I'd say my brother was smitten with you."

"It's just sex," I say dismissively, realizing it came out automatically and without thought. I've already steeled myself to think of this as casual and nothing more, initiating a protective mode over my heart.

"I don't know," Willow says slowly.

"Well, I do," I counter, then reach out to touch her arm. "Are you sure you're okay with that part of things? I didn't mean for it to happen. He didn't either. The first time, alcohol was involved and—"

Willow stops me by putting her hands on my shoulders. "It's fine, Regan. You're an adult, and well... Dax can act like one sometimes, so there's that. It's none of my business. I just don't want either of you to get hurt."

"We won't," I assure her. "We love each other. In a friendly way, I mean. Our bond is too tight to mess up, and we're both aware there are boundaries, so it's good.

I promise."

Willow's smile conveys understanding and acceptance, but there's no hiding the slight tinge of worry that's still there.

The doorbell rings, and I immediately start for it. When I open the door, I'm blinking at a huge bouquet of white roses.

"Delivery for Miss Willow Monahan," the man behind the large vase says.

"Oh, wow," I say as I take them from him. "Thank you."

I turn, cross the threshold, and kick the door closed since it takes two hands to carefully hold the huge arrangement. I can barely see where I'm walking, so I guess my way back to the kitchen and put them on the table.

Willow stares at them with wide eyes. "I didn't think Dax had it in him."

"He doesn't," I say with a grin. "They're for you."

"What?" she exclaims in disbelief as she strides to the table. She snatches the envelope tucked in among the blooms out and removes the card. While she scans the words, her lips curve slightly upward as she shakes her head.

"Who are they from?" I ask breathlessly. I've never seen that many roses. There has to be three, maybe four, dozen.

"Dominik Carlson," she says flippantly. She hands me the card to read.

Last night was incredible. Please come to L.A. with me next weekend.

My mouth hanging open in shock, I say, "Last night was incredible? What did y'all do?"

"What didn't we do is the question," she says with a saucy smile. "God, that man has it going on between the sheets."

"You slept with him?" I ask, aghast at her naughtiness. "But you only just met him."

Willow shoots me a look that tells me to grow up. "Regan... love... you will one day learn that sex is awesome, and it's totally okay to occasionally engage in casual affairs. I know you can't see that right now, but I'm comfortable with the fact I met an incredibly handsome, charming man and took what I wanted from him."

"Am I a prude?" I ask impishly.

"Little bit," she replies, holding her thumb and forefinger up with just a small space between them.

"I'm sorry," I say earnestly, but then curiosity strikes. "Soooo... how was he?"

"Girl," she says, stepping in closer and lowering her voice even though no one is here to eavesdrop. "The man knows what he's doing. Like... he's a master at it. I'd venture to say he may even be the best I've ever had."

"So you're going to L.A. next weekend then?" I conclude.

"Um… no. I most certainly am not."

"Why? Are you crazy? Why wouldn't you?" I ask, peppering her with questions.

"Because there's no sense. Nothing would ever come of it. Besides, I'm visiting my parents. I want to spend as much time with them as I can before I head back out on assignment."

"But—"

"No buts," she states with a firm tone and a hard gaze. "I'm not interested. That's all there is to it."

"Oh-kay…" I say slowly, taking the hint she wants me to back off.

But I have to wonder why she's lying to me. Because she can deny it all she wants, but she is most definitely interested in Dominik Carlson.

CHAPTER 19

Dax

I GLANCE AT Regan where she sits in a waiting room chair perpendicular to me. She's flipping through a magazine as we wait to meet with the case manager from the pharmaceutical company. This is the person who greases the wheels with the insurance company for approval... as well as controls the purse strings for additional financial aid if needed.

It's not, of course. I'm more than able to cover Regan's out-of-pocket expenses, but since she's being stubborn and insisting on paying me back for everything, we need to ask about it. But I think once they realize her husband has a lot of money at his disposal, they're not going to offer her any additional help.

She doesn't seem quite right, though. I noticed it this morning when we woke up.

Which was again naked and wrapped in each other's arms.

This was preceded by a night filled with off-the-charts sex that was even better than before.

First, though, we'd had a rather fun, but slightly frustrating evening at The Sneaky Saguaro with Willow and many of my teammates. Fun was a given as we'd won our game. I'd scored a goal and fed an assist to Bishop, who in turn scored. It was frustrating because despite all the frivolity and celebration, I felt out of sorts around Regan. To the outside world, we had to put on a show. That we were just family friends instead of lovers. I lost track of the amount of times I saw her laughing at something someone said, which had then made me want to pull her close and put my arm around her. Made me want to tell everyone, "See this woman right here? She's mine." I hadn't even been able to touch her, and it made me crazy.

This morning, she'd been different from the fun-loving girl of the night before.

Sluggish. Hard to wake up. I thought it might have been too much alcohol, but then I remembered she only had two beers before she switched over to water. After I'd turned the alarm off, I'd given her a little shake. She'd just groaned, rolled over, and tried to pull the covers over her head.

My inclination was to let her sleep, but Willow planned to leave for the airport early, and I'd known Regan would want to say goodbye.

When I finally got her to open her eyes—there was a lot of blinking and dedication to focusing on me—I couldn't help but notice the bluish tint on the fragile skin below her lashes. She'd looked like she could use about a dozen more hours of sleep.

"I'm going to take Willow to the airport," I'd told her after deciding she was going to see my sister at the end of the week anyway when Regan traveled to Michigan for our Detroit game. "You stay here and get more sleep."

But the stubborn thing wouldn't just roll over and fall back into slumber. She'd grumbled and yawned, moving like she was stuck in molasses, but she managed to roll out of bed. Like a zombie, she'd moved to the bathroom. At one point, I swear she fell back asleep while we'd stood under the hot spray of the shower.

It hadn't been until we were actually heading out to the car a bit later, me carrying Willow's duffel, that I looked at Regan and realized… this wasn't just a late night out.

It had to be her illness.

It's confirmed as I continue to watch her in the waiting room. She's flipping through a magazine, but I can tell she's not reading anything. Her eyes appear glazed and unfocused. When I ask her something, she's a little slow to respond. I try for funny, but it seems to take forever for her lips to curl into a smile.

"Regan," I murmur, leaning closer toward her so no one else can listen in. "You okay?"

She slowly raises her head to meet my eyes, smile wan as she admits, "I'm really tired, Dax. It's just one of those days."

"Do we need to take you to the doctor?" My internal alarms are starting to chime. I don't know how seriously I should take her fatigue. It's a symptom, but I'm not sure about the magnitude.

She shakes her head. "No. It's not bad. I mean, it might seem bad to you because this isn't my normal but compared to how it could get before I started on the Salvistas, it's manageable. It's just... after we finish here, I'm probably just going to want to go home and sleep if that's okay with you."

"Of course it's okay with me," I say with an exhale of relief. I reach out and take her hand. "You just have to walk me through these things... teach me the difference between simply being tired and 'okay, we better get to a hospital right now'."

She chuckles, her eyes brightening slightly. "Trust me. I don't play around with this stuff. If I needed to go to the hospital, I'd be out the door and driving myself there."

"Correction," I warn sternly. "I'll be driving you there."

"I stand corrected," she replies with an incline of her

head. "Unless you're gone to a game. Then I'm perfectly capable of getting there myself."

Now... I don't like to think about her being in a situation like that. Sure, I feel in control now while sitting beside her, promising to take care of her, but what happens when I'm gone?

Fuck... how had Lance handled being so far away from her, knowing she could be fine one moment and in the hospital needing a blood transfusion to save her life the next?

How in the fuck had he lived with the knowledge that he might one day get a call from a hospital to tell him that she'd died?

My stomach turns, and I feel slightly nauseated.

"Mr. and Mrs. Monahan," a voice calls. I'm still staring at Regan. She doesn't look over and neither do I, because of the unfamiliarity of the titles in relation to us. It hasn't sank in to either of us that we are now a unit. A husband and wife team.

She's Mrs. Monahan, and it's the first time I've heard her called that.

I snap out of it first, turning to see a woman who looks to be about my age standing in the doorway that leads back to the inner offices. Manilla folder in hand, she scans the handful of people in the waiting room.

"Regan," I say as I take the magazine from her hand. She lifts her head, blinking at me slowly. "They just called us."

"Oh," she replies softly, attempting a smile. She appears to be too tired to even manage that.

I push up from the chair, drop the magazine on the corner table that was between our chairs, and hold my hand out to her. She slips hers in mine, and we both turn to the woman who called our names.

She beams a cheery smile. "Hi. I'm Monica Sanders, and I'll be handling your case."

We approach her, shake hands, and then follow her through a maze of cubicles with five-foot divider walls in between the desks. The air is filled with the chatter of dozens of customer service reps on the phone helping people to navigate the world of insurance denials.

Monica leads us to the far end of the room to a glassed-in office. She's clearly someone above the cubicle workers as she rates an office, and I take this as a good sign. We are here, after all, to make sure Regan gets her treatment with no hassles.

We're invited to take seats as Monica moves around to sit behind her desk. She puts the folder down, flips it open, and does a quick scan of the top page before giving her attention to Regan.

"Mrs. Monahan, it looks like we have the necessary documents filled out and the approval by Dr. Marino in place, but your health insurance company hasn't given the approval for the Salvistis yet."

"Why not?" I ask, noting Regan just seems to stare listlessly at her. I'm so fucking glad I came with her as she doesn't look like she has an ounce of "give a fuck" in her right now.

Monica turns to me. "The red tape is sticky, Mr. Monahan. Especially when you're dealing with a drug such as Salvistis."

"You mean when your company charges almost half-a-million dollars for a medication I'm sure costs a fraction of that to produce? Yeah… I get why it takes a while."

"Dax," Regan says, finding the strength to chide me.

I ignore her, keeping my eyes pinned hard on the representative assigned to help my wife. "That's unacceptable. She has to have her treatment this week."

"Yes, well, I'm sure you can understand we have certain protocols—"

"All I understand is my fucking wife has a life-threatening condition," I growl as I push up from my chair and slam my hands on her desk. Monica jerks backward, eyes opening wide. "I want her treatment set up, and I want it set up now."

Granted, Monica seems like a nice person who is just doing her job. And granted, it's a dick move to go all alpha controlling on her. I just met her less than a minute ago.

But I'm not in the mood. Particularly when she

opens her mouth and spouts off a smart-ass response of, "Well, Mr. Monahan... I'd be glad to set it up if you want to shell out thirty-five thousand for the dosage."

Regan's head drops, and she presses her fingers to the bridge of her nose. I study her a moment, livid she even has to be put through this stress.

Eyes hard, I pull my checkbook out of my back pocket and cock a brow at Monica. Taking a pen out of a cup holder on her desk, I ask, "Who do I write the check out to?"

Monica's mouth drops open, and Regan's head pops up. She reaches a hand out, touching her fingers to my forearm. "Dax... no."

I don't spare Regan a glance, just state firmly, "Yes, Regan. You're getting your fucking treatment this week."

My stare off with Monica continues for just a few more seconds before she finally averts her attention to a drawer where she pulls out a form. "I can set this up as a self-pay. If and when the insurance approves, you can get reimbursed."

"That will be fine," I say, softening my tone as I take my seat again.

I look at Regan, who stares at me incredulously.

"What?" I ask curiously, a small smile playing at my lips.

She shakes her head. "Nothing. It's just... well,

thank you."

"My pleasure," I say and then turn to Monica. "Now... if we could get it set up before Thursday as she's flying out of state."

And it was my absolute pleasure. In fact, I can't quite figure out why I feel so fucking accomplished and satisfied I could do that for Regan, but I do know I like the feeling.

I SET THE tray of food on the bedside table, not really keen on the fact it's in the guest room where Regan had originally been put when she moved in. I had thought the fact she slept in my bed the last two nights would have meant something to her, but when we got back from the meeting with her case manager this morning and she said she wanted to take a nap, I didn't think much about it then.

I went and worked out, stopped by Legend's house to visit Pepper who is recovering nicely from her run-in with a bullet at the hands of a madwoman, and then came home.

It was just after lunch, so I whipped up some canned vegetable soup and a peanut butter and jelly sandwich for Regan. I'm not the best cook in the world, but I'd put it on a tray and carried it to my room for her.

Only to not find her not there, but instead asleep in her own room.

I was hesitant to wake her but realizing she needed to eat and could go right back to sleep if she needed spurred me to rouse her.

Sitting on the edge of the bed, I put my hand on her shoulder and give her a tiny shake. She's beautiful in her sleep, and the peacefulness on her face is something I relish.

Eyes fluttering open, she focuses on me. "Hey," she says, her voice all groggy and husky. Kind of sexy. "What time is it?"

"About one," I say. "I figured you should try to eat something."

Regan pushes up in bed to lean against the headboard, wiping her eyes with her fingers. She gives a long yawn before glancing at the food on the table. "You made that for me?"

"Yup," I say with a smile. "Impressed?"

"Incredibly," she says, and I note her eyes are a lot brighter and more focused.

"You feel better?"

"I do, and I'm kind of hungry," she replies.

This is my cue. I reach over, grab the tray, and carefully lay it over her stretched-out legs. She grabs the spoon and leans over, pulling some soup to her mouth with a sigh of contentment. I watch her eat for a few moments, satisfied knowing she feels better.

Also in knowing it's not a chore taking care of her. I

always thought commitment and relationships were a drain on my own time and energy, but not so much.

At least not with Regan.

She pauses the soup slurping to reach for the sandwich. I had cut it in half, on the diagonal to be fancy, but I left the crust on. She takes a bite, chews, then after swallowing, she says, "I totally forgot to ask you... but how did your meeting go yesterday morning regarding that lawsuit?"

I had forgotten about it, too, as it was resolved to my satisfaction. The team's attorney had met with me, Erik, Sebastian Parr—our director of merchandising who was also named in the suit—along with Christian Rutherford, the team's general manager. Word had come down from the head honcho—that would be Dominik Carlson—that he didn't intend to pay a dime to the woman since her claims were bogus and generated only to try to squeeze some money out of lucrative pockets.

The risk was in if we refused to pay, she could continue with the lawsuit and it would be a long, arduous process to go through. However, we all agreed we'd rather stick to our guns since we were in the right and she was in the wrong. We were all in agreement with the decision to not offer a single penny at the mediation that was coming up in a few weeks.

I relate all of this to Regan while she steadily eats—

alternating between her soup and sandwich, sometimes even dipping the latter into the aforementioned.

"So why would she even make such a claim against so many different people in the organization? I mean… how could she even think it's credible when you guys weren't even involved with her?"

"I guess that's all relative to what you mean by involved with her?" I say dryly, thinking of the lengths this woman went to set things up for her "lawsuit". "She had a job interview with Sebastian, then claimed he told her he'd give her the job if she gave him a blow job."

"Eww," Regan says, wrinkling her nose. "What did she make up about you and Erik?"

"That we slept with her and used our leverage as team players to get her something within the organization in exchange for sexual favors."

"What did she do? Just like… pick you guys off the team roster and target you?" she asks in disgust, clearly incensed on our behalf.

And I wasn't expecting these direct questions. Suddenly, I'm feeling a little hot under the collar.

"Not exactly," I admit.

"Not exactly… what?" she inquires with her eyebrows drawn inward.

"Well… I actually kind of slept with her." I watch her expectantly, wondering just how low I've sank in her opinion by admitting that.

"You slept with her?" she demands, her eyes now flaring with heat and indignation. "Dax... how could you?"

I know I should feel angry and defensive over her tone, but frankly, it's cute as fuck. I can't help but mess with her a bit. "Are you jealous, Mrs. Monahan?"

"No," she snaps.

"Are you sure? Because it sounds like jealousy."

"I'm not jealous," she growls.

"That's good," I chide while trying to hide a smile. "Because that was long before you became Mrs. Monahan and before anyone even knew what a nut job this lady was. She came on to me, Regan. She was hot. And while you might not want to admit your husband was such a bad boy, I really didn't turn my nose up at that sort of thing."

Regan huffs and grabs onto the tray, attempting to swing her legs off the bed, but I'm still sitting there and blocking her way. I lean over her, plant a hand on the mattress, and put my face into hers, grinning down. "Don't be jealous, baby. You are so much hotter than she was."

"Oooohhh, you big jerk," she snarls, trying to figure out how to push me away without spilling the half-full bowl of soup.

I can't help but laugh, taking the tray off her lap and setting it on the table. She uses this as an opportunity to roll the opposite way off the bed, but then I'm on her.

I've got her flipped on her back, underneath me in the middle of the mattress. My hands go to her wrists, and I pin them above her head. She glares, tries to buck, and I start to get hard that she's fighting me.

What a sick fuck I am.

"I think this woman targeted us," I explain. "In hindsight, that's what I believe she was doing. The night I met her, she was flirting hard with both me and Erik. She went home with me. Later, she tried for Erik, but I'd warned him off her as something wasn't quite right about her. She targeted Sebastian Parr, our director of marketing, for sure. Set up a job interview with him, then later claimed untrue shit. It's an unfortunate situation we're all in, but at least the team is standing behind us on this."

Her face softens a bit as she takes it all in.

Dipping my head, I press my mouth to hers. She tries to turn away from me and I let her, using the opportunity to put my lips to her ears. "No one compares to you, Regan. No one. Not ever. And you can't possibly be mad at me for something I did months ago before I ever came to find out how amazing you are. Long before I ever thought we'd be married. So stop being mad and kiss me back, okay?"

She totally deflates. When she turns her face to me, her look is chagrined. Pursing her lips, she mutters.

"Still… gross you'd be with someone so manipulative."

"Didn't know she was manipulative then, babe," I reply smartly. "Fact is, we didn't do a whole lot of talking, so—"

"Okay," she says quickly to interrupt me. "Don't want to hear details."

"Can I kiss you now?" I ask with a grin.

Regan's eyelids droop slightly, her mouth curving into a sexy smile. "Depends on where you want to kiss me?"

"Do you have a preference?" I ask, my voice having dropped an octave on its own accord.

"Between my legs," she whispers. "And take your time with it."

My cock goes from tingling in anticipation to full-on hard in about a nanosecond. "Jesus, Regan… you're learning things awfully damn fast."

Her straight teeth flash as she wiggles under me. "Well, what are you waiting for?"

I'm not waiting. Not for another fucking moment.

CHAPTER 20

Dax

F EBRUARY 25TH.

Trade deadline.

It's nineteen days away.

For some players, it's a time of stress. Other times, it's a time of hope and excitement. I expect the Vengeance management is going to be looking at all offers quite seriously as we head into the playoffs as one of the top-ranked teams in our division. Our shot at the Cup is as good as any, which means management will take any and all serious offers that will bolster our team further.

This is causing a bit of speculation as well as stress as the biggest player at risk on our team is Tacker. He currently stands suspended from our team for being drunk and driving his vehicle into a concrete barricade. While on the ice, he was playing at his best, but his emotional instability is a liability no one can overlook.

On top of that, no one knows if management has even given Tacker a way to try to make it back onto the team, and if they have, if Tacker is even interested.

The unknown can make it difficult to put our heads in the game, until well... we're actually in the game.

Like we are now.

The Chicago Bobcats are giving us a run for our money, and this game is coming down to the wire.

Rafe Simmons has moved permanently to the first line, replacing Tacker as center. Rafe was replaced by a pretty damn talented player from our minor team in Denver, and there's a chance he and Rafe could claim those positions for the rest of the season if the powers-that-be determine Tacker just isn't fit to stay with our team.

I'll be the first to admit... Rafe is fucking good at his job. He's now the center glue that holds Bishop as the right wing and me as the left wing together on the ice. By way of example, Rafe intercepts a pass down low, then whips it backhanded to Bishop as we all take off toward the Bobcats' goal. Bishop, Rafe, and I execute what some would call an almost-choreographed dance as we weave in and out of players, passing the puck between us.

Bishop to Rafe to Bishop to me.

The Bobcats' goalie pitches left and right on his skates, his eyes darting fast as he tries to get a slight lead on our plan.

We don't really have one, but we have drilled many breakaways before.

I give a short tap to Rafe, then he passes to Bishop and starts to wind up his shot as Bishop does nothing more than snap it right back at him. He connects solidly, the puck whizzes to the top right, and I crash it to the net.

There's a loud "clang" as the puck hits the pipe and ricochets right at me. I raise my stick no higher than my hip, turn so the blade catches my prize right on target, and I direct it right over the goalie's left shoulder.

The red light blazes, the Chicago fans groan, and our own Vengeance allies go crazy over the play. It took no more than five, six seconds from end to end to score that goal.

My teammates all converge with pats to my head with gloved hands or taps on my calf with a stick. It's a fucking awesome feeling that never dulls over time. I've been playing professional hockey for a decade now, and the thrill of scoring is still one of the best feelings ever.

I would even go so far as to say it used to be the top-ranked feeling I've ever had the pleasure of beholding, but that honor now goes to Regan. Scoring a goal comes second, and I wonder if Regan is watching on the TV right now. It was tough leaving her this morning, especially after the rough day she had yesterday at her case manager's office.

She seemed good this morning. Was right there with me when I took her after we woke up. Her legs over my shoulders, panting in sharp, tiny bursts as she orgasmed so hard I felt it in my balls. I left her not long after with a satisfied smile on her face as she drifted back to sleep in my bed, and I left to catch the team plane to Chicago.

I had a smile on my face, too.

"To Dax," Erik shouts as he holds his mug of beer up high.

"To Dax," Bishop and Legend echo.

We all tap our beers before taking a sip. I set mine down, then pick up a nacho. The four of us decided to go out after the game for some food and beers. I scored a total of two goals and had an assist, which also landed me the MVP of the game in our three-two win over the Bobcats.

I called Regan right after the game from outside the bus while everyone was loading. It was hard to have any privacy, but damn if I didn't need it.

We chatted about the game—she had indeed watched, and I liked it maybe a little too much how much she gushed about how well I played. We chatted about how she was feeling—she said she felt so much better than the day before, and she was excited about her treatment the next day thanks to the thirty-five-thousand-dollar check I'd written out.

And then… she asked me how big my cock was, and I couldn't have been more shocked.

Except she hadn't said it like that.

She'd said, "How many inches is your… um… penis? You know, when it's fully hard."

I had to take about five steps farther away from the bus, then turn my back on it lest anyone see the expression on my face.

"Excuse me?" I'd asked.

"How big is it?"

"Well, darling," I drawled. "You've seen it up close. Had your hand around it. Your mouth on it. You should know."

She fucking giggled into the phone, and I smiled as big as I did when I'd scored those goals tonight. Seems there are even better things than hockey.

After some digging, turns out Regan had been talking to another woman—my money is on Willow, but Regan wouldn't give her name up—and the dick size came up. I had to tell Regan I had never actually measured myself, so she was just going to have to be left wondering until we were together again.

"I'd give a hundred bucks to know what you're thinking right now," Erik says, his voice vaguely penetrating through my pleasant thoughts of Regan.

I blink before giving a blasé shrug, then reach for another nacho.

"I know that look," Erik says with a leering grin as he points a finger right at my face. My eyes dart over to Bishop, who's smirking as he watches.

"What look?" I ask as I give my attention to Erik.

"I know that look, too," Legend pipes up. He's also grinning. Frankly, it's nice to see on his face. He's been through the fucking ringer here lately since Pepper had been shot and Charlie kidnapped. But he's on to brighter days for sure.

"What fucking look?" I growl.

"You're seeing someone," Erik says emphatically with a nod. "Someone special."

"Am not," I mutter as I take a sip of my beer. "And mind your own business."

"Totally seeing someone," Legend drawls, rubbing his jaw in contemplation. "He can't hide it."

"So who is she?" Erik asks, leaning his elbows on the table. "What's her name? Where did you meet her? When should we schedule a group date with all of us?"

My head snaps toward to Bishop. "What the fuck? Did you say something?"

"Didn't say a word, dude," he replies, but now I've just totally outed myself.

"Christ," I mutter as I glance between Erik, Legend, then back to Erik. Exhaling, I admit, "It's Regan."

Both men blink in surprise, and Legend says, "You're fucking kidding?"

I shake my head, digging through the plate of nachos for a loaded one. "Not kidding. And in the interest of full disclosure, I married her already."

"Holy shit," Erik drawls.

Legend whistles low in amazement. "You don't play around, do you?"

"There's a good reason I had to marry her so quickly," I explain before realizing how that sounds when Erik and Legend both go quite pale. I rush to explain what I can to them. "She's not pregnant, so get those expressions off your face. But there is a very good reason we needed to marry, but I can't tell you what it is. Just know I believe Lance would have approved."

"Okay," Legend says with his head tilted in confusion. "I believe you when you say it's a good reason. Even more so that you can't tell us what it is, but there's no mistaking the look on your face. You care about her."

"Of course I care about her," I snap. "I've known her since she was born."

"You're totally having sex with her," Erik says, and Bishop elbows him in the ribs. He shoots him a glare before giving me his attention again, his tone a little more subtle. "What I mean is you look totally smitten with her. An intimate type of smitten, and I think I'm safe in saying this to be true since I've had that same damn look on my face when Blue is around. Same for Legend and Bishop, I'm sure."

"Well, congratulations, Sherlock. You have me all figured out."

"Why so bitter about it?" Legend teases. "This sounds like cause for celebration. Another beer at least."

"I'm not bitter about it." My denial is fast and strong. There is absolutely no bitterness for my situation.

Confusion? Yes.

Regret? Maybe. I mean, if I end up hurting Regan, sure.

Curiosity as to what more could be? Abso-fucking-lutely.

"Look," I say with a sigh. "Can we talk about something else? No offense, but things are just new and confusing and I'm figuring shit out. When I know something, I'll let you assholes know. I promise. But for now, I have to keep some stuff close to the vest with regards to Regan."

There's silence around the table as they share exchanged glances of concern but acceptance of my request.

"Whatever you need, bud," Erik assures me. "We got your back."

"You bet your ass we do," Legend adds.

"Always," Bishop intones, then snags a passing waitress. "Can we get four more beers?"

"Since we're changing subjects," Erik says as he picks up a chip, studies it, and determines there isn't enough good stuff on it so he drops it. "Everyone's coming to Billy's party on Sunday, right?"

There are resounding "yups" around the table. Billy is Blue's brother who has a form of cerebral palsy that has him confined to a wheelchair. He lives in a really nice group home—his choice—but spends a great deal of time at Erik and Blue's house as they've spent a lot of money and effort into making it handicapped accessible. He's a great guy—funny, smart, and always a joy to be around.

"Guess who else is coming?" Erik asks with a huge, knowing grin on his face.

"Tacker," I guess, but I bet Legend and Bishop were thinking the same thing.

Erik nods enthusiastically. We've all been struggling to find ways to spend time with Tacker. He won't come to any team events, and he'd shunned my invitation to dinner. But Tacker really likes Billy. They sort of have a bond that none of the other players have with him. The one thing we've all figured out with Tacker is he has a soft spot for those who can't help themselves, which puts Billy and Charlie on his list of people he'll actually leave the house for.

This is, of course, great news. We need to make a concerted effort at Billy's party to make Tacker understand he could still be a very vital part of this team if he just wanted to.

CHAPTER 21

Regan

THE MILES AND the Monahans hail from the outskirts of Ann Arbor, just west of the city. I flew into Detroit, then took a thirty-five-minute Uber ride to the Monahan's house.

Dax had wanted to pick me up. He'd played in Chicago last night, and the team flew into Detroit this morning on their fancy private plane. He has the day off, so he rented a car and headed straight to his parents' house to wait for me to arrive.

To say I'm a little nervous is an understatement. Which is silly, I get that. The Monahans are like family to me. I've known them my entire life. Our parents were best friends. As we kids all played, went to school, and spent holidays together.

When my parents died in a car accident, Linda and Calvin Monahan, and their kids, were as devastated as Lance and I were. I know Lance, Linda, and Calvin spent a great deal of time talking about whether I should stay with them rather than move to New York where Lance was playing for the Vipers. We all gave it serious consideration, but when it boiled down to it, Lance was my brother and I wanted to be with him more than the Monahans. He changed so much of his life to take on the role of my legal guardian, and we became tighter than ever.

But Linda, Calvin, Dax, Willow, and Meredith all stayed a constant presence in my life. We visited as often as we could and talked almost daily either via social media, text, or phone.

So yeah… silly I'd be nervous to see them.

But I am because they know the whole truth of what is going on with me. Well, not the entire truth but enough. Dax offered to fill his parents in ahead of time about my illness and how he'd married me so I could get insurance benefits. I felt like such a chicken, but I gladly took him up on it. He assured me they would be totally fine with it, which deep in my gut I already knew to be true. I think my fears stem from the fact we've been duplicitous for a time so there's some anxiety in finally coming clean about things.

My Uber driver pulls up in front of the Monahan home. It's two story, the bottom done in brick and the top in white fiber cement siding with blue shutters. The color of the shutters has changed over the years, and I like this new shade. Our neighborhood would be what I call classic lower middle class, with most of the houses built in the sixties and remodeled over the years to remove shag carpeting and replacing it with laminate. My childhood home was remarkably similar, except it was all cement siding done in a beige color with black shutters and sits one block east of here. I haven't been back there since my parents died and Lance sold it. We used that money to help pay for my undergraduate degree.

Which is funny. Lance made enough to pay for my education ten times over, but we both sort of felt Mom and Dad would have wanted the money from the house to go specifically toward that. They worked hard to give us a good life, and those fruitions helped me to become a nurse.

When the Uber comes to a stop, I thank my driver and slide out of the seat. He pops his trunk but doesn't make any effort to help me get my suitcase from the back. It's no big deal as it's just a rolling carry-on and easily manageable. When I have it out and the Uber is rolling away, I turn to see Dax emerging from the front door of his parents' house to greet me.

He's got on jeans and a thick cable-knit sweater in dark gray. It's freezing out, but he didn't put on a coat to come out and meet me.

I wait on the sidewalk as he comes nearer, struck

almost stupid by how ridiculously handsome he is. A wave of giddiness crashes through me as I realize... this man is mine.

For now, anyway.

It amazes me that someone like him could be interested in someone like me. Attracted to someone like me.

Let's face it... I come with a whole slew of messy problems—and who wants to be saddled with someone who faces such a serious medical condition?

For now, I just accept it for what it is, letting myself be struck by the enormity of how much Dax Monahan dazzles me.

"Bout time you got here," he says gruffly, and I'm stunned when he wraps his arms around me, lifting me in a big hug. My arms go automatically around his neck, and I squeeze tightly as he buries his face in my neck. Lifting my gaze slightly to the house, I see Linda and Willow with their faces pressed against the glass peering out at us. Calvin wouldn't dare to be so nosy, but I'm sure he's just waiting on a report from the women.

When Dax loosens his hold and lets me slide to the ground again, he gives me a critical once over with worried eyes. "How are you feeling?"

"Good," I reply with a confident smile.

"No side effects from the treatment yesterday?"

"Nope."

"You'd tell me if so?" he prods.

"Nope," I reply with a sassy grin.

"You need a spanking," he mutters as he picks up my suitcase. "But I better get you inside. Everyone is dying to fawn all over you."

"So you told them everything?" I ask, worrying at my lower lip.

"Well, I told them about the PNH and us getting married. Willow had already blabbed about us."

"What about us?" I inquire.

Dax takes my hand. Squeezes it. "That we're not just friends."

I'm fairly sure my hand just turned sweaty. "And how did they take it?"

"A lot better than you having a serious medical condition. Mom's obviously worried about you, so you should be prepared... she's in full-on mothering mode right now."

I sigh with relief that it's now all out in the open. "I'm okay with that. In fact, that sounds a little nice actually."

"Then come on," he says, then tugs me across the front yard, up the porch steps, and into the house.

No one is there to greet us. Probably didn't want to get busted spying on us. Dax sets my suitcase down, and I follow him to the kitchen at the back of the house.

Linda, Calvin, and Willow are all there waiting.

Linda moves on me first, wrapping me up in a warm

hug. I inhale the familiar floral perfume she always wears, and it feels a little like coming home to me.

"You poor, sweet girl," Linda croons as she just holds onto me super tight. "What you've been through. Had I known, I would have insisted you come back home and let me take care of you."

She releases me, leans back, and locks her eyes on me. "As it is, I'm proud of how strong you are, and of my son for stepping in to help you. He loved Lance and he loves you, and I'm so grateful for all of it."

I was not expecting words like that, and they punch me in the chest. In a good way. Painful, but good. Touching and relieving and reassuring all at once. It was probably the fact she said Dax loves me that caused the most feels, but I have to remember there are several types of love and his is born of obligation and duty.

"Come here, you," Calvin says gruffly, then I'm pulled away from Linda and lifted into a big bear hug that has me laughing as I squeeze him back.

Calvin was a lot like my own dad. Short on words, big on actions. So when he lowers me to the ground and then bends so he can peer straight into my eyes, I'm surprised when he says, "We all have your back, Regan. We're your family now."

My eyes immediately flood with tears, but then I'm being jerked into another hug by Linda, Calvin enveloping us both in his arms. We all start laughing when Willow rushes in saying, "Let me in on some of that action."

I'm stuck in the middle of a Monahan hug, and it feels good and right. I glance past Linda's shoulder and see Dax leaning against the counter, hands pushed down into his front pockets. The smile on his face is like nothing I've ever seen. It's packed full of emotion and maybe even a bit of pride in his family at this moment.

We break apart, Calvin giving a gruff, semi-awkward cough as he steps away to lean against the kitchen counter beside his son.

"Meredith will be coming over in a few hours after the kids get out of school," Linda says as she moves over to the coffee pot. They always have some hot and ready to serve.

"I was actually hoping to go to the cemetery," I say, shooting a glance at Dax as I had not told him before of my desire to do this. "Think I could borrow your car?"

"I'll take you," Dax says, smiling as he pulls the rental car keys out of his pocket and twirling them on his finger.

MARYBETH AND JUSTIN Miles share a headstone, their ashes mingled and interred together below it. I kneel in the dried grass browned by winter, brushing a few stray blades from the granite. Dax comes to stand beside me, close enough his leg brushes against me.

I was just fourteen when they died. Such a fragile age for a girl. Yet, Lance did an amazing job at making me feel safe and secure. I didn't have to fear the future because I trusted in him to take care of me, which left me able to grieve my loss along with him.

"I'm not sure I ever really thanked Lance for all he did for me after they died," I say quietly as I stare at the headstone.

"He knew," Dax replies, squatting beside me.

I nod, hopeful he's right. "I need to make arrangements for his ashes to be buried here."

"I'll help with that," he replies, the strength in his voice infusing me. "Just tell me what you want, and I'll handle it for you."

I look over at him. "Thank you."

He smiles, reaching out to tuck a strand of hair behind me ear. "It's nothing to thank me for. It would be my honor because I loved him, too."

"He loved you right back." My nose stings, and I inhale a sniffle.

It's enough to have Dax's arm come around my shoulder, then he's pulling me to my feet and wrapping me in an embrace. It reminds me of just over four weeks ago when we stood in Lance's apartment and Dax pressed me to tell him what was wrong in my life. I had shred myself into a thousand tears in his arms. He made it so easy for me to let go and just grieve. I had been trying so hard to be strong and bear everything with dignity and grace, and in just a matter of moments, Dax let me fall apart. I know he would never let me completely shatter.

Standing here on my parents' graves, having lost my brother not all that long ago, he makes it easy once again and I begin to weep. His arms tighten as I turn my face into his chest. Dax's hand presses to the back of my head, a silent command to let it all out.

I do, trying not to worry about leaving a snot trail on his coat.

I snicker, then start laughing at the thought. Crying and laughing is a weird basket of emotions, and I decide to give in to more laughter since it's the better of the two.

"What's so funny?" he asks, and I can hear the amusement in his voice.

"I was just worried about leaving snot on your nice wool coat. I'm sure it's expensive."

"I'm sure the dry cleaners can get it out," he replies dryly.

Giggling, I pull away to look up at him. His smile is soft as he gazes at me, and I almost melt when he wipes a tear from my face with his thumb, the chilly air turning my cheek frosty.

"I'm sorry I'm such a mess," I say sincerely. I don't like feeling weak or like I need to be cared for, yet this feeling of security he gives me feels too damn good to walk away from.

"Don't apologize, Regan," he replies in a low voice. "You've been through so much this past month. Lost a brother. Gained an unexpected husband. Faced an uncertain future without lifesaving medical care, moved to a different state. I don't know many people who wouldn't be a complete mess. Yet, you keep trucking along with such a positive attitude. I'm proud of you. If you decide to break down periodically in my arms, just consider it a husbandly service I'm glad to perform."

"A service you were not looking to sign up for," I point out. "I don't know if I'll ever be able to thank you enough for what you've done for me."

Something flickers through Dax's expression. An uncomfortable look, but it's gone before I can even really analyze it. His lips curl up, his eyes sparkling with mischief. "Oh, I don't know. There's been some benefits. Not exactly hard to hold a beautiful woman in my arms when she's all soft, pliable, and susceptible to suggestion."

I grin at him, blinking back the rest of my tears and sadness so I can tease him in return. "Yeah... not a hardship to be held by a totally hot and muscular man with what I'm guessing is a good eight to eight and a half inches of a pure pleasure machine."

Dax blinks, sucks in air, and coughs as he starts

laughing. His arms go tightly around me, and I'm being squeezed hard as he laughs his ass off. "God, you're fucking funny, and that also turns me on just a bit. And I'm totally weirded out by the fact we're standing on your parents' graves while having this conversation."

Laughing, I snuggle deeper into his hold, trying not to let this good feeling slip away as I wonder how much longer this is going to last.

CHAPTER 22

Dax

OUR WIN OVER the Detroit Cardinals was pretty fucking awesome. But it's not going to be the highlight of my night. That goes to the fact I am in my home state, near my hometown, and with my entire family all together. I had snagged tickets for everyone, including my niece and nephew, to attend the game along with Regan. My brother-in-law is a Cardinal fan, but I still got him a ticket.

The last two days have been both surreal and just like old times. Surreal because I brought home a surprise wife, and everyone was amazingly accepting and supportive. Just like old times, because we were all back together again with the exception of Lance. There was comfort in the fact my family banded together in support of Regan and everything she's going through with the PNH.

We had chosen to gather after the game at restaurant near the Cardinals' arena. I'd even invited all of my teammates as well. Unfortunately, we had to take the team bus back to the hotel following the game, but then Bishop, Erik, Legend, and I grabbed an Uber to the restaurant.

It's late and most of the diners have left, but the bar area is hopping as we walk in. I scan the crowd, immediately locking on Regan. I head straight for her as she winds her way through the crowd with a particular destination in mind. I step in front of her, halting her progress as I grin down at her. She blinks in surprise before delight floods her face and she throws her arms around my neck. "Oh my God… you played amazingly tonight, Dax. What a victory."

I give her a return hug before we break apart, and I'm not going to lie… it feels good to know she is now my personal fan and cheerleader.

"Where is everyone else?" I ask.

"I was just coming back from the bathroom. They're on the other side of the bar." She points in that direction before taking me by the hand and pulling me through the crowd. I glance over my shoulder to see Erik, Legend, and Bishop following behind us with knowing grins on their faces. I guess there was no hiding how much I like being around Regan, and they are clearly liking my enjoyment.

As I follow along behind her, I call above the noise

of a bunch of rowdy patrons, "How were the seats I got for you?"

"They were really good," she says as she glances at me briefly. "But we got invited up to the visiting owner's box, so they got even better."

My body goes tight. I start searching the crowd with a sneaking suspicion gnawing at my gut.

"Why were you invited up to the owner's box?" I ask as I tug her to a halt, and she turns to me in question.

"Dominik Carlson came to the game, then sent an usher down for all of us. Invited the whole family up to the box to watch the game. There was all kinds of food and alcohol, although I only had one glass of wine because I wanted to concentrate on the game. It was amazing, and you could see everything so good. Plus, they had TVs so we could watch the replays and—"

"Carlson is here? And he invited everyone up?" I ask, confused as to why he singled out my family.

But deep down, I know it's not the entire gang that has caught his fancy.

It's only my sister, Willow.

"Come on. Everyone's just over here." Regan starts pulling me again, and I follow.

The crowd breaks apart to show my family standing in a tight circle. Drinks in hand and laughing. My mom and dad. My sister, Meredith, without her husband Tim who took the kids home since it was so late, and besides... he's a Cardinal fan. Willow is there with a glass of bourbon on the rocks in her hand, and yes, Dominik Carlson.

Regan pulls me into the group, and everyone breaks into smiles and congratulations as hugs are given. Everyone knows Bishop since he played with me and Lance for a time on the Vipers. I introduce Erik and Legend around before finally giving my attention to the team's owner, Dominik Carlson.

He stands there in his fancy designer suit with what looks to be a bourbon on the rocks in his hand as well, although I bet it's the most expensive brand. There's a slight smirk on his face and a challenge in his eyes as if he realizes I know what he's doing and he's completely unapologetic about it.

He holds a hand out to me, and I shake it. "Great game, Dax."

Dominik releases my hand and turns to congratulate my teammates, then everyone starts conversing again.

Erik claps me on the shoulder with a, "What are you drinking, buddy?"

"Sam Adams," I reply, watching as Legend and Bishop follow him up to the bar.

By the time I turn around, Dominik has launched into a story about some foreign business deal that is apparently funny by the way everyone seems to be laughing.

Everyone except Willow.

She stands opposite of him in the circle, watching Dominik with a certain detachment that surprises me. There's definitely interest in her eyes, but there is a healthy layer of skepticism as she listens.

Now *that* is interesting. Dominik Carlson would be on the front page of the catalog entitled "Dream Man". He's the poster child for everything a woman could want.

I stand quietly and observe. My teammates return and hand me my beer, which I sip casually. Dominik carries most of the conversation, but after his funny business deal story, he turns the focus on my family, asking questions of everyone in an attempt to get to know them better. He's gregarious, charming, and I can tell everyone is taken in by him.

Everyone except Willow, who smiles only faintly at him when the attention is turned her way.

There comes a moment when Dominik's drink runs dry and he asks if anyone would like a refill. He turns to the bar after getting everyone's order, and I step up beside him.

"What do you think you're doing?" I ask as I sidle in beside him at the bar.

He twists to see me with a bland smile on his face.

"Isn't it obvious?" he replies dryly.

"Yes. You clearly have a thing for my sister. Everyone can tell you're trying to impress her."

"It's not working," he mutters.

"I'm glad you're smart enough to see that."

Dominik nods, glances to the bartender who is still busy serving someone else, then regards me pensively. "Any words of advice?"

"Yeah, stay away from her."

This does not offend the man. If anything, I see a measure of respect on his face. Still, he is not put off in the slightest. "Willow doesn't seem to be the type who needs protecting from her older brother."

"She's not. But that doesn't make me any less protective as her brother. But I'm telling you… you might as well give it up. She's not into the lifestyles of the rich and famous. Money won't impress her."

Dominik straightens up and leans an elbow on the bar. He smiles in what I would term to be triumph. "Interesting. Tell me more. What will impress her?"

I stare at him incredulously. "I'm not giving you advice to help you out."

"Why not?"

"Because you're my boss," I growl. "That's my sister. It's weird and creepy and just… leave her alone, okay?"

Dominik snorts. I have clearly amused him. But then his eyes turn hard as he leans towards me. "I could just trade you."

That gets my attention. "You wouldn't."

Dominik stares at me for a long, thoughtful moment, and I wonder just how far this immensely powerful man would go to get my sister. But then he shrugs and turns to the bartender. "No, I wouldn't trade you. But I also don't take orders from you. Until your sister tells me to stop, I'm going to keep on trying. My apologies if it bothers you."

Well, fuck.

He is effectively putting me in my place and telling me not to whine about stuff I cannot control. But I think he's also smart enough not to really piss me off as I can make things more difficult for him.

He needs to keep me on his good side.

I decide to use it as an advantage, changing the subject in an effort to catch him off-guard. "What is the team going to do about Tacker?"

Dominik's head snaps my way, his eyes narrowing. "That's private."

I just stare at him, not willing to accept that.

Dominik glances at the bartender, then leans into me slightly. "Without giving details, we've offered him a means to stay on the team and we're hoping he takes it. We think he's necessary to help us win the Cup this year. The deadline for him to give us an answer is Monday."

I think that's terrific news, but I don't show my jubilation. Instead, I say, "I'm going to see him on

Sunday. He's coming to Blue's brother's birthday party. We'll all encourage him as best we can."

The bartender walks up, interrupting our conversation. "What can I get you?"

Dominik starts rattling off the order, including another Sam Adams for me. I had not told him that's what I was drinking, but he must've been observant when I had asked Erik to get me one earlier. I try not to be impressed by his level of attentiveness.

I step away from the bar, rejoining the group. Taking Regan's hand, I give it a tug, pulling her a few feet away.

Bending so only she can hear me, I point out the obvious. "I was just thinking this is sort of the first time you and I are together as a couple in front of the team."

She cocks a perfect eyebrow at me. "I hadn't realized we were acting as a couple here tonight."

I hate to tell her, but I really like that smart mouth on her. I grin before giving her a kiss. When I pull back, I say, "If anyone was watching right now, they would know."

"So we're going to be open about this?" she asks cautiously.

"Not about your illness. Of course, we'll still keep the marriage a secret since that sort of goes hand-in-hand with that. But I don't see why we can't be open about us being together."

"If that's what you want to do," she replies hesitant-ly.

Putting my arm around her, I pull her into my side before I usher her to our group. "Yeah, that's what I want to do."

CHAPTER 23

Regan

ERIK AND BLUE'S house is pretty magnificent. It's huge, of course, which means despite the fact the entire team is here for Billy's party, it doesn't feel overcrowded.

This is good because despite the fact our time together following the game in Detroit was our first official "outing" as a couple, it feels as if I'm more in the spotlight here. Probably because it was late and in a dark bar in Detroit, so not everyone saw Dax and me together. Plus, we didn't really engage in overt affections being as his family was there and it was still a little awkward with us being "together" in front of them.

But here in Blue and Erik's house, where it's broad daylight and not overly crowded, it feels like there's a spotlight on us. That might be because since we arrived, Dax hasn't left my side. Hasn't stopped touching me for that matter.

It might be an arm around my waist, or maybe he'll pull me down onto his lap. Several times, he's leaned over and kissed me right in front of people. No one has said a word.

Well, no one except Blue herself. After we arrived and Dax introduced us, she immediately pulled me away from him, asking if I'd give her a hand in the kitchen with a few things.

I was delighted to help as I'd heard wonderful things about her from Dax. She's a flight attendant on the team plane, and Erik fell hard for her. Blue didn't really want much to do with him, but he was persistently charming according to Dax and finally won her over. It sounds like such a romantic love story, especially with how Erik has become like a brother to Billy.

Once I was away from Dax, Blue proceeded to grill me—in an incredibly nice and overly friendly way—about how Dax and I came to be together. She knew from Erik that he and Lance were best friends and we're longtime family friends. I guess a friends-to-lovers story was just too intriguing for her to ignore.

I stuck to the truth as much as I could. That Dax offered for me to come to Phoenix to be around a longtime family friend during my grief. That we'd gotten drunk one night and one thing sort of led to the other. That we had doubts and then regrets, but then ultimately decided to "go for it" so to speak.

Blue listened with a dreamy smile on her face as we sipped wine in the kitchen. I'd found out the party was catered, and she didn't have a damn thing to do to get ready, but just wanted to get to know me.

Dax showed up not long after, and he whisked me away to meet some of the other players and their significant others. I'd met Brooke, who is engaged to Bishop. Sadly, I didn't get to meet Pepper who was still recuperating from her injuries, although Legend came to wish Billy a happy birthday.

And, oh my gosh… Billy. The sweetest man ever. I loved seeing how at ease the players were with him and vice versa.

Best of all was watching the mysterious, reclusive Tacker interact with Billy. Dax had told me they bonded months ago at Dave & Buster's while playing video games, and that Tacker often visited him at his group home. I observed him carefully for a while. He smiled easily and talked without restraint to the young man who looked to be about my age, and he did all this without Billy being able to actually talk back. But he did respond with smiles and nods, communicating with hand signals and grunts. They sat in front of Erik's big-screen TV in the basement and played *Mario Kart* together.

The party is a smashing success. And after the cake and opening of presents in the large great room upstairs,

which was more than enough to accommodate every-one, I finally have a moment to take a long overdue bathroom break. The two upstairs restrooms are occupied, so I make my way down into the basement.

That restroom is thankfully open, and I go in to do my business. After washing my hands and drying them, then checking my makeup and popping in a breath mint, I exit the restroom and make my way to the staircase that leads up. Just as I raise my foot to take the first step, I see something from the corner of my eye. Pivoting to the large sectional sofa in front of the TV, I see Tacker sitting by himself, staring blankly at the darkened screen.

My first instinct is to ignore him and head upstairs, only because I've been told how much he doesn't like interacting with people. I don't want to make things awkward for him or cause him distress.

But there's something about the slump to his shoul-ders and the slightly haunted expression on his face that has me reconsidering. It's like looking at myself four weeks ago, and I recognize something of myself within him.

I make my way around the long side of the sectional sofa until I come into his view. He blinks at me in surprise, then just stares.

We had not actually been introduced yet, so I take the moment to step up to him and hold my hand out

with a bright smile. "We haven't met yet. I'm Regan."

Tacker raises his hand to give mine a brief shake. "Dax's girlfriend."

I can tell by the flat tone of his voice that this conversation is not welcome.

I'm not welcome.

For the life of me, I can't think of one interesting thing to say that could engage this taciturn, withdrawn man.

Except…

"I'm not his girlfriend. I'm his wife."

Tacker's large body physically jerks at my proclamation, his eyebrows flying upward. He doesn't say a word, but he can't hide the interest I find within his eyes.

"Actually, I'm quite ill," I say in another surprising burst of honesty. "I have paroxysmal nocturnal hemoglobinuria. It's a deadly blood disease. Dax married me so I could be put on his health insurance because there's a lifesaving treatment, but it's over four-hundred-thousand dollars a year to get it."

I cock my head at him expectantly, hoping what I have said is enough to make a connection. Why I feel the need to do this I have no clue, other than I guess I just feel sorry for somebody who seems so lost. Perhaps forming a bond with someone—no matter how tenuous—will give him some sense of belonging.

Tacker remains silent so I say, "No one knows what

I just told you. It's a secret. Well, some people know.
Dax. His family. Bishop. I think Erik and Legend know
we're married. And now you. But that's it."

"Why tell me?" Tacker mutters, and I'm overjoyed
upon hearing those three words.

I take it as an invitation to keep talking, moving
next to him on the couch. Shrugging my shoulders, I
explain, "You just kind of look like a guy who doesn't
go around telling secrets."

Tacker snorts. "Unlike you, who clearly has no
problem with dropping all kinds of secrets."

I grin. "It's my secret to tell so I get to choose who
knows it."

Tacker regards me unblinkingly. Not a flicker of
emotion on his face.

"Want to tell me a secret in return?" I ask. "As a
means of returning trust?"

I don't expect a response. My energy for engaging
this man is starting to fizzle as he has proved to be
perhaps too reluctant to overcome.

The silence gets a little awkward, and I consider
standing up to leave when sweet words come out of his
mouth. "I've been ordered to do therapy by the team. If
I don't do it, they're going to cut me loose permanently.
I need to give them an answer by tomorrow."

My heart is hammering over the unexpected admission. There's no doubt it's a secret that no one else

knows. I nod in understanding and sympathy. "I'm sorry about what happened to your fiancée. I remember when it happened, and I can't even imagine going through that."

His face softens minutely, and he murmurs, "Thank you."

Tacker's gaze slides off to the side, and I feel like we're losing the connection.

"So are you going to do the therapy?" I blurt out.

His eyes snap to mine. "Don't really want to."

"Why not?"

I get a mirthless laugh in return that comes out more like a staccato grunt. "Pretty sure I'm going to have to talk about my feelings, and that's sort of not my thing."

"And look where that's gotten you," I point out.

Tacker stares at me blankly for just a moment before his head tilts back and he lets out a long, deep-bellied laugh.

At that same moment, Dax comes trotting down the stairs, obviously searching for me. What he finds is me sitting with Tacker, who is laughing with deep amusement. Dax's jaw drops slightly as his eyes roam back and forth between Tacker and me. I grin at him, clearly pleased at my breakthrough.

"Who are you and what have you done with my teammate, Tacker?" Dax accuses, tongue in cheek, as his eyes focus on his laughing friend.

Tacker's laugh turns to a chuckle before fading away. His eyes are still bright though when he answers. "Your wife told me all her secrets. So I told her one in return."

Dax's eyes now bug out of his head as his face morphs into disbelief that I'd outed our marriage. I shrug and say, "I thought I should share something personal to get him to open up."

Dax blinks.

I grin. "And it worked."

Knowing I won't reveal it unless given permission to do so, Dax raises an eyebrow at Tacker. "And what exactly is your secret?"

"Management has ordered me into mandatory therapy if I want to keep my place on the team. My suspension will be lifted as soon as I start meaningful counseling sessions, whatever the hell that means. I have to give them an answer tomorrow."

I'm shocked he gave that information up to Dax so easily. I almost feel a little betrayed, but not really. I'm actually thrilled he's brought my husband into the fold.

"So," Dax drawls, taking a few steps closer, his gaze pinned on Tacker. "You're ready to hug it all out and open up to your pain?"

"Fuck no," Tacker growls as he pushes from the couch. He holds his hands out, looking baffled. "Last thing in the world I want to do is discuss my 'issues' with some stranger. It means I have to move on, and I don't feel ready to."

"I sense a 'but' in there," Dax murmurs. I hear it, too.

"But…" Tacker continues, scrubbing a hand through his hair. "I'm also tired of feeling shitty. I'm ready for these toxic, wasteful feelings to get the fuck out of me. And… I miss hockey. It's one of two things that have given me purpose lately."

"What's the other?" I ask curiously.

Tacker darts a glance to me and he flushes, as if realizing he's truly opening up and ruining his reputation or something. I tilt my head, eyes imploring him to trust me with another secret.

He sighs, gaze dropping to the floor as he rubs the nape of his neck. Finally, he raises his head, looking first to me, then to Dax, before he admits, "When you and I were riding around, searching for Charlie… I felt so fucking awful for Legend. I was expecting the worst, and my heart was fucking bleeding for him. And that made me realize I cared about you fuckers a lot more than I'd given myself credit for. So yeah… you guys give me purpose, too."

"That's wonderful," I exclaim, having to restrain myself from clapping in delight. "So you're going to give it a try. Good decision, Tacker."

His eyes are flat when they return to me. "I appreciate your enthusiasm, Regan, but I haven't made my final decision. Still have some thinking to do."

And with that, he nods at Dax and moves around the couch, heading to the staircase. He doesn't say another word, just leaves us staring at each other, more confused than ever.

CHAPTER 24

Dax

CHECKING MY WATCH, I see the reporter is technically only two minutes late. I try not to be
annoyed. I'm a stickler for punctuality, but even I admit
things can sometimes throw schedules off.

I stir my club soda and lime. The reporter—a woman by the name of Chelle Markinson—suggested we
meet for drinks. I never quite know what that means
coming from a woman, which might be interpreted as
sexist by some, but I always tread with caution these
days since I got sued by Nanette Pearson for sexual
harassment. It still burns me up so bad knowing a
woman can just lie like that and take a man to court.
But because the woman doesn't have a shred of proof
and Dominik Carlson is taking a tough stand against
her, I'm just not going to worry about it. At any rate, I
suggested a restaurant/bar I had intended to take Regan
to dinner at tonight. She should be arriving within half

an hour. She had a job interview this afternoon close by, so this was about her convenience as well.

I check my watch again. Now two and a half minutes late.

Lifting my glass to take a sip, I see a woman walking in dressed semi-causally in jeans, a white t-shirt, and a navy blazer. Her hair is pulled up into a high ponytail, and she's carrying a cross-body satchel. She scans the bar area, which only has a handful of people and zeroes in on me.

When she smiles and raises a hand, I return the motion.

The woman holds her hand out after she approaches. "Chelle Markinson."

"Dax Monahan," I reply as we shake. I nod to the stool beside me. "Have a seat."

Chelle hops on the barstool, putting her satchel on the bar top before pulling out an iPad. It's equipped with its own keyboard and she takes a moment to set it up, commenting, "I hope you don't mind if I type my notes."

"Not at all." While she gets set up, I take a moment to ask, "So what magazine do you work for again?"

I should know this and ordinarily I would before I agreed to give an interview, but Brooke had asked me to do this as a favor as Chelle was a friend of hers from New York. She works for a company called LWW

Enterprises, which is launching a new sports magazine for women.

Shooting me a quick glance, Chelle smiles. "Right now it's just an online blog called *Sporting Insights.*"

"And it caters to women?" It's a fascinating concept, and I was intrigued enough I didn't mind doing this little interview for Brooke.

Chelle nods and turns to me with an enthusiastic sparkle in her eyes. "We cover all the mainstream sports—and even those that aren't—but we focus more on what women want to know about the sport."

I can't help but tease. "Like they want to know stuff like what fashion labels I wear or what cologne I use? Stuff like that?"

Snorting, Chelle rolls her eyes. "Please... give our women readers some credit. You'd be surprised how many women out there are deeply rooted in sports, which are dominated by male players. Some of them know the ins and outs of a sport far better than many men do. But we do focus on some of the lighter things like home-life balance, dealing with notoriety and pressure, and mental health awareness issues."

I blink at her stupidly, effectively put in my place. "That's actually some serious stuff. Have to tell you, most men readers just want to know stats and what my workout routine is."

Chelle laughs and replies, "Hey, you don't have to

convince me the female species is the deeper of the two."

A bartender comes up and asks Chelle what she's drinking.

"Bottled water," she replies efficiently before she asks me, "Are you under any time constraints? Shouldn't take more than half an hour."

"I'm getting ready to meet my wi—" I catch myself, give a cough. "My girlfriend for dinner here. But we've got about twenty minutes."

I half expect Chelle to seize on the opening and ask me something personal about my "girlfriend," but she doesn't.

She merely gives me a brisk nod, references something on her iPad, and then shoots her first question. "The Vengeance is doing what no other expansion team has ever done... entered the league and shot straight to the top. What's the secret to your team's success?"

I launch into a recitation of the perfect recipe that sort of came together on this team. Unmitigated talent, great coaching, and a team owner who believes in his men. We talk for fifteen minutes straight, and I am incredibly impressed at the level of awareness Chelle has about the depth charts as well as a pretty damn good analysis of our chances in the playoffs.

She asks a few follow-up questions. I find her to be thoughtful as she prods way past the surface of most interviews I've done.

She also stays aware of the time. As we're winding up, she says, "One last question. I have to ask you about the lawsuit that's been filed against you, Erik Dahlbeck, Sebastian Parr, and the team as a whole for sexual harassment. The responsive court documents I've looked at show an adamant denial of all of her charges, and I don't expect you to tell me anything different than that. But I am curious as to your feelings on the matter."

Any veteran professional athlete has got to be ready for tough questions in any interview. I had suspected this was going to come because it is pretty buzzworthy news around the sporting world.

I try to temper my answer as best I can while still making clear my disgust over the whole matter. "You are correct we have categorically denied all of her allegations. When it's all said and done, you will see she has absolutely no proof to back up her claims. And while I can't speak for the team or the other men named in the lawsuit, I can tell you that I will never, ever pay her a dime. If I do something wrong, I'm man enough to admit it and accept the consequences of my actions. But in this instance, Nanette Pearson is flat-out lying about us harassing her."

The reporter cocks an eyebrow. "Can I quote you on that?"

I nod. "You can quote me on anything I've said here today."

"As this case progresses and is eventually resolved, do you mind if I contact you for a statement?"

I flash her a confident smile. "I don't mind at all."

I give Chelle my direct email address that is set up through the Vengeance organization. She offers to send me a copy of her article before she publishes it, and I gratefully accept. While she seems on the up and up and it sounds like she's going to put out a really interesting piece, I don't mind taking a gander at it first.

We shake hands. As she's exiting the bar, I pull out my phone to call Regan. However, I see a text from her that she's running about fifteen minutes late, so I ask the bartender to bring me a beer while I wait for her.

A couple comes in and sits down to my left at the bar. The guy nods in greeting, then his eyes go wide as he recognizes me. He doesn't make a big deal out of it, though, and I lift my gaze to one of the TVs behind the bar to watch a basketball game they have on.

A few moments later, someone takes the stool to my right. When I glance that way, I see it's an attractive woman who is roughly my age. I can tell by the way she's staring at me that she knows exactly who I am. She has on a dress that slits right up the outside of her thigh when she crosses her legs. By the way she is pointedly staring at me, I can tell she's looking for a reaction.

I give her a polite smile before turning my attention back to the basketball game.

She asks the bartender for a glass of wine. Once she has it in front of her, she unfortunately attempts to make conversation with me. "You are Dax Monahan, aren't you?"

It would be rude of me to ignore her, so I give her my regard along with a polite smile. "You got it."

She holds a limp hand out sideways. "I'm Tara."

Again, it would be rude to ignore her, so I give her a quick shake and another smile.

"Can I buy you a drink?" she asks.

I pick up my beer mug, holding it up to show her it's still three quarters full. "I'm good, thank you."

"Your next drink then?" she persists.

I manage another smile. It slides off just as fast as she takes the tip of her index finger and runs it down the center of her chest to the low-cut V of her dress. It's a move that's highly sexual and meant to convey she's offering more than just a drink. I try to figure out the most nonconfrontational way to stop this in its tracks.

A month ago, I would've made a move, but today I am completely uninterested. "Look, you seem like a nice—"

I'm completely stunned when she leans on her barstool toward me and puts her hand on my thigh, moving it quickly upward. Of all the times I have been hit on by women eager to fuck a hockey star, I have never had one touch me so intimately and so quickly after having just been introduced. She almost reaches my dick, but my hand moves light and fast to latch it around her wrist.

The woman grins as I remove her offending appendage. "Oh, come on. I know you're not a shy, schoolboy virgin. I also happen to know you're single. I follow the Vengeance very, very closely, and you, Dax Monahan, are as single as they come."

I open my mouth to respond. Instead, Regan's voice comes from behind me. "He is most certainly not single. And if you put your hand back on him, I am going to break it."

I jerk my head up to see Regan, who is absolutely and perfectly glorious in her fury directed at this woman. For the first time, the woman appears to be off balance as she stares at Regan with a healthy dose of fear in her eyes and an unflattering pallor to her face. Her eyes slide to me in question.

Nodding, I gesture at Regan with a thumb. "She's really scrappy. I wouldn't mess with her."

The woman wraps her hand around her wineglass, then picks up her clutch purse. "I'll just go find another place to sit."

I push up from my barstool as I grab my beer. "Don't bother. We're here to have dinner."

Turning to Regan, I put my hand behind her neck and pull her to me for a soft kiss. "You hungry, babe?"

"Starved. And I've got great news to tell you about."

And just like that, the woman at the bar is forgotten as we walk over to the maître d' stand.

We're given a nice table by the window. Once we get settled in, Regan nods toward the bar area. "Is that pretty typical?"

I grimace. "It's typical for women to hit on professional hockey players, but I've never had one move that freaking fast. I feel violated."

Regan snorts. "Puh-leeze. What man doesn't enjoy a beautiful woman putting her hands on him?"

"This man." There's no teasing in my voice, and Regan blinks at me as I clarify. "Unless it's your hands."

She stares at me a long moment, appearing slightly confused. "How do you do that?"

I tilt my head. "Do what?"

I know she doesn't mean it, but her tone sounds almost angry. "Sound so goddamn convincing."

"Because what I said to you is true, Regan. I don't want another woman's hands on me. I have no interest in that. Why is it so hard for you to believe?"

She gives a tiny growl of frustration. "Because I'm just me. Just Regan Miles. College graduate and former nerd who you've never looked at twice while growing up. And on top of that, I'm sick and my future is uncertain."

Reaching across the table, I take her by the hand to give her a tiny squeeze of reassurance. "You are the most beautiful, sexiest, and intriguing woman I have ever known. I'm not going to lie to you—you weren't always that way, Regan. You are so much younger than me. At the age I was starting to notice women, you were too young, but I'm looking now. And what I see is what I want."

I expect her to have some follow-up questions. Perhaps she might need some additional reassurances. At the very least, I kind of expect her to tell me how much she digs me in return. Instead, she changes the subject.

"Willow just texted me a little bit ago. She's going to come visit next week before heading off to her next assignment in Kosovo."

Great. Just perfect. Willow is going to come in and take all of Regan's attention from me. Can't wait. There will probably even be a side dose of Dominik Carlson drama to go with it.

I don't use my inside voice, though—because I really do love my sister—and instead, I convey an enthusiasm that is truly there. "That's awesome. I'll take any chance I can to see her since she travels so much."

"Oh, and I had a fantastic job interview this afternoon," she says, then starts chattering on about a pediatric office she applied to that needs a part-time nurse.

I sit back, listening to my wife tell me all about her day, knowing I could get very, very used to this.

CHAPTER 25

Dax

W E HAVE A home game tonight. On game days, we usually only have a light skate practice. But a team meeting has been called by upper management. Since it is the day after Tacker was supposed to give his answer to the organization about whether he wanted to meet their demands to stay on, I have a fairly good suspicion that's what the meeting is about. I did not tell any of my teammates about the conversation Regan and I had with Tacker at Billy's party. This included my best friend on the team, Bishop, who has been acting as team captain since Tacker got suspended. Prior to that, we had shared the co-captain title, but I singularly own that since Bishop has been promoted.

Even though Tacker hadn't said the information was secret, I chose not to tell anyone what he'd revealed to us at the party. It was such a deeply personal issue, and it's just not my place to share it. Regan and I sure have talked about it a lot the last two days, wondering what he was going to do.

The team meeting is held in a large room with stadium seating and a podium at the front. All the chairs have flip-top desks used for a surface to write on. There's a large electronic screen that drops from the ceiling where we can watch video of game footage for analysis and discussion. When I enter, I see I'm one of the last to arrive, with a few guys trickling in behind me. I take a seat next to Bishop in the front row, giving a quick scan around the area. I'm disappointed to see Tacker isn't here.

While everyone is settling into their seats, I lean over and ask Bishop in a low voice, "Do you know what the meeting is about?"

I figured since he's the team's captain if anyone knows it would be him. Unfortunately, he just shrugs while he drums his fingers on the desktop. He has an open notebook turned to a blank page with a pen sitting there ready to jot down whatever pearls of wisdom are going to be handed to us.

If I had wondered who would be talking during this meeting, I need not wonder any further as Dominik Carlson walks into the team meeting room followed by Coach Perron and the rest of the coaching staff. Following up the rear is Christian Rutherford, the team's general manager.

The minute Dominik steps into the room, though, a respectful hush falls over the players. He's endeared himself to everyone by coming to the rookie party and being incredibly cool by paying a huge amount of money down on the tab. He's also done some personal favors to a few of my buds—including lending Bishop his private jet to chase after Brooke when they broke up.

Dominik walks right up to the podium while the rest of the team management stands behind him. Legs planted slightly apart, hands clasped in front of them, and dour expressions on their faces. This is not looking good.

"Thank you all for coming in to this team meeting," Dominik says as he glances around the room. "I know your time is precious, particularly on game days, so I promise not to take long."

His gaze lands briefly on me, but there is no flicker of recognition.

Nothing on his face tells me he's inappropriately interested in my sister. Certainly no leftover amusement I called him on the carpet about it or he threatened to trade me.

Right now, he is all business.

"As you all know, Tacker Hall has been on an indefinite suspension from the team." He lets those words hang in the air, heavy and oppressive on us all. "I am, however, pleased to announce he will be returning to the ice as a team member next week. This will be for practices only until he can get his legs back underneath him and time for the fracture in his wrist to heal up."

Dominik continues, "We anticipate Tacker will be able to return at game capacity within two full weeks."

There is a low-level of chatter rippling through the room, a tone of joy within it. I don't think there's a single player on this team who didn't want Tacker to return, despite the fact he is so closed off from the team.

"While I'm not going to share with you the details of the discussions we have had with Tacker, I will tell you that his return to the team is contingent on him not drinking any alcohol. This is obviously because he had an alcohol-related driving incident, and we do not tolerate that on this team. Tacker has some other conditions he has to satisfy to remain a member of our organization. If he chooses to share those details with you, that is fine. Suffice to say, we are incredibly happy he is returning and has agreed to abide by our demands for him to stay on this team. Thank you for coming in for this team meeting. Good luck tonight. I'm going to stay in Phoenix to watch you guys play, and I'm incredibly proud of every member of this team."

Without another word, without a glance at his coaching staff, me, or any other player, Dominik turns from the podium and strides out of the meeting room. There's a smattering of applause as he leaves.

Coach Perron steps up to the podium. He gives a slight cough, scanning his players to make sure we are all paying attention. His gruff voice automatically instills within us a need to listen carefully to what he says. "I want to talk a little bit about Tacker's compliance to stay on this team. What Mr. Carlson did not tell you is if Tacker has so much as one drop of alcohol, he's going to be released from the team immediately. No second chances. It is not something we take lightly. And while I cannot dictate your own behaviors, I would suggest you do your best not to let Tacker enter into any circumstances that might involve drinking. I've never known Tacker to be a big partier, but we can't discount the fact he has abused alcohol.

"If I may be so bold as to suggest it, please consider moderating your behavior accordingly if you want him to be on this team. I know that is asking a lot of you. You men are young and in your prime, and there is a certain element of fun that comes along with your job. All I'm asking is for you to be considerate of Tacker's demons. I ask this not only for his benefit, but also for this team's. The reason Mr. Carlson, Mr. Rutherford, and I have worked so hard to get Tacker to stay with us is because we believe he will be instrumental in winning the Cup this year. So if you men can taste that victory, if you want to hoist that cup above your shoulders, I suggest you do whatever is necessary to keep this team

DAX

whole, motivated, and driven. With that, I'll see you all at the team skate in a few hours."

Coach doesn't stick around for questions. He and the coaching staff, along with Christian Rutherford, promptly leave the room.

The players all start exiting right behind them. Bishop and I stand from our chairs, and he looks at me pointedly. "You got any plans for the next few hours until the team skate?"

I was actually going to go home and see if I could talk Regan into a little tryst with me. Not that I would have to "talk" her into it. She is so fucking responsive to me. When I give her the barest of touches, she just melts for me. But fuck... all she has to do is look at me a certain way and I get hard. The chemistry between us is red hot, and it doesn't need much to ignite.

But I also take heed of the serious undercurrent within Bishop's tone, so I say, "No plans. What do you want to do?"

"Let's go to Tacker's place and talk to him."

IT TAKES US about twenty-five minutes to make it to Tacker's crappy apartment. We can't tell if he's home because he hasn't responded to the text Bishop sent him inquiring as to his whereabouts before we left the arena. Of course, there is no telltale sign of his truck in one of the parking spots since he totaled it. I imagine Tacker is going to be one of Uber's best customers for a while. While none of us have been given details, nor would I ask for such, I'm going to assume he's going to lose his license for that little stunt he pulled.

Since I have been here before, I lead the way up to Tacker's apartment, not hesitating to pound on the door once I get there. I glance over my shoulder at Bishop, who is rocking on the balls of his feet. No clue if this is going to be confrontational or not, so there might be a little anxiety involved.

We hear the snick of the door unlocking from the other side, then Tacker has the door open, staring out at us. He keeps one hand on the doorknob and the other up on the door casing, with no invitation to invite us in.

That's really not going to work for what Bishop and I intend to talk to him about, so I say point blank, "We'd like to come in and talk."

Tacker sighs long and heavy, appearing incredibly put out as he turns to the side to grant us entrance. I enter his living room, completely stunned by what I see.

He's such a recluse and doesn't give a shit about anything, I expected his home to be an utter mess. I glance into his pristine kitchen. I thought there would be a mountain of dirty dishes with flies buzzing around them. His garbage can is empty, and I expected it to be filled with empty liquor bottles. I sniff hesitantly at the air, but only find it clean and lemony.

What actually doesn't surprise me is how minimalist everything is. It's a low-budget apartment with worn and threadbare carpet. It's clear to see this because he has no furniture except for a single reclining chair in the corner with a floor lamp beside it. There's no TV, no couch, no coffee table. In the kitchen, there's not even a table to sit at to eat, nor are there any appliances out on the counter. In fact, as far as I can see, his apartment consists of only the chair and the lamp I had first laid eyes on. I'm going to go out on a limb and say his bedroom probably consists of a single air mattress on the floor.

Tacker moves past us, deeper into the living room, then turns to face us, crossing his arms over his chest. He doesn't look angry to see us, but he doesn't look friendly either. "So what's up?"

"Dominik Carlson called a team meeting. He told us you're going to be coming back to the team," Bishop says.

Tacker doesn't respond, but that is hardly surprising. He isn't the most engaging person I've ever met in my life. The only exception to that is when he is out on the ice. Then he is like a different person who has no problem communicating with his teammates or providing critique or encouragement. If there was ever any reason why this man needed to come back to the team, it's because of that. It's the only place he truly seems to have any life left in him.

"We want to know how we can best support you," I say, taking over the efforts to get a conversation going. "While they didn't tell us any details, the only thing they did make sure to reiterate is you are not allowed to have any alcohol. What can we do to help you with that?"

There's no anger or offense from him. But there is a slight annoyance in his tone. "I'm not a goddamn alcoholic, and I don't need an intervention. I got drunk one lousy time and made a stupid decision to drive."

"Technically," Bishop drawls. "That's still an abuse of alcohol."

"No shit, Sherlock," Tacker mutters before taking in a breath. "But I don't need any supportive help if that's what you're asking. I don't crave alcohol. I've never been a big drinker to begin with. I certainly don't need the rest of the team to forgo alcohol in some form of stupid-ass solidarity with me. I just want everyone to be normal around me when I come back."

"But everything isn't normal," I point out quietly. "Going to be a lot of people walking around on eggshells with you, brother. People aren't going to know how to act around you."

Tacker shrugs and turns away from us, walking into his small efficiency kitchen. He opens the refrigerator and pulls out a bottle of water, closing it without offering us anything. He untwists the cap, takes a sip, and then says, "Everyone just needs to go on like we did before. I will be a professional out on the ice. Won't be anybody's fucking friend off the ice."

Bishop shakes his head and snaps, "You see, that right there probably isn't going to work, Tacker."

I blink in surprise at my friend for the anger in his tone. Everyone always treats Tacker with kid gloves, but I'm thinking they've just been pulled off.

Bishop continues, "You see, I want to win the fucking Cup. In order to do that, everybody on this team has to be playing at their maximum. You have to give forth every effort. And you have to rely on your teammates to do the same. That involves a certain amount of trust. And if you can't open yourself up to the men on this team who would probably lay down their lives for you if asked, it's not going to fucking work. So I suggest you get your head out of your ass and figure out how to not only be a professional hockey player, but also how to be a comrade to the rest of your teammates. It's time to move the fuck on, Tacker. Figure it out."

And with that, Bishop pivots on his foot and storms out the door.

I stare after him a moment before turning to Tacker warily. The expression on his face is stunned, and there's a tiny bit of red in his cheeks. His attention comes to me slowly, and he sort of shrugs. "I guess I just got fucking put in my place, didn't I?"

"Appears so," I reply.

I turn to leave, but Tacker's hand on my shoulder stops me. Turning around, I look at him questioningly.

"I have an appointment with a counselor tomorrow. Tell Regan, okay?"

It's a chore to keep my lips from crawling into a smile, because Tacker just gave me a gift. He opened himself up without prodding or pushing. He volunteered personal information that could have invited a lot of feedback from me. He put himself out there.

It's a start.

I smile at him. "You got it, buddy."

CHAPTER 26

Dax

JESUS CHRIST.

I'm hot under the collar. And I mean that literally.

I tug at the knot on my tie as I walk up the porch steps to my condo, thinking it feels just a little too tight. I'm wearing one of my best suits, and I have never remembered it feeling so uncomfortable. I'm thinking it has something to do with the fact I'm walking up to my own home getting ready to pick my wife up and take her out on a Valentine's Day date.

I hit the top of the porch, stopping to appraise myself. A dozen red roses clutched in one hand and a black jewelry box in the other. Fancy restaurant reservations have been made, and I even preordered a bottle of the most expensive champagne to be waiting at the table for us. I'd told Regan I wanted to come pick her up like a real date even though we live together. So I had everything prearranged and planned except for the roses I'd needed to pick up for her. While she was in the shower, I put on my best suit and jetted out of the house, calling out I'd be back in about half an hour.

Earlier today, I spent a torturous two hours with Bishop, Erik, and Legend as we all went out shopping for gifts for our honeys on Valentine's Day. I imagine we'd looked lost and out of our elements.

Over the past six months, we have methodically fallen for a woman. All four of us were previously irrepressible, confirmed bachelors and never once considered buying a Valentine's Day gift for the female persuasion. We finally ended up at a jewelry store where a kind, matronly woman who had been in the jewelry business for thirty-five years—or so she said—helped us each pick out what she deemed to be the perfect gift.

This came after we each tried to outdo one another, which meant we kept finding ridiculously more expensive pieces of jewelry to buy. I just about had my mind made up on a twenty-thousand-dollar bracelet when the clerk showed me a stunningly simple yet elegant necklace with a diamond pendant hanging from it. It was significantly cheaper than the bracelet, but that had nothing to do with my decision.

I'd just known Regan would love it. She's not into flashy, ostentatious bracelets, but this necklace was understated elegance. It's exactly how I would describe

Regan.

As for right now, I should just walk in my own house and call out Regan's name to see if she's ready. Instead, I ring the doorbell as if I were picking her up for a first date and about to meet her father. It takes her a few minutes to open the door, but the wait is so worth it.

She's got on a cream-colored dress that hugs her body like a second skin, but it isn't in any way trashy-looking. The material is actually kind of thick and cut sharply across her collarbone. The skirt is long and comes down to about mid-calf, her narrow waist encircled with a gold belt. Her hair is loose in choppy flowing waves, and she is absolutely breathtaking.

She takes in my appearance, and I expect a little smirk in return over how over-the-top and ridiculous I must look standing on my own front porch. Instead, she stares in wondrous awe. I have to wonder if she has ever been picked up for a date before in her life. Her gaze flicks to the roses, then over to the necklace box in my hand, before wandering over my suit. I force myself not to reach up and tug at the tie again.

"Wow," is all she says.

When my eyes roam over her, she blushes. I bring my gaze up to her face, repeating the sentiment. "Wow."

We just stare at each other, both of us now grinning

like fools. Finally, I shove the roses forward. "These are for you."

Regan takes them gently in her hands, then brings them up to her nose to sniff. "Mmm."

And yet, I still stand on the porch and she still lingers in the foyer as we stare at each other over the red petals.

Finally, she snickers and steps backward. "You might as well come in. I'll need to put these in some water."

I enter my own home, now clutching the necklace box with my eyes pinned on Regan's shapely ass as she sashays into the kitchen in search of a vase. I'm fairly sure I don't have one, and I realize that was a fail on my part. Should have gotten flowers already in a damn vase.

I commit that to memory for next year.

Except it will be two dozen.

I follow Regan into the kitchen, watching in amazement as she immediately pulls out a plastic pitcher from the cabinet beside the sink. Regan has been here long enough to know I don't have a vase, but she immediately fills the substitute with water and arranges the flowers within it.

She fluffs and primps the arrangement. Plucks a worn petal here, a wilting leaf there. She raises some of the flowers up higher than the others, then continues to fret over them. I think they look perfect, but she keeps working at it.

Until I finally realize she's avoiding me.

She's overwhelmed by this, and she doesn't know what to say.

I step up behind her, one hand going to her waist while I rest my chin on one of her shoulders. "Did I make this weird?"

Regan twists to look at me with the softest expression. "Not weird at all. In fact, it's incredibly wonderful. I just don't want this moment to end."

I've never been an overly romantic guy. Truth is, I wouldn't have thought about roses until the clerk suggested them to me. But I swear to fuck Regan's words to me right now produce an almost-swooning sensation within my head. I have to place my other hand on the edge of the sink for balance.

To cap things off perfectly, Regan goes to her tiptoes and plants a kiss on my cheek. "Thank you, Dax."

My skin actually tingles when her lips pull away.

"Want to see what else I got you?" I ask with a grin.

She nods her head fervently.

I turn her body so she's facing me, and I place the black velvet jewelry box in her hands. The clerk had also suggested I stop and get a gift bag as well as a card to go with this, but I ran out of time.

Regan's hands shake slightly as she opens the square flat box, then peers at the necklace I bought her. She places a fingertip on the edge of the chain, following its path gently to the pendant.

"Oh, Dax," she breathes out as her eyes lift to meet mine. "It's so very beautiful."

Taking the box from her, I gallantly offer, "Let me put it on you."

Smiling, Regan lifts her hair up in a big pile as she turns to expose her neck to me. I manage to work the clasp of the necklace and get it on with little fuss. She spins to face me, lifting the diamond drop pendant up to examine it. "It's perfect."

"No, you're perfect," I say.

She grins then, a slight sparkle of mischief in her gaze. "I got you something, too."

"Oh yeah?"

Her lids droop slightly, her smile turning coy. "I'm wearing it. Under my dress. You'll have to wait until later to see it."

Jesus.

Instantly, my cock jumps to attention, wondering exactly what she has on under that dress. Regan isn't into a lot of fancy, sexy lingerie, but I'd like to change that one day. The fact she's gone out and bought something designed to drive me crazy makes me want to say to hell with dinner reservations. I know exactly what I want to dine on, and it's standing right in front of me.

Instead, I man the fuck up and mentally tell my dick

to get itself under control. Leaning into her, I press a soft kiss on her mouth. "I cannot wait to unwrap my present," I promise, loving the slight shiver that takes hold of her body. "But first… dinner. You ready to go?"

"I'M COMING AGAIN," Regan moans as her fingernails dig into my shoulders.

Those are the best fucking words in the world. It's number three for her tonight.

I am not going to last much longer. I'm on the edge as it is. We are face to face, pelvis to pelvis, torso to torso. My hips drive into her in long, luxurious thrusts. I have never fucked—made love—this slowly and deliberately before. It's been the best thing I've ever felt. I've never been more connected to another human being in my life.

Regan's fingers twine within my hair, and she puts her lips near my ear. "I want you to come, Dax. Inside me."

She's never urged me along before, and I find myself helpless to ignore her request. I drive in one more time, rest my cheek against hers, and unload a monstrous orgasm inside of her with a long groan of relief.

"Yes, baby," she murmurs, reveling in my pleasure.

When I come down from my high, Regan has already drifted off into a semi-sleep. I roll to the side, my spent cock slipping out of her, then gather her closely to my body.

"Sleepy," she murmurs, then lets out a huff of air against my chest that tells me she's fallen straight to sleep.

This is a good thing.

The way I'm feeling right now—the overwhelming strength of the emotions I have coursing through me right in this moment—I was probably going to say something to her that I'm not quite sure I'm ready to admit.

That is, I am fairly sure I have fallen helplessly in love with my best friend's little sister. It sounds overly clichéd, yet incredibly right. I can only conclude that I have loved her in some form or fashion her entire life, and that has led to the development of a different—*deeper*—type of love. I don't want Regan to be my wife in name only. I don't want her to be with me for my insurance benefits. I want her to be by my side for the rest of my life. I want to have children with her. I want to fuck her morning, noon, and night—in a perfect world, of course.

I simply want Regan in every conceivable way a man could want a woman… and I want her to want me in return.

Which is why it's good she fell asleep. I'm fairly confident in my feelings for her, but I honestly have no clue how she feels about me. I know there has to be some level of distrust given that first time we were intimate together. When I'd gotten scared, gotten even more stupid, and then called the relationship over before it ever got started.

Yes, I know Regan has to doubt me in more ways than one.

Which means I'm just going to have to work harder to get her to trust me—to believe I'm going to always do right by her.

And along the way, if I can get her to admit she loves me in return, things will be just fine.

CHAPTER 27

Regan

MY FINGERS TRAIL along the line of dresses hanging from the metal rack. Spring is just around the corner, so they are all in pastel colors. Willow is a few paces ahead of me, eyeballing blouses that are on sale.

I approach her, then start flipping through the rack. "I'm really glad you came back to visit us before you head off to Kosovo."

She shoots me a glance before holding up an olive-colored shirt for inspection. "Me too. I'm worried about you."

"I'm fine," I drawl, picking up a rust-colored T-shirt with golden bumblebees embroidered into it. Too cutesy for me, so I put it back. "And please find a different color. You wear too much khaki, brown, and olive to begin with."

Willow re-racks the T-shirt with a tiny shrug of indifference before pinning me with a direct glare.

"You're fine, huh? Then why have you been coughing all morning?"

We start meandering along the department store's aisles, lazily looking at items we have no intention of buying. Neither one of us have bought a thing all morning. We are just enjoying being out and chatting.

"I just have a cold," I explain. "Your brother gave it to me."

Willow slips her arm through mine, then gives me a little squeeze. "That's what you get for sucking face."

My head snaps toward her, and she grins.

I've been sucking more than that, but I will keep that to myself. I return her smile but ruin it with a short coughing fit. It's pretty deep and hacking. We halt our progress until I can clear my throat, but I'm left panting as I try to get air in my lungs.

"That sounds really bad." Willow's face is awash with concern.

I suck in a deep lungful of air, but it doesn't feel like it's enough for some reason. I let it out slowly. "Honestly, it's been this way for a few days. Doesn't seem to be getting any worse, but it's definitely not getting any better. I forgot to take cough syrup today, though. That's all."

Willow gives me a critical once over, as if she doesn't trust what I'm saying.

"I'm fine," I promise, then loop my arm through

hers, urging her to walk forward again.

"So how are things going with Dax?"

I duck my head, trying to hide a smile as I study the shiny tile floor. Perhaps I hesitate too long because Willow stops and pivots toward me. I'm forced to raise my head to find her grinning like a Cheshire cat.

"Oh, things are going *very* well," she drawls. The tone of her voice is slightly taunting, but in a fun way. "I can see by that expression on your face."

I could deny it. I could downplay it. Wipe my face blank.

But why should I? Willow is my friend. My sister-in-law as well.

So, I choose honesty. "Things are going well. Too well, actually. So well, I doubt it's real. This wasn't supposed to be anything more than sex."

Willow laughs as we start walking again, heading toward the shoe section. "Nothing is ever really just sex, Regan. There's always something more. But that's a good thing for you and Dax, I'm thinking."

I open my mouth to respond, but another coughing fit hits me. This time, it doesn't last very long, but I'm left almost gasping for breath at the end. Before Willow can say anything about me being sick, I say, "Anything more than sex is too complicated right now."

"No way," she tells me. She waves her hand up and down, indicating my entire self. "You practically glow when I talk to you about my brother. You've got it bad for him. It's more than just sex for sure, and that's a complication you should relish in."

I turn to pick up a pair of taupe-colored sandals. They have little leather daisies running along the strap that goes around the ankle. They're adorable, and I don't want to talk about Dax anymore.

I don't want to talk about him because it makes me hope for too much. These last few days—really since Valentine's Day—I've started to think he might be developing deeper feelings for me that go beyond our initial friendship as well as beyond the bedroom. But then I start doubting myself because it seems way too good to be true.

Dax is way too good to be true.

"Cute shoes," Willow says. "And you ignored my last question, so I am guessing Dax is off topic for now."

"For now," I agree. I put the shoes back on the stand, and we start meandering again. "So let's talk about you. Are you going to hook up with your big-dicked photographer friend?"

Willow shakes her head. "I don't think so."

She then spies a pair of strappy high-heeled sandals in a pearly champagne color and nabs them. She holds them out toward me. "These would look fantastic on you. I bet Dax would find them incredibly sexy."

I hold back a chuckle since I know it will instigate

my cough. Shaking my head, I smile. "When I win the lottery, I'll buy them. But right now, I'm pinching pennies. Until I finish my master's degree and can work full time, I don't have room for luxuries like that."

Although I will have to say I didn't mind digging into my meager savings account to buy the lingerie I wore for Valentine's Day. Dax went crazy when he saw it. For the first time in our sexual relationship, I felt a measure of power over him. It had felt nice, but I also like that it was short-lived. Truth be told, it's better when Dax holds the reins.

And I realize Willow has effectively turned the direction of the conversation back to Dax and me. Sneaky woman.

I feel compelled to turn it around on her. "I think you should hook back up with the guy with the big dick. Will he be in Kosovo?"

Willow just shrugs as she picks up a hideous pair of purple pumps. She holds them up for my inspection, and I shake my head while wrinkling my nose.

"They are pretty ugly," she mutters as she puts the shoes back.

"Could it be you're interested in someone else?" I ask, and her eyes flick to mine for a moment before turning away guiltily.

Willow refuses to look at me, seemingly intent on another pair of shoes, but asks innocently enough,

"Who would I be interested in?"

"Dominik Carlson, of course."

Willow looks at me blankly. We engage in a stand-off, our eyes locked on each other. She doesn't so much as blink, even lifting her chin a bit in defiance.

"Oh, come on," I blurt out to break the silence, ignoring the tickle in my throat telling me another cough is brewing. "That get-together in Detroit... it's obvious he's interested in you. And you were playing it all cool, and I thought maybe a little too hard to get. You really—"

Willow cuts me off snappishly. "I am *too* hard to get because I don't want him to get me."

"Why? You had a great time with him. It was unparalleled sex from what I remember you saying. I don't believe for a second—"

"We're not compatible," Willow says gently, the soft tone cutting over my tirade and stopping me in place. I can't even think to come back with a good argument.

All I can ask is, "Why not? The sex is great. Isn't that enough?"

"It was great, but—"

Willow's words are drowned out as another coughing fit overcomes me. It feels like razor blades are shredding my lungs. Disgustingly, I bring up a huge glob of phlegm I'm forced to swallow down again.

And then.... a wave of dizziness hits me. I reach out,

pressing my palm onto a table that holds several shoe displays. Closing my eyes, I try to get my bearings.

"Are you okay, Regan?" It's Willow's voice, but it sounds like it's coming through a tunnel. But then it seems to get louder and clearer. "Regan... look at me."

Slowly, I flutter my eyes open, Willow coming into immediate focus. The dizziness is gone. "Yeah... I'm fine. Maybe the cold has just gone into my head."

"You look a little pale," she says with worry. "Why don't we leave?"

My initial instinct is to deny I'm sick and insist we keep shopping, but I suddenly feel exhausted. I'm also dying of thirst.

"Yeah," I say as I hook my arm through Willow's once more. This isn't a sign of camaraderie. Rather, I want to use her for balance in case I get dizzy again. "I think I could actually use a nap before we leave for the game tonight."

Willow stops dead in her tracks, turning to me with both hands gripping my shoulders. Her eyes are swimming with worry. "Regan, there's no home game tonight. It's away. Dax is in Dallas, don't you remember?"

Dax is in Dallas?

Dax is in Dallas. He left this morning. I remember now.

Fear strikes in the pit of my stomach.

I smile sheepishly, trying to keep my voice steady. "Oh yeah… that's right. I'm sorry. I think I might be a little dehydrated. Maybe we could stop and get me a bottle of water somewhere?"

Willow stares at me a moment, the concerned expression on her face not budging an inch. Finally, she gives me a slow nod and ushers me toward the exit of the department store. Our arms are once again linked, and I can feel her holding me steady. As we get nearer to the entrance, another wave of dizziness hits me. "Willow."

My legs seem to turn to Jell-O, and I start to sag. Luckily, there is a bench just a few feet away with an old man sitting on it. He has several bags at his feet. I'm guessing he's waiting for his wife who must be on a shopping spree.

Willow leads me over to it, and I sit next to him. Raising my eyes to hers, I swallow hard. "I think I need to go to the hospital."

Willows voice quavers with fear. "Is this something more than a cold?"

I know exactly what she's asking me. And it's not something I had actually considered until that moment of confusion about Dax's game. I nod, fairly sure I'm in a hemolytic crisis. My blood cells are being destroyed faster than they can be made. They're necessary to carry oxygen throughout my body. I've been in this situation before, and I recognize it.

I give a slow nod, speaking past the dryness in my mouth. "I think so."

"Do you want me to go get my car?"

I shake my head, my gut instinct telling me that's a bad idea. "I think you need to call an ambulance."

"Shit," Willow mutters, then whips out her phone. Before she can even attempt to unlock it, I reach out and touch her elbow. "Don't call Dax. He's got a game tonight, and I don't want him to worry."

"I'm calling 9-1-1."

"I know that," I say with a wan smile. "I'm saying after... don't call Dax."

Willow gives me an exasperated grimace. "He will kill me if I don't let him know what's going on."

I know there's an important point I should make to her, but between the dizziness and fatigue, it's a little hazy. I shake my head. My words are so weak sounding. "He can't do anything. He'll only worry."

Willow's words are clear... I think. I sort of understand what she's saying. But I'm not sure I really care as I begin to feel very, very tired.

"Dax is a big boy," she replies briskly as she unlocks her phone. "He'll just have to worry. That's life. And it's not fair to keep this from him either."

I give a wan wave of my hand to indicate I have no energy to argue with her. Right now, I have to depend on Willow to get me to the hospital.

I sink onto the bench, watching as Willow calls 9-1-1.

CHAPTER 28

Dax

"**C**AN YOU GO any faster?" I growl at my Uber driver from the backseat.

"We're almost there," he tells me reassuringly. Even though I can see he's already going fifteen miles over the speed limit, it's still not fast enough for me. "Just one more block."

I do see the hospital up ahead. Oddly, my anxiety increases the closer we get.

Willow told me Regan was stable and resting well. She's told me that several times in fact, via text as well as several phone calls over the last twenty-four hours.

There is nothing worse than being several hours away from someone I care about who is ill. In Regan's case, her illness can lead to death. I have never felt more wretched, out-of-control, and terrified in my entire life than when Willow called me yesterday to tell me that Regan was being taken to the hospital by ambulance.

There was so little information. I really had no clue what was going on. She said Regan was coughing a lot, then got incredibly dizzy and confused while they were out shopping.

I'd known Regan had a cold. I'm pretty sure I gave it to her. Whereas mine never amounted to much more than a minor sore throat as well as a few days of a light cough, Regan's seemed to come on strong and hold steady.

And yet, I wasn't worried when I left her yesterday to get on the team plane to head to Dallas for an away game.

It was a cold. That has nothing to do with her blood disease. Besides, she was getting her treatment, and she was stable enough for me to travel away from her with no worries.

It's why I cannot wrap my head around what Willow told me yesterday. All I know is things are serious when she had to take an ambulance ride to the hospital.

When I hung up the phone, I immediately told Bishop what was going on and informed him of my need to get back to Phoenix. Thus ensued a ten-minute argument where he tried to talk me out of leaving. There were a lot of F-bombs dropped, mostly by me.

Eventually, he got me to at least agree on waiting until Regan could be evaluated in the emergency room to determine how bad things were. He pointed out she could merely be dizzy from dehydration from a bad cold.

That I could not assume the worst.

So I agreed to wait. I'd stewed and fretted. And I called Willow about every ten minutes, who kept telling me that they were still going through the emergency room process.

In that time period, I had to attend a light practice skate with my team. I couldn't concentrate, and I was an asshole to most of my teammates on the ice. Bishop told Coach Perron what was going on with me, but that didn't earn me any concessions. As professional players, we are supposed to know how to put everything out of our head and concentrate on our jobs.

I hated to tell him, but my head was not in the game, nor would it ever be, until I knew Regan was going to be okay.

Four fucking hours before I got a solid update from Willow. As it turned out, Regan did indeed have an upper respiratory infection. But those types of things could cause an acute hemolytic crisis because of her PNH, and she needed to have a blood transfusion. Two units actually.

My immediate thought was to hang up the phone and rush to the airport to grab the next flight to Phoenix. Before I could do such a thing, though, Willow said, "Regan wants to talk to you."

This shocked me. After all, I had thought she was probably near death's door if she had to have a blood transfusion. As it turns out, she'd already had a unit of blood by then and sounded fairly strong.

"I absolutely forbid you to come back to Phoenix," she had told me in no uncertain terms. "This is entirely manageable, and we caught it early. I'm going to be fine, so you are to stay there, get your head in the game, and bring home a victory."

Those were her words. I wanted to tell her to go fuck herself, but that wouldn't have been appropriate, of course. I'd also known I was being driven by emotion and a distinct lack of the ability to control anything. The only thing I could use for guidance was Regan's own words telling me everything was under control and I should stay to play hockey.

So I did.

And I hated every fucking minute.

We won, but not because of anything I'd done to help. It had been one of the worst games I can remember playing.

The team plane was not set to leave until the morning after the game. As luck would have it—and I'm talking about piss-poor luck—there were no flights available for me to take by the time we finished the evening game, so I hadn't been able to get to the airport early. I'd been stuck waiting to catch the team plane back to Phoenix. Luckily, the plane left early this morning.

It was a two-hour-and-ten-minute flight. By the time we taxied and I was able to get an Uber, I didn't make it to the hospital until almost ten. I jump out of the Uber without saying a word, slamming the door behind me. I make a mental note to go back and add a tip for him, but truth be told, I will probably forget until the next time I log into the app for a ride.

I rush through the hospital, trying not to bowl people over in my haste. Regan's room is on the seventh floor, and I choose what must be the slowest elevator in the entire world.

I half walk, half trot through the halls, searching for her room until I finally come to it.

7209.

I realize I'm actually panting. While some of it might be that I'm a bit out of breath from my rush to get up here, I can tell by the pounding of my pulse that it's also anxiety.

I don't know if I'm prepared to see her in a hospital room.

With IVs sticking out of her arms and the beep of machines.

In fact, I'm pretty sure I'm terrified.

I take a deep breath in through my nose, then let it out slowly through my mouth. I do this two more times until I actually start to feel a little calmer, then push her door open.

She doesn't look as bad as I had built up in my mind. A little pale, with dark circles under her eyes, but when she sees me, I'm hit with a bright smile and her teasing, "Well hello, Mr. Monahan."

A huge wave of relief hits me so hard my knees feel a little weak. I shore up by concentrating on the kernel of anger deep in my gut that she's lying there in that bed, battling a disease she doesn't deserve.

Willow sits in the corner in a recliner chair covered in blue vinyl. She's surfing on her phone, but glances at me with a chin lift. "Welcome home brother."

I walk to Regan's bedside, putting my hands on the rail to lean over and brush my lips across her forehead.

"How are you doing?" I ask as I pull away to see her.

"I feel much better from the transfusions," she says reassuringly. "They're probably going to keep me for another day just to make sure I'm out of crisis."

I straighten, scrubbing my hand through my hair, and the anger in me flares a bit. "How did this even happen? Does this mean your treatment isn't working? Because if that's the case, I want my thirty-five-thousand back and I'll find something else that works."

Regan's eyes go soft with understanding. She knows I feel lost. "The treatment is working fine. It's doing what it's supposed to be doing. But you have to remember, all it does is decrease the risk of my red blood cells being damaged. Unfortunately, infections can cause this to happen. The upper respiratory infection just tipped me over into crisis."

That is not what I wanted to hear.

"Is this going to happen again?" I demand.

She shrugs. "It could. Or it may never happen again."

I growl at her lackadaisical attitude. Turning away, I pace. I give an angry glare at the opposite wall before pivoting to face her with an incredulous expression. "How are we supposed to live with that?"

None of this is fucking fair.

Regan gives a small sigh. "You mean how are *you* supposed to live with it? I already live with it every day, Dax. I've made my peace."

I'm not sure what I'm supposed to say to that. I think I've actually been put in my place, but I'm not sure I was really out of my place. Willow pushes up from the recliner, then starts around the bed toward me. She puts her hand on my upper arm, then starts pushing me toward the door.

"What are you doing?" I ask.

She glances over her shoulder at Regan before saying, "We need to talk."

With a huff of frustration, I follow Willow out of the room and into the hallway. She gently pulls the door behind her until it clicks shut. My sister turns, puts her hands on her hips, and scowls at me angrily. "What the hell is wrong with you?"

"What is wrong with me? Isn't it clear I'm fucking freaked out that my wife is in the hospital and could've potentially died while I wasn't even here?"

Willow takes in a deep breath, then lets it out. Her eyes turn gentle. "Look, I get you're freaked out, but you are not helping matters by showing that to Regan. You need to calm down and be strong for her."

"I am being strong for her," I snap.

"No. You were not. You acted like a big, whiny baby."

"I did not." But even I have to admit my tone sounds whiny right now.

Christ.

I want to punch my fist through the wall. It's made of cinderblock, though, which will just result in a broken hand. I regard my sister, feeling incredibly helpless. "I don't want her to die."

My sister doesn't respond. Instead, she wraps her arms around my waist. She squeezes me hard, pressing her cheek against my chest. Reluctantly, I hug her in return.

"None of us want her to die, Dax. And she's fine now. She's going to be fine."

"Until this happens again," I mutter.

Willow pulls back from me, her eyes solemn. "Maybe. But like Regan said, maybe not. Until that time, you need to get in there and treat this like a tiny bump in the road. You need to be reassuring and supportive of her."

My sigh is long and heavy. I hate when my sister's fucking right. But still, because she's shown good wisdom as well as patience with me, I admit, "I hear you."

"I'm going to go get some coffee," she says with a kind smile. "Want some?"

"Yeah."

I watch until Willow is out of sight before returning to Regan's room. I fortify myself, promise I will do right by her, then push the door open.

There's a confident smile on my face when I walk in. She watches me carefully, so I turn up the wattage.

I stride to her bed and take her hand, squatting beside it. "Sorry I got a little wigged out. It's my first time dealing with this type of crisis, but I am well aware it's not yours."

She smiles tenderly, her thumb stroking the back of my hand. She's reassuring me when I should be doing the same for her.

"I understand this is scary stuff. But it doesn't have to be. You just need a little time to understand how all of this works."

"This scared the shit out of me," I say truthfully. "But you have once again shown me how so incredibly brave and strong you are. I'm just really proud of you, Regan."

"I'm sorry you have to go through this," she replies. "I'm sorry I'm a burden—"

"Don't you ever fucking say that to me again," I snap harshly. She blinks in surprise, her mouth falling open. I gentle my voice, but reiterate, "You are not a burden. You will never be a burden. Please don't ever feel that, because, if you do, that means I'm not doing a very good job of taking care of you."

Regan stares, her eyes blinking slowly.

"You understand what I'm saying, Regan?" I press my point. "You coming back into my life is one of the best things to ever happen to me. A burden is the furthest thing from the truth of what you are to me."

Slowly, she nods and whispers, "Okay. I understand."

CHAPTER 29

Regan

GOD, IT'S NICE to feel human again. I actually trot down the staircase, my stomach growling with hunger.

As I turn the corner and the kitchen comes into view, I see Dax and Willow sitting at the kitchen table, both huddled over cups of coffee and talking.

I've been out of the hospital for two days, and I'm feeling so much better. The heavy antibiotics knocked out the upper respiratory infection. My blood has been replenished and is manufacturing my red blood cells nicely.

Dax doesn't quite understand that. He's been too overly attentive, hovering, which admittedly was nice at first but has now become slightly annoying.

As evidenced by the fact he jumps up from the table and asks, "What can I get you? Sit down and I'll make you some breakfast."

I merely point my finger at his vacated chair and order, "Sit back down. I am more than able to get my own coffee and breakfast."

I shoot a glance at Willow, who smirks at me. I think she has secretly been enjoying watching Dax flutter around me.

Dax reluctantly sinks into his chair, and I can feel the weight of his eyes on me as I saunter over to the coffee pot.

As I'm pouring my coffee, I ask Willow, "What time are you heading to the airport today?"

"Not until about noon," she replies.

I'm going to be sad to see her leave. She has been such an amazing support to me not only these past few days when I got sick, but also in her general acceptance of me and her brother being together. On the flip side, there's a part of me that will be glad to have Dax back to myself. While Willow is a pure joy to have around, I can't be free to act the way I want to with Dax.

For example, Dax has not touched me sexually since I got out of the hospital. I understand his reticence. He is new to learning the limits of what I can and can't handle due to my illness. What I would have liked to do this morning as I walked into the kitchen in my bathrobe after having just gotten out of the shower was to go and drape myself across his lap and give him a kiss that might prod him to do something. The fact Willow is sitting across the table totally nixes that idea.

With the coffee pot in my hand, I swivel and hold it up. "Anyone need a refill?"

Both shake their heads.

I set about making a couple slices of toast with some butter and jelly. While I make my breakfast, I ask Dax, "What are your plans today?"

"Going to get a quick workout in and then come home to do my laundry for the road trip. We have a light skate at noon followed by a team lunch, then I will probably just stay at the arena."

Dax has a game this evening, which means he'd normally get to the arena around four or so. I'm really looking forward to going to the game tonight. But then he'll leave with the team tomorrow morning for six days to cover three away games.

I'm totally going to miss him, but that's part of this business. As a kid growing up with Lance as my guardian, it was the same... having someone I care about travel for fifty percent of their work year. It's definitely something that has to be adjusted to.

I grab my plate with toast, then head over to the table. As I sink onto the chair, I tell Dax, "I've got your laundry covered so don't worry about that."

Dax shakes his head. "I want you to take it easy. I'll do all the laundry today, yours included."

I push my plate forward, crossing my arms on the

table. Leaning slightly toward my dear husband, I give him a small shake of my head. "You see… this isn't going to work."

His eyebrows shoot upward. "What do you mean?"

"I mean you coddling me when I don't need coddling," I say gently. "I feel really good. I've got strength. I can do laundry. And Dax, I *need* you to let me do it."

Strangely, Dax doesn't reply immediately but instead shoots a look across the table at Willow. She just stares at him, giving away nothing on her expression. It's almost as if they were talking about this very thing and Dax is waiting for her to say, "See… I told you so."

Reaching out, I touch his arm to get his attention, sucking in a breath when he focuses on me. God, I love that face, even if he is completely irritating me this morning. "I am fine. I promise. Now, in addition to the laundry, is there anything else you need me to do to get you ready for the road trip?"

Dax is completely adorable as he tries to fight his own annoyance and alpha tendencies to want to take control of the situation. His jaw is locked tight and there's a slightly hard glint to his eyes, but he eventually nods and gives me a smile. "We're out of headache meds, and I always like to have a bottle with me when I travel. Do you think you can swing by the drugstore and get me some? That will save me a trip."

I grin broadly, giving a squeeze to his forearm just

before reaching for a piece of my toast. "I would love to."

"Are you excited about starting your new job to-day?" Willow asks.

I nod before taking a sip of coffee. "I'm not actually starting. Just going in to fill in the employment paperwork. They'll show me around, maybe have me shadow one of the nurses for a little bit. But I don't technically start until next Wednesday."

I had actually been given a formal job offer from the pediatric office I had applied to the week prior. It was a good thing I had been honest and upfront with them during my interview about my PNH, as they had wanted me to come in right away to fill in the employ-ment paperwork so everything could get processed for me to start next Wednesday.

Of course I couldn't because I was in the hospital, but they were very understanding. I know exactly how lucky I am to have such a compassionate employer. Frankly, though, their business model makes it so I shouldn't put any hardship on them. They have several part-time nurses who rotate a schedule, and there is usually always somebody willing to cover if somebody is out sick. They assured me it wasn't a problem, so we made plans for me to come in today.

I finish my toast and drink my coffee while Dax and Willow argue over the best fight scene in *Game of*

Thrones. We're all super fans of the show, although I've also read the available books.

Dax is insistent it's the Battle of the Bastards. Willow is partial to Daenerys torching the Lannister army and their wagon trail with her dragon. I'm a little bit more subtle in what appeals to me.

I think the best battle or fight scene is when Arya practices sword fighting with Breinne after she returns to Winterfell. It's not a real battle, but in my opinion it's completely epic. A waif of a child pretty much gracefully defeats a giantess who has battle experience. Dax and Willow think I'm completely crazy for that opinion, but whatever.

I glance at the kitchen clock, noting I need to get a move on. I push up from the table, then take my empty plate and coffee mug to the sink where I just place it in there, intent on cleaning the kitchen when I come back from my job a bit later.

Turning, I move to Dax, then lean down to place both my hands on his shoulders. This is an overt act of affection, which I'm slightly uncomfortable doing in front of Willow, but I want to give him one more reassurance.

Leaning in, I brush my lips across his cheek and put my mouth near his ear so I can whisper, "When I say I am fine, I mean I am fine in *all* ways."

When I retreat, I'm rewarded with heat flashing

through Dax's eyes as he understands my meaning. I've just guaranteed we are going to have a nice catch-up session in bed before he leaves tomorrow for his away trip.

Straightening, I start to leave, but give a tiny, surprised yip when his hand comes out and pops my backside pretty hard. Willow snickers as I shoot a mock glare at my husband over my shoulder.

God, I really want him to be my husband. Not just in name. Not just as an excuse to have sex with someone I'm insanely attracted to. I want every bit of him, because he already has my heart.

Now if I could only figure out if he's willing to give me his in return?

I make my way upstairs, then run through my regular routine to go to work. This means I blow dry my hair and put it into a ponytail. No makeup. After putting on scrubs, socks, and my nursing shoes, I am ready. I grab my purse and make my way downstairs, but when I'm halfway down the staircase, something catches my attention and I freeze.

It's Willow's voice, and she sounds pissed. "You need a damn attitude adjustment."

My hand goes to the rail on the stairwell, and I lean forward a little to try to hear a bit clearer around the wall that separates us.

"Trust me. I know," Dax mutters, and I can hear

the frustration in his voice. "But it's hard, Willow. The constant worry about her. I can't fucking concentrate on anything else. Every damn text or phone call I get now, I wonder if it's someone calling to tell me she's sick or dead. And I'm terrified to leave tomorrow. You're not going to be here. What if something happens to her?"

There's a dull ache in the center of my chest, and I think it's my heart constricting too tightly in response to Dax's pain and worry. No one should have to feel like that.

I take a step backward, then another, not really wanting to hear more.

"When I took Regan in and got her to marry me, I felt like a fucking hero for helping her out. Got her insurance for a lifesaving drug. It was awesome. But I didn't know then what I know now. That her life is still in danger. That this is very fucking real, and I wasn't prepared for how terrifying it would be."

I can't take another moment of listening to this. Hearing Dax and his regrets for what I've brought to his life… It hurts to know I've hurt him.

I start down the stairs again, this time stomping hard enough they hear me coming. The conversation goes silent in the kitchen. I know I can't face them, because they'll read it on my face. They'll see the guilt I'm now bearing.

So rather than turn their way, I head straight for the

door. I strive for overly bright but incredibly rushed as I call out over my shoulder. "I'm running so late. Willow... I'll try to be back before you leave."

I dare not even glance behind me. After I open the door, I jet out onto the porch, only to realize once the door shuts behind me that my car is in the garage and I've gone out the wrong way.

Fuck.

What a moron.

I open the door and walk back in, having no choice but to look at them as they have clear line of vision from the kitchen. They haven't budged an inch, but merely stare at me in surprise.

"Spazzed out for a moment," I say with a sheepish grin as I nod toward the mudroom off the kitchen that leads into the garage. "Forgot my car was in there. Guess I'm just overly excited about the new job."

Willow moves first by standing from her chair, and I'm terrified she knows I overheard them. I feel like I'm walking the plank as I head toward the kitchen, but she merely hurries over to give me a hard hug.

"Just in case you can't get out in time before I leave for the airport," she tells me, squeezing extra tight. "Promise we'll text every day, okay?"

"Promise," I whisper as I squeeze my eyes tightly shut so I don't cry.

We break apart, and I shoot a glance at Dax, who is

still sitting at the table with a slight smile on his face, as if my silly escapade out the front door amused him.

Or maybe it's trying to cover the awkwardness of me having heard what he said. Maybe he knows I heard him say he pretty much detests the situation we're in.

Stop it, Regan.

Stop dramatizing. Dax is merely talking about his frustrations. He doesn't detest you. He cares for you. Well, for most of you. He hates the part that's sick—

"I've got to get going," I blurt out, mainly to stop my rampant thoughts before I crumble into a million pieces.

"Bye," Willow chirps before she snags one more hug, her eyes a little moist.

"Bye, babe," Dax says. This time, his smile is warm and fond, and he actually looks like he'll miss me for the next few hours.

I try to memorize his face right now, as it almost dulls the pain of what I just listened to. He actually looks like he might love me right this moment, but I know my doubts will creep back up the minute I walk out of here.

CHAPTER 30

Dax

I WATCH REGAN leave, a funny feeling welling inside of me. Willow sits back down at the kitchen table.

"Did she seem all right to you?" I ask, staring at the closed door to the garage. I can hear the door lifting and then Regan's car start.

"For God's sake, Dax," Willow snaps. "She's good. Stop worrying."

"No," I say with a firm shake of my head as I give her my regard. "I mean... did she seem weird?"

"Weird how?" she inquires.

I shrug. "I don't know. I can't put my finger on it."

"I think you're just overwhelmed, and you need to get things sorted out. So let's get that shit done so I can leave for Kosovo and not worry about you two numb nuts flaking out on each other."

"Then please figure out how to reduce my anxiety and stress about Regan," I demand with a healthy level of sarcasm. "I mean… what the fuck do I do about away games? I can't be here with her all the time to watch her."

"Neither could Lance," Willow points out. "He lived in New York while she lived in California after she was diagnosed. He figured out a way to live with the fear and anxiety."

"Well, I wouldn't know, would I?" I snap. "The fucker never shared Regan's illness with me. Kept that all to himself and died with whatever pearls of wisdom he might have had for his best friend."

"Bitter much?" Good thing she's a girl, or else I'd be tempted to knock that smirk off her face. Downside to growing up with smart-ass sisters.

"I'm not bitter," I insist. "But it does make me wonder how he did it."

Willow's tone gentles. "He did it one day at a time. He figured it out through trial and error, I'm sure. He got more confident as he learned about her disease, and I'm sure even more confident once she started the new drug therapy. One thing I can tell you, it was not an overnight process. You're just in the beginning stages of this, Dax. If you really care for Regan and want her to be a part of your life, you're going to need to be prepared because it's going to be hard."

I just stare at my sister, because right now, I might be overwhelmed with respect for her. That might be the soundest advice I'd ever received in my entire life, and I've been handed some good stuff over the years from my parents and friends.

"Dax," Willow says as she reaches out and grabs my hand for a squeeze. "You have a choice to make. Either you grab what might be only thirty minutes of wonderful and hang on tight for the ride, or you slug through a lifetime of nothing special."

"Jesus," I murmur in awe. "That's really good. Where do you come up with this shit? You should write a self-help book or something."

Willow snorts, pulling her hand away from me. "Most of that's just common sense, although that wonderful versus nothing special analogy is from *Steel Magnolias*."

"*Steel Magnolias*?" I ask, moving from clarity to confusion quickly.

My sister rolls her eyes, as if she can't believe I don't know what it is. "It's a movie. Like the best movie ever."

"Who's in it?"

"Sally Fields, Julia Roberts, and Shirley MacClaine," she says, as if this will make me decide I have to drop everything in my life to watch it right now.

"Are there aliens in it?" I ask.

"No."

"Big battle scenes?"

"No."

"Sports?"

"No."

"Then why the fuck would I know what it is?" I growl.

"Because it's so iconic. I mean… everyone knows that movie."

"I doubt everyone. Bet none of my teammates know what it is."

"Bet the married ones do," she counters. "Or the ones with serious girlfriends. In fact, I bet Erik, Bishop, and Legend do."

"No way."

"Twenty dollars per guy," Willow says with a flash of challenge in her eyes. "Text them right now and simply ask if they know what *Steel Magnolias* is."

"You're on," I reply as I whip my phone out. I shoot a group text off to the fellas. Within moments, my phone is dinging with their responses.

Looking at my screen in disbelief, I lean on one hip to pull my wallet out of my back pocket. I pull out three twenty-dollar bills, then push them across the table to my sister. I also make a mental note to see if Regan wants to watch the movie with me sometime.

"Thank you," Willow chirps as she waves the money at me.

Sighing, I push up from the chair, taking my empty coffee cup to the sink. I place it in there on top of

Regan's dirty dishes, thinking I should clean the kitchen, but Regan always insists on doing it as her part in contributing to the household. She said she's feeling fine, so I need to let her do things to make her feel accomplished.

I need to let Regan be strong. To do that, I have to be strong with her. I have to help her believe she can beat this disease.

My eyes go to Willow, and I decide to release something out into the universe I've been holding in close. "Even though this shit with Regan is hard and scary, it's still the best thing I've ever done in my life."

Willow blinks at me in surprise. She can hear my tone and the reverence within it for my wife. I lay it all out to her. "Better than hockey, Will. Despite everything with Regan's illness and the worry that comes with it, she's still the surest thing in my life. Nothing has ever felt better or more right to me."

"Wow," Willow murmurs, my admission hitting her hard.

"So yeah… I'll get my head out of my ass because when it boils right down to it, my life has turned out more amazing than I ever thought it would be once Regan stepped back into it."

"Holy shit," my sister drawls in amazement. "You love her."

"Fuck yes, I do." I think it became very real when I got the call from Willow that Regan was on the way to the hospital and I realized my entire happiness was wrapped up in one woman.

"Have you told her?" she asks.

"No," I reply with a healthy dose of shame about that oversight. "I've been a little wrapped up in my head, trying to come to terms with everything, that I think that got lost."

"If you love her, she's the most important thing to you. It's only natural your worry is going to sort of take over things. But if you want some advice, you should tell her sooner rather than later."

"I will. Before I leave tomorrow, she won't have a doubt as to how I feel. If I'm lucky, I'll hear it back from her."

Willow's smile is secretive but knowing. "Oh, I'm sure you'll hear exactly what you want."

Yeah... she knows something, but what I cannot say. I should press her for the details but really, I'd rather wait to hear it directly from Regan's lips.

Still, I can't help but ask, "You really think so?"

"I do," she replies simply with no elaboration, and I'm okay with that.

But she does spur an idea.

A really great fucking idea as a matter of fact.

"I need to run an errand, and I need you to go with me," I say. "Do you mind?"

She gives me an exuberant smile. "As long as I make my flight, I'm good."

CHAPTER 31

Regan

I DRIVE WITHOUT thought through the neighborhood I live in with Dax. It's all upscale townhomes with a communal pool and gym, and it's gated for security. It's amazing how quickly I have come to think of this as home. I left my new job—which I can tell I will adore—and stopped by the drugstore for a bottle of pain reliever for Dax. But despite having to keep present and alert while I filled out forms and shadowed another nurse this morning, my mind was actually racing with a million different things.

First… how do I even take what I heard between Dax and Willow this morning? I heard probably less than fifteen seconds of a conversation, but I was making my own conclusions. I'm just not sure which are the correct ones. Was he making a plea for help, venting normal frustrations, or does he have a desire to cut me loose?

And let's say he's merely frustrated... I should probably go ahead and break things off with him. Make things easier on him. I don't ever want him to be unhappy because of me.

Things just got too complicated once we introduced intimacy into our relationship. It brought a whole new level of care that made it inherently more difficult for him to deal with my issues.

But how would I even break things off with him?

I could move back to California. Put distance between us. But I just started a new job. It would be highly unprofessional to quit before I even really got going. Besides, I can't afford to move.

Could I even think about staying here? I could move back into the guest room. Would Dax even go for that? Would he be grateful for the suggestion?

I'm not sure how I could continue to live in the same house with him, knowing what I had and watching him go back to his normal life without me. Sure, we would maintain our friendship. It's lifelong. That's a given. But it would be torture to stay here and watch him move on without me. Given my money situation, though, that's the most reasonable thing for me to do. I can't afford to do anything but stay.

The thought crosses my mind to ask Dax for a loan. Enough to get me back to California and help me get back on my feet. We could stay married, so I could keep the health insurance until I didn't need it. That would definitely work, but the thought of it is frightening. I have come to depend heavily on Dax just for moral support. Just having a "family" member who I can talk to has become a lifesaver in and of itself.

This is how my thoughts have been all day. I keep coming back to one thing, though. It's clear I should break things off. The thought of Dax being in any way, shape, or form unhappy kills me. The easy thing would be to stay here but if I really buckle down, I can talk myself into leaving. I lived far apart from Lance for years, and even a year on my own after I got sick. I don't want to, but I *can* do it on my own.

The real question is how will Dax react to whatever I decide to do?

He would be too gallant to let me go without a fight. A strong argument at the least. Even if it's the best thing for his happiness, he is going to feel too much loyalty and obligation to me just to let me walk out the door.

Of course, I could just pack up and leave. Not tell him. It's a completely shitty thing to do even if it's what's best for him. He would be so upset, though. He would follow me to California, of that I have no doubt. Maybe not to drag me back, but to at least let me know what a shitty thing it was that I did to him.

There's no easy answer. I sigh as our townhome

comes into view. I'm stunned when I see Dax's car sitting out on the curb. He always takes one of the parallel spots there to leave the single-car garage in the front open for me.

As I'm pulling into the driveway, I glance down at the clock on my dashboard. Twelve fifteen. He should be long gone by now as the team skate was supposed to be at noon, followed by a lunch.

I open the garage door, then pull my car in slowly. Turning it off, I sit there in silence and wonder what in the hell he is doing here.

I may have had a million questions before pulling up, but I didn't have a single answer. What I did have, though, was a little time on my side. I'd thought I had hours before I would see Dax again—which would technically be after the game tonight—to decide what to do. I am not prepared to walk in there right now and confront this issue with him.

But maybe he's not even in there. Maybe he got a ride with someone else.

A wave of relief rushes through me as I realize it's the most logical explanation. Bishop probably came by to pick Dax up. Hell, maybe it was even Tacker. While it doesn't appear he's any more socially engaging with the team as a whole, he has opened up to Dax at the team practices this past week. If by opening up, complaining about his new therapist he has to see counts. So maybe he grabbed an Uber, came by to get Dax, and they rode to the arena together.

Sounds a little foolish, but not implausible.

Yeah, either Bishop or Tacker or hell, even Legend or Erik came by and gave Dax a ride to the arena for some reason. No way he is in that house because there is no way he would miss a mandatory team event.

I feel much better as I exit my car after grabbing my purse and the pharmacy bag. Letting my mind roam ahead to what's in the refrigerator that I can make for lunch, I start for the house as my appetite is back in full force following my brief illness.

We don't lock the door leading from the garage into the mudroom, so I turn the knob and push it open. I can see into the kitchen—the portion that contains the table at the breakfast nook and part of the small island.

Brows knitting in confusion, I creep slowly through the mudroom, more of the kitchen coming into view. There are lit candles on the table. It's formally set with plates, silverware, and linen napkins.

Linen napkins? What the hell?

I smell something in the air. Italian maybe? Red sauce for sure.

My purse slides from my shoulder, and I drop the pharmacy bag on the small counter to my left as soon as I enter the kitchen.

Dax waits for me there.

He looks nervous. Shoulders tight, legs locked, and face pinched.

"Have I interrupted something?" I ask slowly, wondering why in the world he thought it was a good idea to have a romantic dinner with someone knowing I'd be coming home.

Dax's own brow furrows in confusion. "Um… no. I thought we'd have lunch together since I'm leaving tomorrow for almost a week and we haven't had any time alone with Willow visiting."

Okay… that just adds a million more questions to the already-long list I'd made under the theory Dax is unhappy with our situation and needs to be cut free.

He's certainly not making it easy.

My eyes roam over the romantic table setting before returning to him. "But… you should be at the team skate right now."

"I got a pass," he replies, taking two steps toward me. His hand goes to my elbow, and he leads me over to one of the chairs. "I got some lasagna from Bella Italia. I know it's your favorite."

Yes, it is. In the short few weeks I've been here, I've already found a favorite Italian place. I am touched by his thoughtfulness in—

"No, wait a minute," I say as I come out of the haze of being wooed. I pull my arm away to glare at him. "You can't just get a 'pass'. You have obligations. It's mandatory you be at the arena. What the hell is going on?"

Dax blinks at me over the vehemence in my voice, but he mildly says, "I want to spend time with you, Regan. I talked to Coach, and he gave me a pass."

"I don't fucking understand any of this," I cry out in frustration as I wheel away from him. I take two steps toward the living room, thinking flight is the best thing to do, but then no… I just spent all morning going over the possibilities in my head, so maybe we just need to hash this out right now. I wheel back around to face him. "I heard you and Willow talking this morning right before I left."

Complete understanding flows over Dax's face. "I thought something was going on when you walked out the wrong door."

"Yeah," I say with challenge. "I was a little upset to learn how horrific things are for you with me around."

That sounded totally childish and petulant, but now I'm being driven by pure emotion. My future happily ever after is getting ready to be put to rest right now.

Dax's expression softens with sympathy, and I hate that look. When he steps toward me, I backpedal.

He stops, giving me some space, but says, "That's not what I said, and you know it."

I shake my head, not wanting to hear the reason in his voice. "You said this was too hard."

"Not too hard," he corrects me. "Just hard."

"Well, I don't want things to be hard on you."

"That's my problem, not yours." Ugh, he sounds so fucking in tune with his feelings, like he has this all figured out. Calm, rational, and not easily susceptible to my arguments.

"It makes me feel bad you feel bad about me," I say truthfully. It's the closest I can get to boiling this down to simple words. "And I can't have that on me. You've done so much for me, and I cannot have this disrupting your life. It's more than I can bear."

"I'm sorry," he tells me, taking a tentative step toward me. "I never want to make you feel bad. It's why I talked to Willow and not you. Yes, it's hard. It's terrifying watching the woman I love face the things you're facing. I want to make everything right for you, and I can't. It makes me feel weak and powerless and a failure to you."

"But you're not," I rush to assure him. "You've done more than—"

"Did you even hear what I just said, Regan?" he cuts in over me. "You're the woman I love."

I blink a moment, then hesitantly drawl, "Yes. I heard that. You've known me forever. Of course you love me."

"Jesus," he mutters in frustration. Then, somehow, he's right in front of me. His hands go to my shoulders and he gives me the tiniest of shakes as if it's needed to clear the cobwebs from my head. "I don't love you as a fucking friend. Well, wait... I do. But I love you as *more*. I am *in* love with you. Like my heart is fucking gone. It belongs just to you, and it will never belong anywhere else again. So that's why things are scary and terrifying. I don't want to lose you. I've just now entered into a life that has become the happiest I've ever been. It adds so much promise to my future because I have you, and I don't want to lose it. I want to be a husband to you for real. For the long haul. I want to have children—assuming you can with your condition—and if not, we'll adopt. I just know I want my life to be with you forever. So yes, I'm scared. Yes, I'm frustrated. Yes, I'll probably always be that way, but I'll learn to be strong and supportive about it. I'm sorry you overheard that, but if this is what's come out of it... a talk about our feelings, then I'm glad you eavesdropped."

I just stare at him.

"Which is never really cool to do by the way," he adds.

My brain swims as I replay the words he just spoke. I get a little dizzy, pulling away from him to sink down onto the edge of the couch.

Dax stands there, hands loose at his side, and watches me warily. "Are you okay?"

I nod dumbly. He loves me? Like really loves me?

Wants to be married for real? Kids?

Holy shit. I don't know if I've ever been more stunned in my life. Not even when I got my PNH diagnosis.

"Regan," he asks again, taking a step toward me. "Are you okay?"

I nod slowly, my voice thick. "Just a little overwhelmed."

Dax's lips curve upward, his eyes twinkling.

He reaches into his front pocket, pulls something out, then drops to one knee before me. My vision actually blurs, my head spinning.

"You're about to be a little more overwhelmed," he says as he opens up a royal-blue velvet ring box.

My head stops spinning, and my eyes focus with utter clarity on the contents inside.

Three rings.

An engagement ring. A huge, emerald-cut diamond that's bigger than any I've ever seen before in my life.

But that's not what has my heart squeezing and my eyes misting.

It's the two wedding rings beside it. A woman's ring crusted with diamonds, along with a man's ring—platinum, thick, and masculine.

A complete set of wedding rings for us.

Tears start slipping down my cheeks, and I don't even bother to try to blink them back. Something tells me they'll just keep coming.

My gaze lifts. Dax is staring at me, and I finally see it.

The truth of all those words he just said.

He loves me.

Like really, truly loves me.

I launch myself off the couch, slamming right into his chest I propel us backward onto the carpet. He lands flat on his back with me on top of him, then I'm kissing him. Dax is laughing into my mouth, his arms banding around me tightly.

When I lift my head to stare down at him, I finally take stock of the incredibly overwhelming flash of pure joy that fills me. It's without a doubt the best feeling I've ever had the privilege of knowing in my life.

"I love you," I say simply. It's all I have to offer at this moment. He skipped a mandatory practice and set up a romantic meal to propose to me. Yes, to propose we spend our lives together. I had come home with the thought I was going to end things.

Nothing is what I expected, and I feel almost small in my appreciation of the wonders of this universe and what it can bestow upon me.

"So you ready to do this marriage thing for real?" he asks with a grin, holding up the box which has somehow shut when I knocked him backward.

My head jackhammers into a furious nod, and I

push up to straddle him. Dax smiles from his position flat on his back, then holds the box up to reopen it. He pulls out the wedding band first. "I believe tradition is that this goes on first as it should be held closest to your heart."

I didn't know that, but it's so sweet. He sets the box on his chest, then takes my left hand and slides the band onto my ring finger.

So weird, but I feel an instantaneous bonding with Dax that was not there before.

I feel… complete.

He then plucks the engagement ring from the box. I'm totally dazzled by its brilliance as he slides it on, then presses his mouth to my palm before releasing me. I hold my hand out to admire the set. It's more than I would have ever thought possible.

My gaze drops to the box still clutched in his hand. I take it from him, plucking his wedding ring out. It's heavy and masculine.

I take his hand, so large and strong in my own, and I put the circle of commitment onto his finger. When I dare to glance at his face, I see his own eyes shining a little with emotion as he stares at the platinum band.

"Dax," I whisper softly, and his attention comes to me. "I love you so much. These past few years, I've never dared to hope for a happily ever after. This is more than I could have ever wished for. I promise I will make you the happiest man in the world."

"And I promise to give you your best life, Regan," he says in return. "I'll never let you down. I'll always be there for you. You'll never walk a single step alone."

And those words we just spoke…

They're our wedding vows.

Completely spontaneous and utterly perfect.

I lean forward, stretching out on top of my husband—for real now—and I seal our vows with a kiss.

The Arizona Vengeance are taking the hockey world by storm! Please visit sawyerbennett.com to see all of the sexy standalones available in the Arizona Vengeance series.

Read on for an excerpt from
Tacker
Arizona Vengeance
by Sawyer Bennett

CHAPTER 1

Tacker

"Three Three December," I say into the headset. "I'm having some issues with the primary attitude indicator. I'd like to climb a bit."

I glance over at MJ. She always used to snicker when I'd say "attitude" indicator. Most people think it should be "altitude" but no... it's called an attitude indicator. She thought that was hilarious.

How many times has she sat in the copilot seat of my Cessna 335, glancing out at the world with pure joy on her face? She loves to fly as much as I do, but she is always content to let me have the controls. Though she loves being up in the air, she's never had a desire to pilot.

I've never seen her look scared before, and it causes my anxiety to skyrocket. She doesn't even look back to me, her eyes squinted and peering through the windshield, trying desperately to locate the horizon.

The radio crackles, and then the controller replies, "I'll be able to issue a higher attitude in two miles. Copy?"

"Roger that," I reply, resolving to hold steady for that

long. I'm at twenty-six-hundred feet, flying through fog as thick as pea soup. My attitude indicator—perhaps the most important instrument on my dash that shows my plane's orientation relative to the horizon—is fritzing out. Without clear skies, I can't find the fucking horizon and I'm at risk for spatial disorientation. My request to climb higher is to get us above this mess.

Get us to safety.

I don't risk taking my hands off the yoke to grab MJ's for assurance. So instead, I say, "Hey... think you'll let me take a little peek at the dress?"

It's the reason for our trip. We're flying from Dallas to Houston for the last fitting of her wedding dress. Then in two short weeks, we'll be married.

MJ—short for Melody Jane—and what I've called her since I first met her in Dallas, tears her gaze away from the foggy air surrounding us and gives me a quick glance. "Not a snowball's chance in hell."

I don't dare look at her, only able to see the sharp twist of her head from my peripheral vision. But I grin, loving her sass even in the face of true danger.

"Cessna 121 Papa Papa," the controller says over the radio. "I'm going to have you make a slow left turn heading southeast, then climb to seven thousand feet. You should have seven miles visibility but some light rain."

"Roger," I reply, glancing down at the attitude indicator. The horizon line sits flat, telling me I'm flying straight as an arrow. I hope to fuck it's working correctly now

because I'm going to have to rely on it heavily in just a moment.

This time, I do take a moment to look at MJ, and she swivels slowly to meet my gaze. This left turn is all going to be dependent on that indicator leading me through the fog.

"I love you," I say solemnly. Not a goodbye. Just a reaffirmation.

"I love you, too," she replies, and I start to turn the plane.

Terror clutches me so hard I can't breathe. I come flying out of my nightmare, soaked with sweat. My mouth is wide open, but no scream comes out. I never screamed as we were going down, but MJ had. It had been loud, piercing, and filled with terror. I can hear it vividly ringing in my ears right now, even though my nightmare didn't progress very far tonight.

Sometimes, I relive the entire crash.

Sometimes, it will only be a loop of MJ's last moments alive. She hadn't been killed instantly. We'd both been trapped in the wreckage, and I had to watch her die a long, torturous death. That's the worst nightmare I repeatedly suffer.

Scrubbing a hand over my face, I wonder what time it is. I don't have a clock, and I don't wear a watch. My phone is plugged into a charger on my bathroom vanity. The only thing I have in my bedroom is an inflatable air mattress covered with a fitted sheet, a fleece blanket, and two pillows.

Judging by the dark gloom with a bluish cast coming through the blinds, I'd guess it was on the verge of dawn. I'm exhausted. If I laid back down, I might be able to drift off to sleep. However, the thought of falling into a vortex of plane crash terrors doesn't appeal to me so I roll off the mattress, careful of the cast on my left wrist. I have a slight fracture to the scaphoid bone, compliments of my idiotic choices of drinking and driving two weeks ago. I've got another two weeks in the cast, although maybe I can talk the doctor into taking it off sooner.

Pushing up to my knees, then my feet, I make my way into the small bathroom across the hall. This apartment complex is a dump, and I'd rented a small one-bedroom when I moved to Phoenix in September after having been picked up by the Vengeance in the expansion draft.

I was a pretty unmarketable player, having sat out most of the second half of last season due to the plane crash. Not because of my injuries, though. I came out relatively unscathed except for some deep lacerations. Rather, I didn't have much spirit of competition left within me and stayed on "injured reserve" with the Dallas Mustangs.

I wasn't surprised they put me on the auction block for the expansion draft. I was too much of a risk, but apparently not to Vengeance. They wanted me on their team, and so I thought.... what the fuck? Why not? At least it provided me some respite from my demons.

What I found when I came back to playing professional hockey was that as long as I was out on the ice, I was able to keep MJ and her death out of my head.

Step foot off the ice and she occupied everything.

I do my business in the bathroom, wash my hands, and then nab my phone from the charger. After I shuffle into the kitchen, I start a pot of coffee. While it brews, I reach into the cabinet and pull out the only coffee mug I have. An Arizona Vengeance one I picked up in the arena fan store when I first moved here. It's the only drinking container I have in my apartment unless the empty water bottles in my recycle bin count.

My phone lets me know it's six forty-five, and I wonder if I'll actually make my nine AM meeting. I have plenty of time. A ten-minute shower and change. A twenty-five-minute Uber ride to the arena—thanks to my license being suspended due to my DUI charge—and probably a five-minute mandatory wait in the front office until I can be granted an audience with Christian Rutherford.

He's the general manager of the Arizona Vengeance and he's expecting me to give him an answer today.

The question?

Will I choose to continue playing with the team?

His offer for my continued employment as a player on the team wasn't made without a lot of thought and care. He met with Coach Perron and the team's owner, Dominik Carlson. They discussed the benefit I could provide, and they weighed it against the terrible shadow I'd thrown over their entire program with my antics.

They are not without compassion, although it's probably misplaced in a man like me.

Regardless, they made me an offer, and I've been considering it. Last week, I got called in to talk to Christian. His terms were simple and nonnegotiable.

First, I was going to be fined one-hundred-thousand dollars for driving drunk. He wanted to send a message to the Phoenix community as well as to the hockey world at large that my type of behavior would not be tolerated and would never be condoned.

Really, it was a punishment designed to make me think twice if I were to ever do something so stupid again.

The second requirement was no big deal. I was not allowed to drink alcohol anymore. Not a single drop. If evidence was presented that I had partaken, I would be released from the team with a forfeiture of my contract. This didn't bother me. I didn't intend to drink again as it was never really my thing to begin with. MJ didn't drink at all, so neither did I.

It wasn't for any religious, spiritual, or health reasons. Neither of us just liked the way it made us feel. Besides, the morning after my run-in with the concrete barricade, along with the three quarters of a fifth of Jack I had drank, left me vowing never to touch another drop of alcohol again.

The third requirement to my continued employment with the team was I had to attend some sort of grief counseling. The terms were specific. I had to go at least twice a week for the remainder of the entire season, and I was even provided a list of suitable places I could go to. I had to sign a full release so the counselor could communicate my progress back to Christian. If at any time I was not fully participating, he could release me from the team with forfeiture of contract. If I skipped one session, I'd be released. If I didn't make progress in emotional healing, I would be released.

It was all very rigid, narrowly defined, and almost designed to set me up for failure if I didn't know any better.

There's a big part of me that just wants to hand the team a big 'fuck you'. The terms aren't going to be easy. It means I'm going to have to confront my demons.

It means I'm probably going to have to let MJ go, and no matter how fucking painful it is to remember her dying beside me in that plane, they're the freshest memories I have of her. I don't know if I can do it.

I've done a lot of thinking. I've prayed to the only

God I know and one who I never called on much until now. I've searched my soul for the right answer, but there's no clarity.

There seems to be no right answer for me, except…

Except if I hand a 'fuck you' to the team, my hockey career is over. And for better or for worse, it's the only thing in the world that gives me some small measure of happiness.

Maybe happiness isn't the right word, but it sure as hell gives me respite from the pain.

And that has value to me.

I glance at my phone again, noting it's now six fifty-one. Still time to think on this some more, but I know the clock is ticking ever closer to the decision I'll have to make—one that will have a profound impact on my future.

No easy task.

Connect with Sawyer online:

Website: sawyerbennett.com

Twitter: twitter.com/bennettbooks

Facebook: facebook.com/bennettbooks

Instagram: instagram.com/sawyerbennett123

Book+Main Bites:

bookandmainbites.com/sawyerbennett

Goodreads: goodreads.com/Sawyer_Bennett

Amazon: amazon.com/author/sawyerbennett

BookBub: bookbub.com/authors/sawyer-bennett

About the Author

Since the release of her debut contemporary romance novel, Off Sides, in January 2013, Sawyer Bennett has released multiple books, many of which have appeared on the New York Times, USA Today and Wall Street Journal bestseller lists.

A reformed trial lawyer from North Carolina, Sawyer uses real life experience to create relatable, sexy stories that appeal to a wide array of readers. From new adult to erotic contemporary romance, Sawyer writes something for just about everyone.

Sawyer likes her Bloody Marys strong, her martinis dirty, and her heroes a combination of the two. When not bringing fictional romance to life, Sawyer is a chauffeur, stylist, chef, maid, and personal assistant to a very active daughter, as well as full-time servant to her